Malodorous

Del Robertson

Special Edition
Including
My Fair Maiden

Affinity
eBook Press
NZ
2014

Malodorous
© Del Robertson 2014
Affinity E-Book Press NZ LTD
Canterbury, New Zealand

1st Edition

ISBN: 978-1-927282-87-8

Editor: Ruth Stanley
Cover Design: Irish Dragon Designs

Acknowledgements

Thanks to the wonderful women at Affinity for allowing me to do what it is that I do. Thanks also to Kelly, Sherry, and mom for whatever it is that they do. And, thanks to BLR for doing everything else.

Dedication

For Lee. Always and Forever

By Del Robertson

Taming the Wolff
My Fair Maiden
Malodorous

Table of Contents

My Fair Maiden
Del Robertson
Affinity eBook Press NZ LTD

My Fair Maiden

A Novella by Del Robertson

Chapter One

When I entered the tavern I didn't detect anything amiss. Despite that, I was inherently cautious. Being a woman traveling alone vigilance wasn't just a habit, it was also a matter of survival.

As was the swagger and the attitude. I'd learned long ago the best way to stay out of trouble was to not invite it in the first place. In other words, don't look like a victim...or approachable.

Body language goes a long way in taking care of that first part. So does the body. I'm big for a girl, for most men, too. I'm tall, with broad shoulders, and the sort of build that comes from a lifetime of sword work.

That helps with the not looking approachable bit; my sword. Or rather, swords. I wear two of them in a double crisscross harness buckled in the front with dual leather sheaths at my back. Two hilts, one gold and the other silver, ride high behind each shoulder, within easy reach. If the threat of twin swords wasn't enough, the long knife sheathed at my waist and the dagger belted at my thigh offered further discouragement.

Fingers gripped comfortably about the hilt of my knife, I strode through the tavern with a sense of purpose. That was something I'd learned while in the army: always walk like you know where you're going, even if you don't.

Something else I'd learned was how to dress. In other

words, always look the part. I was no longer in the guard, hadn't been for several winters. I still had the tunic, though. The once dark material had faded to a cornflower blue. The golden yellow epaulets from both shoulders were missing, as were the two stripes on my sleeves designating rank. I'd cut the collar from the neck myself to make it more comfortable.

Not that it mattered any. The uniform of the guard was unmistakable, no matter what the condition. Most people took one look and saw what they wanted to see—whether good or bad. Either way, it usually made them think twice before starting trouble.

I passed by several men seated around a wooden table. There were no whistles or catcalls, inappropriate gestures or attempted pats to my backside. Good. The last barbarian that had tried that had pulled back his hand with one less finger attached. Barbarians are stupid cretins not easily deterred by attitude, uniform, or weapons. If anything, they seem to be even more attracted to a woman possessing a sharp blade and a sharper tongue. As for the uniform, their only concern was how fast they could get their intended conquest undressed.

Thankfully, these men didn't appear to be barbarians. None of them were heavily armed or armored and I judged most of them to be villagers or farmers.

I felt a set of eyes watching me as I made my way to the bar. I turned and looked, seeing a lad seated alone and staring. He wasn't a boy, yet he wasn't what I'd term a man fully grown, either. His face held the pockmarks of youth, there was peach fuzz about his chubby cheeks, and light wisps of brown hair sprouted from his chin and lined his upper lip.

This lad was no farmer. His finer clothes, the rings on his fingers, and the feathered cap on his head indicated he was more than a commoner. His coin purse was worn and appeared to be less than half-full, revealing that he wasn't well-to-do nobility, either. Next to the coin purse, on his belt, he wore a knife. It was long and thin, and I doubted if he'd ever used it on anything more substantial than his dinner. He saw me openly appraising him and hastily downed his eyes. I smirked, discounting him as any sort of threat.

I approached the tavern keeper, purchasing food and drink for now and a room for later. I'd had enough walking beside my horse and there was nowhere urgent I needed to be. I decided I'd get my horse's shoes fixed and rest up here for the remainder of the day. A good meal, a hot bath, a full night's sleep, and I'd start out fresh first thing in the morning.

I claimed a corner table by dropping my saddlebags on one chair and my backside on the other. A barmaid brought a tray laden down with a wooden bowl, a trencher of bread, and a mug. I thanked her with a nod of my head. A bronze coin in her palm and a suggestion of more to come ensured she'd return to refill my mug as often as needed.

The venison stew tasted like it'd been left cooking over the hearth for three days. The bread was stale. The ale was bitter, lukewarm, and flat. Still, it was the best meal I'd had in over a fortnight. I leaned back in my chair, propping my boots up on the knife-scarred table, and chewed over a hunk of gristle I'd spooned up.

I sensed someone watching me. I looked up expecting to find the lad's eyes on me again. I was surprised to find him with his head down, his eyes locked on his bowl as he sopped up his stew with his bread. I watched for a few heartbeats to see if he was exaggerating his interest in his meal.

Juice dripping from the bread onto his chubby fingers, he brought his hand to his mouth. He tilted his head back as he shoved his mouth full. Thick meat juice dribbled from his thin lips. Without letting loose the remaining hunk of bread, he swiped the back of his hand across his chin.

It wasn't him. No one could pretend to be that engrossed in a meal. Still, my sword hand was itching. That was always a sure sign of trouble. I rubbed my left palm against my trousers and let my eyes search the room.

She was seated far back in a corner niche, slouched down, her body partially hidden by shadows and the table in front of her. If it hadn't been for the intensity of her stare, I might have overlooked her completely.

I met her gaze. She hastily looked away. A heartbeat later, her eyes drifted my way again.

Oh, yeah. She's interested.

I could tell. I have enough experience with women to know when I've caught an admirer's eye. Even when she tries to hide it. And, believe me, this one was trying her best to keep her desires hidden.

She'd been openly staring at me. Then, the instant she thought I'd noticed, she quickly averted her gaze. She turned her head, making a showing of looking about the tavern, as though she were casually observing everyone, and not just me in particular.

She lifted her mug to her lips. Big, brown eyes peered over the rim of her wooden mug at me. Seeing me watching her, her eyes widened and she looked away. We played this cat-and-mouse game for a while. She'd look at me and I'd look back. Before our gazes could truly connect, though, she'd hastily look the other direction.

Until the time came that she moved too slowly and I snared her with my smile. I'm very proud of my smile. It's one of my best features. I still have all my teeth and I keep them clean by scrubbing salt on them daily and chewing willow bark on a regular basis. I've been told that my smile alone can charm the breechcloth off any girl.

I'm sure the blond hair and blue eyes don't hurt, either. In the south, where most men and women tended to have dark hair and dark eyes, my fair hair made some consider my looks to be exotic. In the north, my looks aren't all that uncommon. There, it's my dimples that garner the attention.

She was still watching, so I extended my tongue, trailing it slowly over my lips, as though they were parched. She choked on her drink, lowering her mug and patting at her throat and upper chest. I waited until she regained her composure before raising my mug and tilting my head at her. She hesitated before offering a timid smile in return. I responded with a brazen wink and beckoned her with a crooked finger.

†

In truth, I wasn't entirely certain she would come. It's rare, but there has been an occasion or two in which a woman has proved impervious to my charms.

Twice. It's happened exactly twice. Both times had left a decidedly bad taste in my mouth.

The girl sat motionless upon her chair, eyes unblinking as she stared at me. At last, she pushed the chair back from the table and slowly rose to her feet. She picked up her mug and clutched it tightly in her grasp. I let loose a little sigh, glad I wouldn't have to add the sourness of her rejection to the bitterness of the ale I was sipping.

She was tall. Not as tall as me, mind you, but she was long-limbed. Her linen skirt ended midcalf, swirling about her legs, emphasizing just how toned they were. Rich, brunette tresses fell over her shoulders. She wore her peasant blouse off the shoulder, cut low in the front and tucked into her skirt, accentuating the trimness of her waist. She was fit, but also buxom and curvaceous in all the right places.

I felt myself salivating and swallowed hard. She crossed the room, her hips swaying with every step. The nearer she drew, the shallower my breathing became. My eyes remained fixated even as she drew to a stop in front of me.

"Hi." Her voice was soft. "Hello?"

I blinked and shook my head briskly, forcing my eyes

from her waist and up. They lingered on her generous bosom before traveling higher. When at last I reached her face, I saw a pair of eyes, the same shade as warm honey, looking down at me.

"I'm Gwendolyn. Gwen." She offered up a shy smile.

"Bodhi," I said.

Her eyes indicated the chair beside me. I reacted immediately, hurriedly taking my boots off the table and my saddlebags off the seat. I used the toe of my boot to nudge the wooden chair toward her.

She slid onto the seat, scooting forward so she could tuck herself in close to the table. She propped her elbows up on the table and wrapped her long fingers about her drinking mug. Above the froth at the top of her mug, her bountiful breasts and generous cleavage were on ample display. She drew in a breath as she lifted her mug to her full lips.

My imagination whispered in my ear that if I watched long enough she might draw in a deep enough breath that her blouse would slip and her mouth-watering breasts would be completely bared to my gaze. Spirits help me if that were to happen. I was already enraptured...and that was with her being fully clothed.

"Bodhi?"

"Hmm?"

"Bodhi? Have you heard a word I've said?"

"Huh?" I shook my head to clear the cobwebs. "Of course."

Of course I haven't. How could she have possibly expected me to listen to a word she'd said when I was busy ogling her? I lifted my mug to my lips in an attempt at stalling long enough to search my mind in case my ears had managed to catch any part of the conversation that the rest of my body couldn't care a lick about. All I managed to discover was that sometime while she'd been speaking, I'd managed to drain my mug of every last drop of that awful ale.

If my obvious leering, inattention, or any of my other ill manners at all offended Gwendolyn, she gave no indication. She just looked at me with those warm honey-brown eyes and that soft smile of hers and carried on speaking.

"I asked if you're visiting family in the area."

"Hm? Uh, no. Just passing through."

"I expect you'll be continuing on your way after your meal," she said.

I shook my head. I spotted the barmaid refilling the pockmarked lad's stew bowl and held my mug aloft. As she gave a curt nod of acknowledgment, I lowered my mug back onto the tabletop.

"Why not?" Gwendolyn asked. "There's plenty of sunlight left. You could put a lot more miles beneath your feet before dusk."

"You're right about one thing—there's plenty of sun left. Too much. I'm tired of getting baked by it. I've decided to rest here for the night and head out either tomorrow..." I purposely allowed my eyes to drift over her desirable body "...or perhaps the next day."

"You could rest now and travel at night when it's cooler."

I looked at her as if she were either daft or mad and ticked off on my fingers the many reasons her suggestion was inane.

"Too dangerous. Too easy to lose your way in the dark. Could ride off the path. Horse could step wrong and go lame, toss his rider, or both. Not to mention thieves on the road."

"You look like you could handle yourself just fine."

I preened beneath her gaze, sitting up a little straighter and puffing out my chest with pride.

"It's not about being able to handle yourself." I snorted. "Only a fool or someone on the run would go traveling about in the dark."

"What if there was no other choice? What if it were a matter of life or..." Gwendolyn's voice trailed off and she lowered her gaze.

Looking up, I saw the barmaid standing beside our table with a pitcher on a tray. As she took my mug and refilled it, her eyes drifted to my companion.

"We've only just met and already you sound like you're trying to get rid of me," I teased.

"Trying to drive away a thirsty traveler?" asked the barmaid. "That would be inhospitable. You weren't being inhospitable, were you, Gwen?"

"No, of course not, Cathryn." Gwen's teeth bit into her bottom lip. "Bodhi must have misunderstood my intent."

"Ah." The barmaid smiled widely as she turned to me. "There, you see, Bodhi? Gwen doesn't wish you to leave. You aren't leaving now, are you, not when you've scarcely begun to quench your thirst?"

Something about the barmaid calling me by name when I hadn't given it to her rankled me. I rubbed my palm with the thumb of my opposite hand as I looked up at her. It seemed to me that although her lips were curved, there was no true warmth or sincerity behind her smile.

"As I was telling Gwendolyn, I'm heading north. I have no place urgent to be, though." I looked directly into Gwen's eyes. "Besides, I can't leave now. I've already paid for a room."

Gwendolyn's indrawn breath was audible. Her eyes darted from me to Cathryn. Cathryn speared her with a look. Gwen paled and she downed her head. Her hand trembled as she lifted her mug to her lips. She kept her gaze lowered as she drank.

The barmaid gave the buxom brunette a long, hard look and breathed heavily through her nose, her nostrils flaring with the effort. Then, as if remembering I was there, she looked to me. She gave me an odd look before reaching for my bowl of stew.

I put my hand on top of her wrist to stop her.

"Enough."

My gaze indicated I was speaking about the stew, but I trusted she gathered from my tone that there was also a deeper meaning. I dipped two fingers into my coin purse and withdrew another bronze coin. Cathryn snatched it out of my grasp and turned on her heel and left, leaving me alone with a clearly disturbed companion.

✝

Her encounter with Cathryn had left Gwen quiet and withdrawn. She sat forward, her shoulders hunched and both hands wrapped about her mug. Her gaze was riveted on the contents of her cup. She made no attempt at conversation. Indeed, it seemed as if she'd swallowed her tongue.

I drank nearly half my ale waiting for her to find her voice. When it looked as if she never would, I decided it was up to me.

"Truth. Is Cathryn the barmaid as naturally sour as the ale she serves, or is she, in fact, an evil faerie sent to cut out the tongues of fair maidens?"

"What?" Gwen's head jerked up and wide, startled eyes met mine.

"That's better." I smiled at her to let her know that I was at least partly teasing. "Now that it's been proven she's not an evil faerie, who is she?"

"Just a barmaid." Gwen released a heavy sigh. "As well as my elder sister."

Ah. I thought they bore more than a passing resemblance.

My eyes flitted about the tavern. I spotted Cathryn at the bar. She was reloading her tray with more mugs. The tavern keeper was opposite her on the other side of the bar and their heads were bent close together as they conversed. They both kept darting looks over at my table.

There was a featherlight touch against the back of my hand. I looked down to find Gwendolyn's fingertips idly tracing the length of a bleached white scar. I'd gotten it more winters ago than I could count. The seasons had passed, the scar had faded, but the wound was one that had not easily healed. Nor would the pain of it ever be completely forgotten.

She turned my hand over, caressing the calluses of my palm. Despite having skin toughened from a lifetime of gripping a pommel, her tender touch sent a shiver right through me.

Gwendolyn's touch drifted higher, traveling over my leather wrist cuff. Her hand stroked over my forearm. I flexed, causing the flesh beneath her fingertips to dance. Her hand slipped beneath the sleeve of my tunic and onto my bicep.

"Bodhi?" Her voice was sultry.

"Ye—" I couldn't believe my voice cracked in reaction to hers. I took a hasty draught of my ale and spoke again. My voice came out at a much more normal, if slightly huskier, pitch. "Yes?"

She silently stared at me for several long heartbeats. Then, she wet her lips as if they were unbearably dry. To me, they looked moist and full. She chewed her bottom lip, as if in contemplation, before finally speaking.

"You've had a lot of experience, with traveling, I mean?"

I nodded and took another sip of my drink.

"I've never been away from home," she said. "Chatham's a small village. Compared to other women, women from large towns, am I considered at all attractive?"

I placed my hand atop the one that had moved back down to my forearm. I leaned forward, looking deeply into her eyes.

"Fair maiden, you are most desirable." I raised my mug for another sip.

"Desirable enough..." Her eyes searched my face "...for you to take me to your bed?"

"Wha—?" I sputtered, ale spewing from my mouth—what little bit that didn't try going down the wrong pipe. I choked, coughs racking my body as I beat my open palm on the tabletop.

Her hand was at my back, pounding. I coughed a few more times, then signaled for her to stop. She lifted her hand away and I drew in several gasping breaths.

Eyes watering, I looked around the tavern. Any eyes that had been staring at my embarrassment quickly turned the other way. Except for Cathryn's. She was looking at me with a hardened expression.

That's when it hit me, like a sword right between the eyes.

"How much?" I asked.

"Pardon?" She quirked a brow and tilted her head.

"How much?" I repeated, determined to know the price before the transaction.

I openly hefted the bag of coins tied to my belt and made a gesture that indicated her.

"You think I'm some common tavern whore?" Her eyebrows rose nearly as high as her voice.

I stroked my chin as I studied her in contemplation of my answer. She made a move to get up from her chair, but resettled herself before I could reach out a hand to stop her.

"No," I said at last, deciding she was much too young, her body far too firm to have seen the sort of things the other women in this tavern had over the seasons. "But, start now and you'll be as used and dried up as your sister by winter."

I wish I could say that I saw the slap coming. I didn't. I felt it, though. From my aching cheek, to my teeth, and all the way down to my jawbone.

I tried rubbing the stinging nettles from my cheek as I studied her some more. I'd seen it before in my travels. A young girl with no means of support drawn into life as a tavern maid, forced to sell her body as readily as the food and drink she peddled. Harsh as it sounded, ofttimes, it was the girl's own kin that had sold her into the lifestyle. Not necessarily because they were cruel or abusive, but rather out of sheer desperation. Sometimes, there were just too many mouths and not nearly enough food at home.

I'd thought that was her situation. I'd thought that Cathryn, being the eldest sister, was tasked with instructing Gwendolyn in the same trade.

"I'm no whore and I don't want your coin." She held her wooden mug in her grasp so tightly that her knuckles were white. Her teeth were clenched even tighter; so tight I doubted a drop of ale could slip between them.

"What do you want, then," I asked, "if not my coin?"

"You. For a single night."

✝

There was a time, when I had more scruples, that I might have reacted slower. Now though, I was full of ale, full of lust, and a plain fool. I had her up the stairs and in my room, with her back pressed against the closed door, before common sense could deter me.

My nose nuzzled against her neck, brushing her brunette tresses aside. I nibbled, licked, and sucked at her tender flesh. I felt her hands encircle my waist.

Her words, *"for a single night,"* reverberated in my skull. No doubt, that phrase delivered in her seductive voice had initially stirred me to rush her upstairs. Now, it rankled me. It wasn't that I was looking for, nor even desired, something more. If anything, I tended to avoid any pairing

13

that appeared as if it might turn complicated. I didn't need romantic entanglements that included a thatched cottage for two and whispered promises of forever.

A single night suited my needs just fine. What irked me was that this maiden thought she would be the one to make the terms of our coupling. It was as if she thought she could have this instance of debauchery and then return to her unspoiled life untarnished. And, while I'm certain there's been many a maid that's had that same plan prior to being bedded, she was the first one to put voice to the deed.

Even though she had made her claim of only the night, I knew she would bear the mark of my passion come the morn. The thought of her dressing, standing in front of the mirror, eyes fixed upon the discolored flesh of her neck, spurred me to suck even harder. I grew determined that it would take more than one morning for my love bite to fade from her reflection. Or her memory. My teeth nipped at her tender skin.

Her arms were about me, her hands splayed across my back. She tilted her head back, arching her neck beneath my sucking lips. She gripped my shoulders. Fingers curled into my hair, pulling me in closer. As my body pressed fully against hers, a gasp escaped her lips, and her heated breath washed over me.

My lips crushed against hers. Her mouth opened for me and my tongue thrust inside. The kiss was long and deep. She met my passion with fervor, sucking hard on my tongue. When the kiss ended, we were both left breathless, taking in heaping gulps of air.

I captured her face in my hands. Fingers caressed her downy smooth cheeks. My thumb dragged across kiss-swollen lips. Her mouth opened, she extended her tongue, wetting my digit. My thumb slipped between her lips, past her teeth. She teased, sucking on my thumb before her sharp teeth nipped me.

I tore my thumb from her mouth and took a step back. Without thinking, I stuck the stinging pad of flesh into my mouth and sucked hard. As I caught my breath, my gaze swept over her.

There was a teasing cast to her eyes that suggested she'd intended playfulness, not malice. There was something else too. Want. The shade of her eyes had deepened, taking on the hue of hardened amber.

Her chestnut tresses fell in waves over her shoulders and down her back. The sleeves of her peasant blouse hung off her upper arms. It seemed she, too, was struggling with her breathing. Her chest lifted with every intake and fell with every exhalation.

I gripped her by the nape of the neck and pulled her to me for a searing kiss. As the kiss ended, I gripped both her shoulders. My calloused palms caressed over her smooth shoulders and down her arms. As my fingers came into contact with the material of her peasant blouse, I tugged—hard—and shoved her blouse down to where it was tucked into the waist of her skirt.

This time, it was my turn to gasp aloud. She was...stunning. I'd already guessed that she was well-endowed. That much had been obvious, even in the dimly lit downstairs tavern. What I hadn't guessed, though, was just how buxom she really was. Her uplifted breasts were fuller and heavier than I expected, given her slender frame. Her nipples were dusted a pale rose and were swollen to stiffness.

My gasp became a groan. I grabbed her and spun her around, away from the door. I pushed her down and she landed with a thump on the bed. With expertise borne of experience, I lifted my dual shoulder harness over my head and hung my swords from one corner post of the bed.

She sat on the edge of the bed, looking up at me. Her hair was disheveled, her lips were swollen from our kisses, and a pink flush tinted her cheeks.

I stood for a heartbeat, just staring down at her, entranced by her beauty.

Her hands closed about my waist. Her fingers gripped my hips as she tugged me closer to the bed. Nails bit through the thin material of my tunic and scraped the coarser material of my britches. She leaned forward, pressing a kiss to my abdomen. Brown eyes blinked up at me.

"Bodhi."

That's all it took. The spell was broken and I was on my knees before her. My hands cupped her breasts, palms lifting, testing their heft. My mouth fell upon her, determined to devour her with my lips, my tongue, and my teeth. I sucked, licked, nipped, and bit. Her fingers twined in my hair. Her hands pulling me impossibly closer and the low mewling sounds she was making urged me on.

At last, I drew back. I looked up, seeing her heavy-lidded eyes looking down at me. Her palms were pressed flat against my shoulders. Still holding her gaze, I extended my tongue. I felt her hardened nipple beneath my oral digit. I licked it, then lifted it with the tip of my tongue, and then sucked it fully into my mouth. Her entire body shivered.

"Oh, Bodhi."

I felt a smile form on my lips.

The sound of splintering wood shattered the moment. I turned my head in time to see the door being kicked open. Several men appeared in the open doorway. Gwendolyn screamed. Before I could reach for my weapons, I saw a close-up view of the sole of a boot aiming for my face.

Then, everything went black.

Chapter Two

When I regained consciousness, I was flat on my back, looking up at the inside of a thatched roof. I turned my head from side to side. The surroundings were strangely familiar. I hadn't spent much time in it, mind you, but it appeared as if this was still the same room that I had rented.

I sat straight up, then instantly regretted the move as the entire room spun about me. Falling back to the floor, I screwed my eyes tightly shut and clutched both hands to my aching face.

I opened my eyes and peered through the spaces between my spread fingers. This time, the room was right side up. Still leery about the floor shifting from beneath me, I rolled onto my side. I made my way onto my hands and knees. From there, I gripped the linens hanging off the side of the bed. I grunted as I used the bedsheets to pull myself up. The room spun again, but I managed to stay upright.

In disbelief, I stared at the bedpost. My harness was still hanging there, my swords resting in their leather sheaths. A quick pat at my waist and thigh assured me that my knife and dagger were also intact. Even my coin purse was still secure on my belt, and from the heft of it, I'd say every coin was accounted for.

The motive for my assault clearly wasn't robbery. I still had my most valued possessions, namely my weapons and my money. *A jealous husband? Overprotective brother? Father?* If their attack was in retaliation for my sullying the fair Gwen, they'd have been better served killing me. They certainly had ample opportunity while I was unconscious.

I frowned and rubbed my chin, wincing as my fingers connected with my battered jaw. Even that damage wouldn't be long lasting. I'd had far worse over the seasons. The lack of serious harm to either my person or my purse was baffling.

The only thing I had lost...was the maiden.

I sighed heavily and reached for my swords, slipping the harness over my head. Practiced fingers fastened the buckles in place. Adjusting the fit of the sheaths against my back as I went, I left my room and raced down the tavern stairs.

Conversation on the first floor died as soon as my boot left the last step. I cast a sideways glance at the bar. The tavern keeper was behind the counter, wiping down the surface with a dirty rag. Cathryn was standing beside him. As soon as they saw me, he downed his head and refused to look up no matter how hard I stared at him while she slipped out from behind the bar and out the door.

I looked around, seeing everyone staring at me, as if waiting to see what I would do. I thought about pulling my knife and scaring the tavern keeper to within an inch of his life, just on sheer principle. It was obvious from his reaction that he knew what had occurred upstairs, perhaps even knew it was going to happen. *I wonder if he got paid to either allow, or ignore, the taking of Gwen?*

I'd wager that Cathryn had. The way she had acted toward Gwen at the table I wouldn't put it past her to sell out her own sister. Just like I wouldn't doubt that she was at that very heartbeat on her way to warn whoever had paid her off. That made Cathryn the more dangerous of the two.

I decided to leave the tavern keeper for later. Hauling down Cathryn and finding Gwendolyn was far more important right now. That didn't deter me from casting a final glare and a low growl of warning in the tavern keeper's direction before I left.

†

After the dim lighting of the tavern, the sunlight was blinding. I shielded my eyes with my hand and looked up and

18

down the street. Cathryn the barmaid proved to be more elusive than I'd anticipated.

The dirt streets were dusty and there was a dry wind blowing, obliterating her tracks. I picked a direction and started walking, hoping I would spot her. After all, it was a small village, not a large town. *How many wandering barmaids could there be?*

The answer was none. At least, none that I could find. Including Cathryn.

I turned the corner of a building and found myself outside the blacksmith's shop. I thought I'd see if the shoes I'd commissioned had been fitted to my horse yet. If so, I'd pay and at least have the luxury of searching for Cathryn and Gwen on horseback.

Thick sand covered the ground in front of the blacksmith's shop to safeguard against flying sparks. Two large barrels, one filled with water and the other with sand, stood nearby a stone furnace. Blistering heat and flames licked at the furnace's open door.

The smith was standing outside his shop, behind a large anvil. Devon was a large ox of a man, taller and wider than me by hand spans. He was shirtless, the muscles in his chest and arms dancing as he hammered out links of chain on the surface of the anvil. The iron rings were still glowing red from the fire as he linked the pieces together.

He saw me and gave a curt nod of greeting.

"Hey. Delay on your horseshoes." He jerked his chin toward the anvil. "Commission from the magistrate."

I gave the length of chain a critical eye. The links were thick and looked heavy. Cast-iron molds for a set of manacles were atop his workbench. A heavy iron ring had already been fashioned and the mold for a key waited beside the ring.

"Dangerous criminal?" I asked.

"Don't know about criminal. Definitely dangerous,

though. Ol' Horace may never walk straight again."

Devon grinned, showing a big gap in his front teeth. His raucous laughter made his whole chest bounce. He spotted my look of incomprehension and pointed.

My gaze followed his finger.

She stood in the center of a wooden platform in the village square. Her hands were bound together with thick rope and she was tied to a whipping post. Thankfully, she was no longer bare breasted. Either Gwen was permitted to or someone else had pulled her blouse back up to where modesty dictated it belonged.

Although she was tied to the whipping post, it didn't look as if anyone had been cruel enough to inflict that torture on her. Yet. Given the set of manacles the smith was fashioning, I could only wonder what the extent of her punishment might be.

"Gwen." I wrapped my fingers about the hilt of my knife and started forward. A restraining hand on my arm stopped me midstep. I turned my head. My entire range of vision was filled with a hairy, sweat-glistened chest. I looked up and up until I could clearly see the smith's face.

"No. It is her punishment." Devon spat upon the ground.

My stomach churned. *For seeking out the touch of another woman. Damn.* I'd forgotten that although love between women was an acceptable practice in many areas, there were still some remote regions that weren't as tolerant.

"Pig-girl!"

Three youths ran out into the street. In their hands, they held dripping tomatoes. Each one took turns shouting and throwing their tomatoes at Gwen. The first one missed completely. The second bounced harmlessly against her skirt before falling to the ground.

The third connected, splattering against her cheek. Gwen's head went to the side with the impact. Red juice ran down her face.

"Hey." Once again, I tried rushing forward, but found myself jerked to a halt by the smith's restraining grip.

"How can you stand by and watch them do that to her?" I craned my neck and looked up at the smith.

"Not my business. Mine is to have these shackles ready by tomorrow. Not an outsider's business, either."

Meaning me.

"Pig-girl!"

I turned in time to see a tossed tomato hit Gwen squarely between the eyes and do a slow roll down her face. With as much dignity as possible she stood up as straight as her confinement would allow and held her chin defiantly high.

"What about her family?" I asked in exasperation as I tried to shake off the smith's grip.

"She's brought shame enough to their doorstep."

I frowned, thinking that was unlikely considering her elder sister was a tavern whore. I ceased my struggling against Devon's restraining hand. As soon as I did, I felt his grip relax, even if it did not fall away completely.

"You can't help her. Her mother can't, even if she wanted." There was a softer tone to his voice. "He can't, either."

I turned to see someone run out into the street. I recognized him as the pockmarked lad from the tavern. His feathered cap fell from his head as he chased after the boys.

"Stop that. Stop that this instant."

One of the boys ran past the lad and bent low, snatching up the feathered cap from the ground. He turned, circling back around. His two friends joined him, completing a circle around the older youth. They tossed the cap back and forth, keeping it away from him as he reached for it.

"Stop that. Give it." The lad pulled his knife and brandished it in the air. Even from a distance, it was clear that his hand was shaking.

"Who is that?" I asked the smith.

"Magistrate's boy, Gerald."

The ruffians didn't look intimidated by Gerald or his knife. Nevertheless, one of them threw his cap back at him, hitting him squarely in the chest with it. They laughed as Gerald juggled to catch his cap. Both his hat and knife fell to the ground at his feet.

He bent to pick up his possessions. Laughing and jeering at Gerald, the trio of ruffians turned and looked around, as if checking for an audience. I met the tallest one's gaze straight on. One of the boys moved in closer, and it looked to me as if he meant to kick the magistrate's son in the face.

Still mindful of the blacksmith at my back, I didn't try to rush in. Instead, I slowly reached up, as if to casually stretch. My fingers brushed against the pommel of one of my swords.

The boy whose attention I'd caught suddenly raced over and pushed the second boy. All three turned to look at me. I leveled my gaze, fixing them with a cold stare. As expected, they bolted.

"Pig-girl! Your mother's a sow!" They taunted as they circled once around the whipping post before running off down the street.

Gerald picked up his knife, tucking it into his belt. He turned round and round in circles, as if not realizing the boys had run off. He dusted off his cap and put it back on top of his head. The feathered plume hung limply, listing to the side, the tip repeatedly brushing against his cheek. He kept shooing it away from his face in agitation.

I watched as he tripped while stepping up onto the platform. He approached Gwen the way I'd approach a skittish mare. Keeping his eyes on her, he bent at the knees, lifting a ladle out of a water bucket. He stepped closer.

Gwen licked her lips. He held out the ladle with both hands. She visibly swallowed and parted her lips. Water dribbled off the ladle and ran in rivulets down her chin and throat.

I found myself swallowing in time with Gwen. I felt a gnawing sensation in my gut. In spite of the maiden coming on to me, and surely knowing full well what the consequences for her actions could mean, I still felt responsible...at least partially so...for her current predicament.

"I'll fix this, Gwen. I'll make it right," I vowed in a low voice. This time, when I tried to walk away, the blacksmith didn't restrain me.

†

It wasn't difficult to find the tract of land owned by Gwendolyn's family. The cruel taunts from the local boys had pointed me in the right direction of a pig farm. Theirs was the third one I visited.

The pigsty had a shed made of stone, with a small forecourt for feeding. Despite the size of the pen, I saw only two grown pigs. Unlike the other farms I'd seen earlier, there weren't any squealing piglets running about.

The house was a cob and thatch, the walls made of a mixture of clay, gravel, and straw. The roof was straw and reed, with a single chimney. In spite of the spring warmth, smoke wafted up from the cooking fire kept continuously burning in the hearth.

I stood in one corner of the kitchen, trying to put as much distance between the unbearable heat of the hearth and myself. Gwen's mother was bent over a cooking pot, using a large wooden spoon to stir what smelled like rabbit stew.

"She's your daughter." I made the argument again.

"Through no fault of my own. Her father's, not mine."

Meredith, who with her excessive weight and unkempt appearance did resemble the sow the lads had compared her to, spat. *What was it with these villagers and their need to*

23

spit, anyway? Her spittle narrowly missed the cooking pot and sputtered into the flames.

"She's your flesh and blood. You can't turn your back on her."

"Always was her father's favorite. He let her tag along everywhere; never made her stay with me to tend the house." Again, a giant blob of spittle went sailing into the cooking fire. "Now he's gone. Gone and left me with a blight on the livestock, a shack in need of repairs, and three more younger than her to care after."

"You didn't want a husband and children."

It wasn't much of a guess on my part. It was clear that was how things worked in these parts. As soon as a girl was of age, she got married, settled down, and had children. Sons were raised to own land, livestock, and women. Daughters were raised to cook, clean, and have children to keep the cycle going.

"Don't punish Gwen for not wanting that, either," I said. "Let her have the chance to make her own choices in life."

Meredith didn't say anything for a long time. She stared into her pot, idly stirring her stew. At long last, she sat the spoon on a stone beside the hearth.

"Too late for that." Her voice was barely above a whisper.

"It's not. She's in the main square. Go get her. Bring her home."

"Naw, couldn't do that. They'd just come for her again tomorrow."

"What? Why?"

"They need her for the offering to the ogre."

"Offering...to...an ogre?" That churning sensation in my gut was back.

"Monster showed up about three nights ago, demanding a virgin by the next full moon."

Ogres are a solitary, dwindling breed, not given to much

contact with other races. As such, their grasp of languages, human in particular, is rudimentary. Primitive beasts, they dwell in dark, dank places and abhor the light of day. Creatures of the night, they live by the lunar cycle.

I frowned. The next full moon was tomorrow eve. That meant the villagers had at least two days in which they could have taken action.

As if sensing my thoughts, Meredith said, "Nearest town with a fighting militia is a twelve- day ride from here. Group of menfolk went off up into the hills, tracking it. None of 'em came back. Filthy beast got 'em all." This time, I didn't fault Meredith for spitting into the hearth. "Magistrate said we couldn't afford to try again; that it made more sense to give up one girl than all our men."

"Don't tell me." It wasn't the first time I'd heard this tale. "The magistrate organized a lottery with the names of all the eligible girls. Your daughter was the one picked, wasn't she?"

"Naw, no lottery. Magistrate offered money outright for anyone willing to put up their daughter." Meredith was grinning from ear to ear and there was a gleam in her eye. "Got five hundred gold coins for her."

I ground my teeth in anger.

"The ogre may be a beast, but you're the real monster."

†

"You never thought to mention you're a virgin?" My jaw was clenched so tight my teeth hurt. "Better yet, that you're a virgin offering for an ogre?"

"Would you please lower your voice?"

Gwen frantically looked around as though embarrassed that I would be overheard. I felt several sets of eyes staring from the cover of late afternoon shadows. Thing was, I didn't care. Let the entire village watch.

25

"Why?" I yelled even louder as Gwen looked like she wanted to crawl under a rock and die. "Everyone here already knows. *Everyone* except me, that is."

"Bodhi, please believe me. I didn't want to involve you in this."

To her credit, there was a pleading look in her eyes and sincerity in her voice. Problem was, I wasn't ready to hear it.

"You didn't want to involve me? How did you expect me to bed you without being at least a little bit involved in the process? I seem to recall being a participant."

The maiden rolled her eyes and let out an exasperated huff that had her hair lifting off her forehead.

"This isn't about you, Bodhi."

"You don't think so? You made me look a fool."

"I think it's more about me." Even with her hands bound together by rope, she managed a gesture that encompassed her entire body from her feet up. "Virgin sacrifice and all, remember?"

"Now that I know, it's not something I'll soon forget." I let out a heated breath. "You should have told me you were in distress."

"As if I were some sort of helpless damsel that needs rescuing by a good-looking, muscle-bound hero?"

"Clearly."

I gave an open-handed gesture that indicated her current, bound state. Then, I turned around in a slow circle, indicating my two swords, my knife, and my dagger to prove how well armed I was.

Her eyes flashed and her nostrils flared at what she no doubt perceived to be an insult instead of simple fact.

"I won't ask you to die for me."

"Good, because I wouldn't save you now if *my* life depended on it."

"Fine." She balled her fist and stamped her foot.

"Fine."

I stepped off the platform and into the stirrup hanging from my saddle. Palms braced on the pommel, I easily pulled myself up. Holding the reins tight in my hands, I held the horse steady long enough for me to send her a final glare. Then, I spat at the ground and rode away.

Chapter Three

—reason everyone in that village spits so much. Women drive 'em to it.

I was still mad enough to curse and spit. In my anger, I held too tight a grip on the reins, an action that my mare protested by fitfully shaking her head from side to side. I loosened my grip, allowing her to navigate the road as she saw fit.

The road was in ill repair, lined with deep ruts and littered with rocks. It curved ever north, leading up through a forest and into foothills blanketed with boulders. In the distance, the snowcapped peaks of a mountain range were just visible.

I had high hopes that the climate beyond those mountains would be far cooler than that of the valleys I'd been traveling through. Barely spring, and already the heat in the south was stifling.

From the distance of the peaks, I judged there were still many days of traveling until we reached the mountains. It was fast approaching dusk now, but my horse had already put miles and miles of countryside between us and that village and...*that damned, stubborn, hardheaded, beautiful...*

Beautiful? How did that thought creep into my head? I blew out a resigned sigh. There was no use denying it, not even to myself. Gwendolyn the maiden was beautiful. I'd desired her from almost the first heartbeat I saw her.

She'd made me look the fool. Worse, she'd hurt my pride. That was what stung the most. An injury from a sword might bleed, but wounded pride scarred.

Why wouldn't she simply ask for my help? Was it because I'm a swordswoman and not some hulking barbarian with a lion skin cloak and a club? Did she think because I was a woman that made me less capable of being a hero?

I shook my head. That made no sense. Gwendolyn was also a woman. From what I could tell, a brave, smart, strong-willed woman that didn't seem at all put off by the knowledge that I was a sword-wielding member of the fairer sex.

Damn. Had I been completely wrong in my judgment of her? It seemed ever since I arrived in her village, I'd misjudged situation after situation. First, I accused her of being a tavern whore. Then, I leapt to the conclusion that the villagers were punishing her for the act of making love with one of her own sex.

I'd fared no better in my assessment of her mother. I'd thought the poor woman was struggling to hold her life together after her worthless husband had abandoned her with more hungry mouths than she could feed. Then, come to find out she'd traded her daughter's life for five hundred gold coins.

I'd half-expected to learn that Gwen had turned herself in for the reward money in some misguided attempt to provide for the rest of her family. I'd only known her for a few candlemarks, but it struck me as the sort of thing Gwendolyn might do. Particularly if she thought she could help others through her sacrifice; and prove her independence in the process.

It fit in with what she had said to me during our argument.

"I won't ask you to die for me."

Not *I won't ask you to fight for me.*

Aw, damn. I pulled up on the reins and turned my horse south.

✝

It was full-on night and it appeared as if the villagers had retired to bed. *Well, why wouldn't they sleep soundly? Their virgin sacrifice was secure and they were safe from the ogre's wrath.*

The faint red glow of the blacksmith's furnace, coupled with the rhythmic beat of a hammer, revealed that Devon was still at his craft. On Gwen's chains, apparently, as she was still tethered by rope and not iron.

"Your father was one of the men that died trying to fight the ogre, wasn't he?" I kept my voice lowered so as not to draw the blacksmith's attention.

She averted her gaze. I gripped her jaw, applying enough pressure with my fingers to turn her head so she was looking at me.

"He was, wasn't he?"

Tears brimming, she nodded. I imagined it wasn't easy for her to allow me to see her so vulnerable. This time, I wasn't referring to the rope or the whipping post.

"I begged him to allow me to go," she confessed in a near whisper. "We used to go hunting together. I'm a fair shot. I could have helped, but he refused me."

"Good thing or you'd be dead now."

I caught her look of indignation and exhaled loudly.

"I don't mean it as a slight against you. I'm sure you're good. Ogres are tough-skinned, really only vulnerable in three places. The eyes, the throat, and their...um..." I pointed toward my crotch as reference. "An arrow wouldn't get the job done. It'd take a sword. A big one."

"Like the one you have."

Even though we were keeping our voices to a whisper, there was still an edge to her words that was as sharp as any of my blades.

"I'm not claiming I could kill an ogre, even with both my swords." I drew my dagger.

"What are you doing?" Her eyes went wide and she moved as far away from me as her bindings would allow.

I reached forward, catching the end of the rope tied to the post. I hooked my dagger beneath the hemp and began sawing. My sword would have done the job quicker, but whoever had tied her hadn't left enough slack to safely allow a clean stroke. In this case, faster might do more harm than good.

"What you should have done days ago; getting you the blazes out of this village."

"Because that wasn't my first thought as soon as I was *chosen*? I hadn't even gotten a mile away before I ran into the magistrate's goons."

"There aren't any sentries on the road now." *Because they believe she's trussed up like a sacrificial lamb.* "I would've helped you. I would have fought for you and gotten you safely away if you'd only asked."

"I tried. In the tavern, I asked if you would be on your way soon."

I lifted my blade away from the rope and looked at her in complete incomprehension.

"Remember, I encouraged you to continue your travels while there was still daylight?"

That did have a familiar ring. "How was I to know? You should have been plainer in your meaning."

"With the entire village watching every move I made? You saw how quickly Cathryn was upon me when I joined you. Then, right in front of her, you had the audacity to ask me to your bed."

"As I recall, fair Gwendolyn, it was you that asked me."

My blade cut through the rope, freeing her from the post. I reached for her bound wrists. Inserting the tip of my dagger between two knots, I worked to loosen her restraints. The position was awkward, forcing me to bend low, the top of my head brushing against her bosom as I struggled to cut through bonds and not flesh.

"Naturally, that's the part of our conversation you remember. I don't know why I expected you'd be gallant and charming."

I paused from my work to blink up at her. She was staring down at me, her eyes focused on a place below my neck. Normally, I'd be flattered. Given Gwen's tone, however, I was positive she wasn't flirting. I frowned and looked down, following her line of sight.

Of course, the uniform. Her eyes narrowed as she stared at my shoulders and the faded fabric where my epaulets were missing. She released a sigh indicative that she'd just realized I'd been stripped of my rank long ago.

"Ah. As with you, things are not always as they seem." I'd intended it as a light jest, but my words came out flat. "If it gives you comfort, many a maid has accused me of possessing both those traits."

"Oh! You are insufferable."

"Me?" Both my eyebrows rose as I turned and pointed the dagger tip at myself. "Insufferable? You—"

"You—"

"Hey, you there. Stop."

We both turned our heads in the direction the shout had come from. The blacksmith was rushing toward us, his hammer clutched in both beefy hands. All about, windows were illuminated as villagers were awakened by the shouts.

I rushed forward, catching Gwen about her midsection. She squawked as I lifted her onto my shoulder.

"Put me down. I don't need your help to walk."

"Escape now. Argue later," I said.

Fists full of fabric, sight obscured by brown tresses, I ran across the platform. I dumped her across the saddle and swatted my horse's rump. I ran alongside, hooking my foot into the stirrup and swinging up into the saddle on the move.

One hand on the reins, the other pressed firmly against Gwen's spine, I spurred my horse into a gallop.

As we rode away, the village bell rang, raising the alarm. Shouts and curses filled the air. An equal amount of these were from the village at my back and the maiden sprawled across the saddle in front of me. I tried not to think about the solid feel of her pressed against my thighs as I rode. Heart hammering in my chest, I instead tried to focus on the sound of the thundering hooves behind us that told of our pursuit.

†

Only a fool or someone on the run travels at night.

My words came back to bite me. Had her shoes been replaced, as I'd intended, I'm certain my horse could have outrun our pursuers. As it was, she lost her footing on one of the many rocks littering the road. The chase was short-lived.

As was the fight. I scrambled to my feet as the first horse drew near. A glance over my shoulder revealed Gwen picking herself up off the ground. She'd landed hard, unable to break her fall due to her bound hands, but she appeared to be mostly unharmed. I drew my dagger, tossing it so the tip stuck in the ground at her feet. She bent, retrieving the weapon, holding it with both hands.

I reached up behind my shoulder with my left hand and smoothly drew my sword. As the first man approached, I ran through a series of drills designed to both limber my wrist and intimidate my opponent.

It worked. He hesitated, backing off until the rest of his friends dismounted and joined him. Together, they found their courage. A half-dozen of them, they approached en masse.

I drew my second sword. I normally only wield one, but just the sight of someone holding two usually gives most foes pause. A slice, a thrust, and a boot to someone's chest had the villagers backing off, no doubt reconsidering their theory about strength in numbers.

"Hold."

I turned to see two men holding Gwendolyn between them, their large hands restraining her by her upper arms. One of them had blood spewing from his nose, the other from a slice on his arm.

The blade of my dagger was at Gwen's throat. Despite that, I could see the tension in her upper body. She was ready to fight, given another chance.

"Surrender or she dies."

I held my ground. On either side of me, I could see the men fanning out so they flanked me. My teeth bit into my bottom lip as I contemplated my chances. I was certain I could take them. After all, they were only poorly armed villagers while I was a trained fighter.

If it'd been just about me, I would take the risk. But, the two men holding Gwen and the knife to her throat—

"Bodhi, no. Kill me and they'll have no offering for the ogre."

Her words were wise. She either faced death now at the hands of a mob or tomorrow eve beneath the ogre's sharp teeth. *Which death was the more merciful?*

It was a choice I couldn't make. In my indecision, the blacksmith rushed forward and swung his hammer at my temple.

Chapter Four

I moaned and rolled over. My movement scattered the rushes spread about on the floor and I heard a rustling sound. Something midsized and fur-covered scurried across the room and into a hidey-hole in the wall. Beady eyes blinked and peered out at me from the shadows.

I braced my weight on the palms of my hands, fingers flexing into the dirt floor. A groan escaped my lips as I pushed myself up into a sitting position. My skull throbbed as if it would split open and when I placed a hand to my head I felt matted blood. Still, I considered myself lucky. If the blacksmith hadn't struck a glancing blow, I wouldn't be feeling anything at all.

Sunlight streamed in through cracks in the daub walls and I recognized the interior as that of the blacksmith's shop. My swords were sheathed in their twin harnesses and hanging from a peg on a wall. My knife and dagger rested on a workbench. Not that it did me any good if I couldn't reach them. My wrists were manacled, heavy chain running from the cuffs to an iron ring fixed to the wall.

A door swung open and I held up both hands to shield my eyes from the bright sunlight. A set of boots crossed the threshold, their owner tripping on the uneven surface of the floor. A tray of food went flying and a pitcher of water went sailing as the lad fell forward.

I surged to my feet and rushed him. At five paces, the slack went out of my chain and I was jerked to a halt. I turned and grasped the chain in both hands and tugged as hard as I could. My boots slid, unable to find purchase on the rushes and I went down, hitting the packed dirt floor.

As I started to get up again, I saw the tip of a blade pointed at my nose. I looked up, recognizing the lad from the tavern. Bits of dirt, straw, and food were stuck to his clothing and chin. His feathered cap was on his head, the plume crushed from his fall. He held his knife at arm's length, using a double-handed grip. Both his hands and his knees were shaking profusely.

"Take another step and I'll…I'll cut you," he said.

I held both my palms up as I slowly climbed to my feet. He shuffled his feet in the straw, but seemed to relax as he realized I had no weapon. I reached out and plucked his knife from his grasp.

Just as I turned the knife on its owner, something blotted out the sunlight in the room.

"Gerald, boy? You done feeding that—" Devon stopped, his big bulk blocking the doorway.

Damn. Spirits knew I could take the boy, even with both hands chained. The blacksmith, though, was something else entirely. I drew myself to an at-ease position.

Gerald took two quick steps forward and snatched his weapon out of my hand. He scurried across the floor, much like the mouse had done. Standing at the blacksmith's side, he regained much of his courage, and stood with the blade of his knife pointed in my direction.

"No more of that nonsense out of you," Devon said, looking me straight in the eyes. "You won't be harmed. We got no quarrel with the guard."

I nearly smirked. Like I said before, the uniform of the guard was unmistakable. Simply wearing it had saved my neck more than once.

"Clean that slop up. My shop isn't a pigsty." He cuffed Gerald, knocking the cap from his head.

Gerald dropped to his knees. He picked up his soiled cap, swatted it against his thigh to dust it off, and tucked it and his knife beneath his belt. He retrieved the wooden bowl he'd dropped and began scrapping it along the floor, indiscriminately picking up food, rushes, and dirt as he went.

"Gw—" My voice cracked. I swallowed against the

dryness in my mouth. "What've you done with Gwen?"

"She's being prepared."

"Prepared?"

"For the offering. You've been unconscious all night and morning. It's well past midday. Wagon will be heading up into the hills soon."

Gerald abruptly stopped scooping the mess up. His face turned red and his entire body stiffened. Knuckles clenched white as he closed a hand about the hilt of his knife.

"You're sending an innocent girl to her death," I said.

"What else can we do? You didn't hear the ogre's demands. It's either one virgin or our entire village."

"Fight."

"We tried that. We've already lost too many. If we try again, it may kill all of us in retaliation."

"So, you sacrifice the maiden and appease the ogre. What happens when he decides he wants another? And another after that?"

Gerald gasped and looked up at the blacksmith. Devon averted his gaze and downed his head.

"And, I'm to be released unharmed?" I asked. With luck, I could guilt him into letting me go in time to intercept the wagon and save Gwen.

"Rest assured, the only reason you still breathe now is because the girl's virginity remains intact."

The voice came from the open doorway. The blacksmith moved aside to reveal an older man, balding and with a paunch. From his manner of dress, I knew him to be the magistrate.

"She's ready. Gerald, get that mess cleaned up, then hitch the horses, and then haul…" He jerked his thumb at me "…this one out to the wagon."

"Amos, you said we wouldn't harm the outsider. Consider what you're doing."

"I am, for all our sakes. She's right; the ogre will ask for another."

"By then, the militia might be here."

"We sent the rider three days ago. Might be that he'll be back with help before the ogre makes his next demand. Might not come at all." The magistrate looked at me. "Either way, we can't let her tell them what we've done."

"She's guard, Amos. We can't kill her."

"Of course we can't. But, the ogre can. Come on, it's getting late."

Oh, damn. Seemed this time, wearing the uniform did me no favors.

The magistrate clapped Devon on the arm and urged him out the door. He paused and looked back over his shoulder at the youth kneeling on the floor.

"Stop your dawdling, boy. There's work to be done."

The magistrate closed the door, leaving me alone with Gerald. The lad stayed perfectly still for many long heartbeats. The tray of slop was braced against his thighs. Suddenly, he let out a tiny wail and tossed the tray away. Food, straw, and dirt flew across the room, splattering the blacksmith's workbench.

Some of it managed to get me. I raised my chained hands, trying to wipe bits and pieces from my face and tunic.

"That has to stick in your gut."

He ignored me, so I tried again.

"Taking orders from the blacksmith. Being the magistrate's son, that should earn you some respect, some entitlement. You shouldn't be doing menial chores, like bringing meals to prisoners. Your dad lets everyone boss you around, doesn't he?"

"What do you know about it?" He swiped a hand at his eyes and the tears forming there.

"I saw the way those boys treated you in the square, when you were trying to help Gwen."

"Gwendolyn. You don't know her. It's Gwendolyn to

you, not Gwen."

"Gwendolyn." I could have argued the point, certain I'd gotten to know Gwen much better in one day than he had in a lifetime. "Too bad. You look like a likely enough lad."

"Likely enough for what?" Suspicion laced his voice.

"You know, just likely."

"No, what do you mean?" He stood up, dusted off his trousers, and came closer.

"You have free run of the blacksmith's shop." I made a point of looking around. "You could take the keys for Gwendolyn's manacles."

"Devon's got the only set and he needs 'em to lock the chains when he leaves Gwen." Gerald shook his head.

"What if you were to sneak them after? You could free the maiden, kill the ogre, and save the village. Wonder how they'd treat you then?"

Gerald got this far-off, dreamy look in his eyes that suggested he was thinking about just that. He gave a lovelorn sigh that left me with no doubt he was imagining how grateful his Gwendolyn would be. He abruptly blinked and shook his head.

"No. All those men died trying to slay the ogre. I can't do it."

He began backing away from me, shaking his head from side to side as he went. When he reached the door, he opened it, and stumbled backward, landing outside. He scrambled to his feet, dusted himself off, and closed the door, leaving me alone to await my fate.

✝

I didn't have long to wait. I was dragged by my chains from the blacksmith's shop and thrown into the back of a wagon. My shoulder took the brunt of the impact as I landed.

There were four horses flanking the wagon. I recognized

two of the riders as belonging to the mob that had chased and caught us the night before. The blacksmith sat atop a large beauty of a black horse, the size of which I'd only ever seen used in the cavalry. He wore a sword belted at his side. He also had both my swords; their harnesses hitched over one of his shoulders.

The magistrate, assisted by his son, hefted his massive bulk into the saddle. The horse stomped its hooves several times, as if in protest of the extra weight. He tightened his grip on the reins, gaining control over the animal before riding to the front.

A whip cracked and the wagon jostled forward. We rode through the village square, past the whipping post. The tavern patrons came outside, most of them still clutching their mugs in their hands. In the group of assembled onlookers, I clearly picked out the tavern keeper and Cathryn. The remaining villagers lined the side of the road, watching as we passed by. If Gwen's mother was somewhere in the crowd, I didn't see her.

Gwen was seated with her back to the driver's seat. Her wrists were manacled, the chain connecting them anchored to an eyelet fixed to a board in the bottom of the wagon. There was dried blood in a ring around her hands, no doubt from chafing caused by struggling against her bonds.

Gone was her peasant garb, replaced by a once-white bridal dress. The material was soiled and one sleeve was ripped, exposing her flesh from shoulder to elbow. Her head was bowed, her dark hair falling forward, hiding her face from view.

A wheel dipped into a rut, causing the whole wagon to shift. I fell forward, my chin slamming into Gwen's upper thigh. She made a mewling sound of protest and I looked up at her from my prone position. Her bottom lip was cut and swollen and one of her honey-brown eyes was framed in bruises.

My hand stretched out to her, my intention to touch her bruised cheek with my fingers. My reach fell short and I discovered that my chain had been shortened and attached to an eyelet on the opposite side of the wagon.

"Gwen, are you…"

She looked at me, the beginnings of a smirk on the curve of her lip as I realized the inanity of my question. Bound by chains, traveling in a cart, her destination to be an ogre's offering. *How could I possibly be about to ask her if she was well?*

Another jostling of the wagon had me rolling back the other way. This time, when I stopped, I pulled myself up into a sitting position.

"I don't understand. We've never had an ogre before. Why now?" Gwen asked.

Despite my chains, I managed a shrug.

"Ogres like solitude, but not cold weather. He probably wandered down from the mountains and found a cave to hibernate in for the winter. Now that warmer weather is here, he's awake and satisfying his carnal desires."

"But, why me? Look at Devon." Gwen's eyes followed the blacksmith as he rode past. "The ogre could make at least two meals out of him. Compared to Devon, I'm hardly a mouthful."

"I'd imagine it's like having a choice between an old goat and a tender lamb. Devon's hide is thick and leathery while yours—"

Someone cuffed me on the back of the head. I turned to see the magistrate drawing his hand back.

"No more talking. We only need the girl for the offering. You needn't be breathing when the ogre comes to eat you."

My mouth slammed shut, my teeth grinding together as I clenched my jaw. The iron manacles cut into my flesh as I balled my fists. If there'd been any way of reaching that balding, rotund man, I would have dragged him into the wagon and choked the life from him.

As it was, I was impotent in my rage. The magistrate laughed and spurred his horse into a trot. I turned and watched him move farther up in the procession that was climbing ever higher into the foothills.

I rode in silence, listening to the sounds of the horses' hooves, the low chatter of the wagon drivers, and the creaking of the wagon. We passed the place my horse had stumbled last night and the patch of ground where Gwen and I'd fought our attackers. It was another candlemark before we passed the distance I had reached yesterday afternoon before turning my mount around.

The incline of the road increased. Riders and wagon slowed with the difficulty of the terrain. The higher into the hills we traveled, the more rocks and boulders littered the path. No doubt, the spring thaw had softened the ground, contributing to landslides.

As we drew near a great mound of boulders, the wagon rolled to a stop. There was a crude marker placed against the stone. Ribbons were tied to sticks and twigs stuck into the ground. Flowers and hand-carved trinkets were scattered about.

The chatter of the wagon drivers fell away completely. Gwen gasped and tore her gaze away from the site where her father was buried. The rest of the trek was made in solemn silence.

†

We were in the ruins of an ancient temple. The cracked marble floor was covered in dirt and leaves. In the center of the temple, there was a series of wooden columns arranged in a semi-circle. They were of equal height, approximately eight feet tall and a distance of no more than three feet apart. It looked as if they may have once supported something.

Images of a great, ceremonial bowl that could have been filled with burning ash, or liquid, or even blood came to mind. Whatever it had been, it was long gone, leaving behind only the wooden framework. Of the remaining pillars, only three were still intact.

Gwen was already shackled to the middle column with her arms stretched high over her head. She hadn't been a willing sacrifice. She'd kicked and screamed and cursed from the heartbeat as they'd dragged her from the wagon. The magistrate, seemingly fearful of her attracting the ogre's attention before nightfall, clamped a hand over her mouth. She'd promptly bit him. Eventually, though, they'd gotten her properly shackled and the fight had gone out of her.

Then, it was my turn. I'd intended to fight as Gwen had, but they didn't take any chances with me. I was dragged from the wagon at swordpoint. The tip of the blade kept pressed against my throat the entire way; I was led to the nearest column.

I was shoved backward, the wood connecting between my shoulder blades as I hit the column. We were facing each other, my eyes meeting Gwen's. I had an impulse to reach out a hand to touch her cheek. We were so close, I'm sure I could have reached her.

Someone slapped my hands away. The action caused my chains to rattle, dispelling the moment.

"Let her go. Bodhi isn't involved in this."

"She was involved the instant you approached her," said the magistrate.

The blacksmith unlocked the chain from one of my manacles. He tossed the chain through an iron ring positioned near the top of the column and back down before fastening it to the manacle and locking it again. Before long, my arms were stretched over my head, the same as Gwen's.

As soon as I was secured in place, Devon lifted my sword harnesses from his shoulder.

"Devon, what are you about…?" The magistrate paused from sucking on the webbing of his hand and shot a look at the blacksmith.

"A soldier should never die without a weapon at their side."

The magistrate's mouth opened and I'm certain he'd intended to protest, but a steely look from the blacksmith had him choose his words differently.

"Be quick about it, then. I want to be well away from here before the sun goes down."

Devon breathed heavily, but didn't waste further time arguing with the magistrate. He stepped in front of me, buckling and fastening both harnesses in place. I felt the familiar weight of my dual swords at my back.

The wagon creaked as the drivers climbed onto the seat. A crack of the whip and they were headed back toward the path to the village. The other riders, including the magistrate, mounted up and trailed behind the wagon. The blacksmith turned to follow.

"Wait," I said. "What good is a weapon without the ability to wield it?"

Devon's back stiffened. He paused two steps from the column, but didn't turn around.

Maybe I asked for too much. "Please. At least leave my sword arm free."

This time, he did turn around. He walked the two steps back to me.

"And risk you escaping? I can't do that."

I cast an eye up at the rusted ring and the length of chain running through it.

"The column is too high. I can't get at a good angle. I'd slice my arm off before I ever cut through the chain."

"When the ogre comes, hacking off your arm may seem like a better option."

"Give me a fighting chance. At best, I'll defeat the ogre.

At worst, I'll give it pause to think about coming to your village and demanding another sacrifice. I'm asking you, allow me to die with my sword in my hand."

He huffed loudly and looked around. The wagon was just disappearing from view, but the mounted riders were still within sight.

He took the ring of keys from his belt and lifted his arms above my head. I heard the *click* as one of my manacles was unlocked. As he stepped back, I made certain to keep both arms raised in case anyone turned to look.

†

Sweat dripped from my hair, getting in my eyes as I squinted up at the darkening sky. My breathing was ragged and I could hear my heart pounding in my ears. The sword in my hand grew heavier with each swing.

"Damn."

Blood ran from the slice on my left arm. I'd told the blacksmith the truth about cutting through my arm long before I'd severed the chain. That's why I'd been hacking at the wooden pillar instead. I'd hoped the wood might be weakened by age and the elements. That, and it was a larger target than the chains.

I cursed as I nicked my arm again. I wasn't doing myself any favors. *Much like the blacksmith.* I'm sure Devon meant well and he probably thought he'd done me a great service by unlocking one of my manacles. I just wished he wouldn't have chosen the one fastened about my right wrist.

He couldn't have known that I'm left-handed. Not many sword wielders are. Usually, that works out to my advantage. Most opponents don't know how to compensate for a left-handed fighter. Like everything else since I'd rode into Gwen's village, things that normally aided me seemed to be working against me here.

Maybe the whole damned village is cursed. I swung and hit the column. A shard of wood broke off beneath my strike. The fragment flew, hitting me in the face. *Maybe it's only me that's cursed.*

"Bodhi, stop. You'll hurt yourself."

"Not as badly as your ogre will."

I took another swing before lowering my sword. The angle was just too awkward and my weapon had grown too heavy. I thrust the blade deep into the ground so that the sword remained standing upright within easy reach. Panting heavily, I rested my back against the column and closed my eyes.

"Bodhi, I'm sorry. I didn't know they'd do this to you. I was only trying to find a way of saving myself."

I opened my eyes and leveled a look at Gwen. She was shivering. It was cooler up in the hills, even with the shelter of the forest surrounding us. It'd get cooler still as the sun set. With the wind blowing against my sweat-soaked hair and flesh, I felt the chill, too. Fortunately, though, I wasn't clad in a lightweight bridal dress.

A very thin dress, I thought, as my eyes locked upon two stiff nipples tenting the material of her gown. My mouth went dry as I remembered how they'd felt upon my tongue. Hair disheveled, bruises upon her face, her dress soiled and torn...and still, I wanted her.

"About that; you do realize you could have fixed everything with a quick tumble from some local lad, don't you?"

I'd meant it as a jest to dispel some of the tension. I'd even said it with a smile. There wasn't a hint of humor in my voice, though. From the look she shot me, I could tell she knew it was no laughing matter. Although, I don't know if she realized how serious I really was.

"You think any of them would have risked touching me, knowing my fate?"

"A youth will risk much if he's randy enough. I think Gerald would, if you asked."

"Ewww." Gwen grimaced. "Not even if he was a Geraldine."

"If not a local lad, I'm sure you could have had your go at any number of wayward travelers."

"In case you didn't notice, Chatham isn't on a main road to anywhere, Bodhi. You're the first traveler to come along in at least a fortnight and before now, I didn't need to *have a go* at anyone."

"Is that why you chose me; because you were desperate and out of options and I was the first fool to come along? It didn't matter to you who I was, did it?"

"Of course it mattered. You think I didn't notice the way you look—the blond hair, the blue eyes, and those dimples?"

In spite of the hopelessness of our situation, I felt my lips curve up.

"You don't have to be so smug about it," Gwen said.

"I'm not being smug."

"Why are you smiling, then?"

"Because I was right. I knew you were interested."

"What?"

"When you were staring at me across the tavern, I knew you were interested."

"Only in asking you to leave and taking me with you."

"You couldn't take your eyes off me."

"As you said, I was desperate and you were my last option. I hadn't even thought of...of..." Her cheeks burned bright red "...until you asked me to your bed."

"You asked me," I reminded her. "You desired me, then. You desire me now."

Her mouth dropped open and her eyes widened.

"What? I did not. I do not," she said.

I grinned, knowing this time, I did look smug.

"Gwen, you may be inexperienced, but I'm not. I know

your body better than you. The shallow breathing, the flush on your cheeks, and the look in your eyes all work against you to give your desires away." My gaze dropped away from her face.

Gwen's eyes followed my line of sight to her breasts and further proof of her arousal. She struggled against her chains and I'm certain if she could, she would have covered herself with her hands. As it was, she could do nothing to shield herself from my stare. She let loose an exasperated breath and I couldn't help but see the way her chest rose and fell with the exhalation.

"Gwen, the solution to your problem is simple." My voice was husky with desire. "The reach of my chain is sufficient. Once I've had you, no one, not even a half-blind ogre would doubt that I've taken you from maiden to woman—"

"Oh! Your arrogance knows no bounds."

"Is it arrogance to speak the truth?"

"Humph!" She turned her head away. Then, as if she could feel my eyes upon her, she turned so that her bosom was no longer in my direct line of sight.

Chapter Five

"Take me."

"What?" I asked, lowering my sword and turning around.

Dusk was upon us and the shadows were lengthening. Even though we were in close proximity, I couldn't clearly read her expression. However, her silhouette was unmistakable. She was standing up straight, her breasts jutting forward, and her chin defiantly tilted.

"You heard me. Take me. Deflower me. Defile me. However you wish to call it."

"I thought you found me to be arrogant."

"I do. You are. You're also cocky, conceited, and jaded."

"We've only just met and already you think you know me well enough to judge me? Bugger you."

"Add *rude* to the list of your traits."

Whether she was jesting or completely serious, I couldn't tell in the waning light.

"Gwen, I may be bold and rude, but you're hardly what I'd term sweet and innocent." I gripped the hilt of my sword, ready to put an end to this conversation and return to my work.

"Bodhi, I didn't fall head over heels for you at first sight and you weren't in that tavern looking for anything beyond a quick tumble. Let's not fool ourselves; neither of us is in love. At this point, we probably don't even like each other very much. Even though it wasn't what I'd originally intended when I set out to save myself..." She stopped speaking and I could hear the leaves rustling on the marble floor as she shuffled her feet. "If sacrificing my virginity is the alternative to being an ogre's offering, I'm willing to allow you to take what you want."

"You're willing to allow me?" I snorted. "Are you certain that's in keeping with your virtuous standards, fair maiden?"

"Night is upon us, Bodhi, and we haven't the time for niceties." She huffed and even though I couldn't see her face, I imagined she was rolling her eyes. "Very well. When you returned for me, you proved that you were also noble and selfless. Bodhi, would you do me the honor of taking my virginity?"

"You sure?" I asked, my voice laden with suspicion.

"Well, I don't see any other heroes rushing to my rescue, do you?"

If my pride demanded I put up the slightest bit of resistance, I didn't pay it any heed. I closed the distance between us. With my left hand and arm stretched behind me and my body turned at an awkward angle, I found just enough length in my chain to reach her.

I reached out, grabbing her behind the head with my right hand and pulling her to me for a bruising kiss. She gasped and her mouth opened beneath mine. My tongue dipped deep inside, tasting her wet heat before withdrawing.

My lips were everywhere—her ear, her cheek, and at the line of her jaw. She tilted her head back and I had access to her neck. I licked, nipped, and sucked at her pulse point. My tongue slathered over the cut left by the knife at her throat and she gasped sharply in reaction.

I lowered my head, kissing my way down her bare neck to her cleavage. I kissed and licked at the flesh left exposed by her bridal gown. My fingers closed on the bodice, determined to tug the garment lower so I could reach her hardened nipples.

"Bodhi. Bodhi."

"Gwen," I murmured in response.

"Bodhi."

This time, I recognized something other than passion in

her voice. There was ardor, of course, but there was also a sound of urgency, as if she were demanding my attention. I drew back. Her flesh shimmered with moisture from my kisses and my fingertips were still hooked within her bodice. I blinked at her, my breath ragged and showing in heated puffs upon the cool air.

"Bodhi, what are you doing?" She was also short of breath and her bosom heaved with each word she spoke.

"Um, I think that would be rather obvious."

"Well, yes, but…"

Oh. "I want to make certain your body is ready for me."

"Believe me, Bodhi, I'm as ready as I'm going to be."

"Your first time," I husked, as my hand cupped her breast, "should be special."

"If I don't die, that'll be special enough."

In a move that surprised me, she rocked her hips, causing her thighs to bump against me. I surged forward, pressing her back against the column. The side of my boot kicked against her shoe, nudging her feet apart.

I bunched the hem of her gown in my hand, roughly shoving it up. My calloused palm traveled up a smooth inner thigh. Fingertips felt moisture as I came into contact with the first downy fine wisps of hair. Gwen groaned as I cupped her fully.

She was drenched. My fingers were soaked with her arousal as I stroked her open. My fingertip brushed against her swollen bundle of nerves and she jerked beneath my touch.

I slipped a finger inside, exploring her heat and moisture. *She's so hot. And, wet.* Her muscles contracted, squeezing about my finger. *And, oh so tight.* I thrust deeply, taking her in one, smooth stroke.

Gwen gasped sharply. Her head was thrown back, her eyes closed, and her lips parted. Her breathing was harsh and ragged and she was moaning incoherently. The scent of her arousal filled the air, invading my nostrils. I inhaled deeply, breathing her in. She rode my fingers until her inner muscles clenched about my digits, she let out a long wail, and collapsed against me.

†

I was leaning with my back against my column, legs stretched in front of me, and my feet crossed at the ankles. My hand rested on the hilt of my sword. If it weren't for the chain keeping my manacled left hand stretched high above my head, I might have been perfectly content.

Except for the fact that night was upon us, the moon was full in the sky, and somewhere, a hungry ogre was waking up and coming in search of his meal.

"Well, that wasn't as bad as I thought it'd be."

"Told you it'd be better if we took our time. Don't think I'm rude for asking, Gwen, but you aren't unattractive. So, how is it you managed to remain a maiden for so long? You must have had offers?"

"Bodhi, you? Rude? Never." Gwen's laughter echoed in the darkness. "You were right earlier when you derided my virtuous standards. There was a time when being a virgin was something special. Being a good girl means the groom will pay more for the bridal purchase. You've heard the saying, *Why pay for the cow if you can get the milk for free?* Same principle applies to maidens."

"Given that, I'm surprised your mother didn't marry you off as soon as you were of age."

"I think she wanted to, especially after what happened with Cathryn. She was scared to death that I'd have a quick tumble in the hay and be as worthless a bride as my sister." Gwen fell silent for a time. When she spoke again, it was in a quieter voice. "My father wouldn't allow it, though. He loved me, even if I turned out wrong."

"Wrong? What do you mean, wrong? I didn't notice you hiding a dragon's tail beneath that wedding gown."

"No, no dragon's tail, Bodhi."

This time, Gwen's laugh sounded forced. She dropped her voice and I had to strain to hear what she said next.

"You know, it's not natural for a good maiden to…like another maiden in that way."

"It's more natural than you might think, Gwen. You'd be amazed at how many women I know that prefer the company of other women."

"Other women, Bodhi, or just you?"

"Perhaps it is just me they find irresistible." I could tell that Gwen was troubled, and this time, I didn't mind playing the fool for her. It pleased me when I heard her snort and chuckle. "You don't kiss like any virgin I've ever known. I take it you discovered another maiden to practice with?"

"The magistrate's niece came for a visit one summer. We became fast friends and went swimming together every day. My father stumbled upon us kissing down by the stream."

"Good thing it wasn't the magistrate," I said.

"True. Papa wasn't mad at me, but he said it could never happen again. After that, he was even more supportive in not accepting any suitor as being good enough."

"You were fortunate to have such an understanding parent. Um, Gwen, about your father and the others?" I hesitated, unsure if I should tell her. After all, the ogre was coming for us, what difference did it make?

"You don't think the ogre killed them, do you?" she asked.

"Uh, no. It looked like there was a rockslide and they were unable to get away before they were crushed. It may be that it's the spring thaw, and not the ogre, that's to blame. But, how did you know?"

"There weren't any ogre tracks at the site," Gwen said.

I thought about what Gwen had said about hunting with her father. Perhaps she really was a good hunter. I hadn't noticed that there were no tracks. I had, however, noticed the abundance of ogre tracks when we arrived at the temple. Clearly, the ruins were a favorite stomping ground of his.

A bush rustled. A twig snapped.

"Bodhi?" came Gwen's whisper.

"I heard it too."

I tilted my head, listening to the sounds of the night and the forest. Leaves crackled and brush crunched underfoot. I strained my eyes, thinking I saw a deeper patch of shadow moving amongst the trees. I followed the beast's progress by the noises it made.

There was the sound of heavy breathing, growing nearer. Something came stumbling out of the forest and tripped in the rut made by the wagon's wheels.

"Gwen? Gwendolyn, are you there?"

"Gerald?" we both asked at once.

"Yes, it's me. Hold on."

Flint repeatedly clicked, causing an impressive spray of sparks. His breathing was labored with agitated huffs as he had trouble getting the sparks to catch. There was a tiny flame and it looked as if Gerald had succeeded—until a tiny gust of wind blew across the clearing. The flame died out. In the darkness, the combined sounds of Gerald's muttered curses, frustrated breathing, and the flint clicking echoed loudly.

At last, the torch flared up, revealing pudgy-cheeked, pockmarked, feather-capped Gerald. He stood there, holding the torch high, and staring at Gwen with a dopey expression on his face.

"Gerald, what are you doing here?" asked Gwen.

"Um, saving you. That's right. I'm rescuing you from the ogre and taking you away from here."

He patted his tunic and britches, as if he were searching

for something. At last, his palm patted against the coin purse tied at his waist and he smiled. He worked the drawstrings loose with the hand that wasn't holding the torch and after much struggling, managed to pull a wrought-iron ring from the pouch. He victoriously held the ring aloft, a set of keys dangling from it, and grinned so wide that all his teeth showed.

"Thank the spirits. Quick, lad, set me free." I was certain I heard something else rustling through the underbrush.

Gerald turned and looked at me as if just now remembering I'd been taken along with Gwen. He made a face, his nose scrunching up as he eyed me suspiciously.

"No."

"What?" My mouth dropped open. I couldn't have heard right.

"No. You said I could be the hero. That's what I'm here for, to save Gwen."

"You can save her. You can save us both, if you like. Just unchain me first."

He did the exact opposite of what I said and rushed to Gwen's side, stumbling over his own feet as he hurried. He jammed the base of his torch into a crack in the temple floor. He held out both hands, as if ready to catch the torch should it fall. Satisfied that it wasn't going anywhere, he stood upright and turned to face Gwen.

He stopped, standing unmoving as he stared up at Gwen.

"Gwen, are you hurt?"

Both Gwen's eyes and mine traveled down her frame, our gazes settling on the stains on the front of her gown.

"Uh, no. It's nothing," she said. We exchanged a look over Gerald's shoulder.

Gerald continued to stare and I wondered what thoughts were running through his addled mind.

"Gerald?" Gwen moved her arms, rattling her chains to get his attention.

"Huh? Oh. Right." He smiled sheepishly.

Gerald gripped the key ring tightly as he raised his arms. It didn't escape my notice that his hands brushed over Gwen's breasts as he did so. Nor that he felt the need to stand nearly on top of her, his body pressed against hers as he stretched to reach her manacles.

It seemed as if it took forever for him to insert the key and unlock that first manacle. As her wrist fell free, he caught her arm in his grasp and lowered it. His hand closed about her wrist, his fingers massaging her tender flesh.

A low growl escaped my lips.

An answering roar echoed from the forest. A horrid stench filled the air. The odor was suffocating, causing all of us to gag. I choked, nearly retching.

Gwen placed her free hand to her throat, as if she echoed my sentiments. Gerald frantically lifted the key ring to Gwen's remaining manacle. His hands were trembling so badly that he kept missing the keyhole.

The ogre crashed through the forest and into the open. He was big and hulking, with a barrel chest and arms and legs the size of tree trunks. He had beady eyes and big, yellow teeth. His long hair hung in tangled strands from his head. Leaves and twigs were matted in his chest and stomach hair.

"Virgin. Smell virgin." His voice was a guttural growl.

He stomped closer. I grimaced. Not being sociable creatures, ogres aren't hampered by civilized sensibilities like wearing clothing. Any clothing. He lumbered forward, obviously aroused by the scent of his offering. His member was grotesquely erect and bobbing obscenely between his thighs with each step he took.

"Gerald. Set me free. Now." I gripped my sword tighter in my grasp.

Gerald turned and looked. He let loose a panicked cry and turned his back to the monster. His hands shook violently and he dropped the ring of keys. It landed in the leaves somewhere at their feet.

"No," Gwen said.

Gerald dropped to his knees, hands frantically shuffling through the leaves.

"Virgin. Want tender virgin."

I gripped my sword, gritted my teeth, and stepped directly into the ogre's path. He halted mere inches in front of me. The wind shifted and I grimaced as I caught a whiff of his foul body odor. I heard a great sniffing noise and saw his nostrils expand as he drew in my scent.

I raised my sword and made a horizontal slash with my blade. He countered with a backhanded blow that sent me flying. I crashed into the column, breaking it in two. I landed hard, my sword falling from my hand and clattering upon the temple floor.

Stunned, I lay sprawled out, my legs and lower body flat upon the floor, my ankle twisted beneath me. My back was arched upon the toppled column and I found it difficult to breathe. I tilted my head to the side, seeing the ogre from an upside-down angle as he stomped past me.

"Not virgin," he grunted. "Want virgin."

Gerald looked up from his crouching position and upon seeing the advancing ogre, shrieked. He scuttled backward, crablike, until his shoulders and back collided with Gwen's legs and the pillar she was chained to.

Feeling Gwen's presence behind him seemed to give Gerald a jolt. He snatched up the torch and climbed to his feet. He held the torch in one hand and drew his belt knife with the other. Holding it in front of him like a sword, he gave a fierce yell and charged.

"Gerald, no! You'll be killed." Gwen frantically struggled, pushing with her free hand against her remaining manacle, as if she intended to force her wrist through the metal band.

"Yah!" Gerald thrust the burning torch at the ogre's midsection.

There was the scent of singed hair upon the air and a cry of pain. Then, the ogre growled and lashed out. The torch was knocked from Gerald's hand. It landed, clattering upon the temple floor, rolling end over end. Gerald gripped his dagger and rushed forward, his arm up over his head as he ran at the beast.

The torch sputtered and the flame went out. The clearing was thrust into darkness. There was the sound of bone crunching, a frightened yelp, and metal falling on stone with a soft *clink*. Then, the sound of retreating footsteps and the rustling of bushes growing fainter and fainter until there was only quiet.

†

The sky had lightened from a midnight black to a dusky gray before I managed to make it completely to my feet. My ankle had been twisted beneath me and stabbing pain lanced up my leg when I tried to put my full weight upon it. I clutched an arm about my ribs, certain a couple of them were broken. A fight with an ogre will do that to a body, I suppose.

The one saving grace was that when he'd thrown me against the pillar, it had splintered and broken in two. Well, I suppose the other saving grace was that he didn't eat me. Matter of fact, it seemed like he could care less about me, other than swatting me away as though I were no more troublesome than a pesky horsefly.

I placed one foot on the fallen pillar and wrapping the chain about both hands, tugged. The eye ring held fast. I turned and limping with each step, dragged the chain and column across the temple floor.

"Bodhi, are you okay?"

"Oh, yeah. Only hurts when I breathe." I squinted at her

through a swollen eye caked with blood.

She still hung as I had, with one arm above her head, her wrist shackled in place. Her hair was disheveled and wild; she kept pushing strands away from her mouth with her free hand. Her dress was soiled and torn, one breast exposed. This time, I knew it to be the chill morning air that was responsible for the stiffness of her nipples.

"Can you find the key?" she asked.

I gingerly slid to my knees. My fingers spread out, fanning over the leaves. By the early morning light, the wrought-iron ring was easy to find. I sat down, unmindful of the damp moisture seeping through the backside of my britches. Dragging the bit of column across my lap, I inserted the key into the lock and opened my manacle. Free, I pushed restraints and broken wood off my lap and kicked them away.

I slowly climbed to my feet, feeling every twinge and ache in my body as I did so. I stood before Gwen and raised my arms above her head. Her breath was chilled upon my neck and I lowered my gaze to find her honey-brown eyes intently studying my face.

At last, the key turned, the manacle opened, and Gwen's arm dropped. She clutched her forearm to her chest and rubbed her wrist. The flesh was chafed raw and bleeding.

"How are you?" I hadn't moved back any since releasing her and now had both hands resting on her hips.

"I'm fine, but Gerald—"

"Is long gone."

Gwen's brow furrowed. She gave me a hard look.

"Bodhi, did you tell Gerald he could be a hero?"

"I told him he was a likely lad."

"A likely lad. Likely for what?"

I shrugged.

She leaned as far away as the column at her back would allow. She folded her arms over chest, hiding her ample bosom from view. Her lips set in a tight line she fixed me with a stern look.

At her unwavering stare, I scrubbed a hand across my face and released a sigh. "You saw him. The pudgy, pockmarked face, the awkwardness, and the dopey, doe-eyed expressions. He just, you know, looked likely."

"Likely as a virgin, you mean. Bodhi, you lured him here as bait."

"I was chained up here with you. I didn't force him to come. He came of his own free will."

"Because you tricked him into becoming the virgin offering in my stead. What did you do, Bodhi, entice him with promises of being able to slay the monster and rescue the suitably grateful maiden? Oh, spirits; you did, didn't you?"

Eyes flashing, she pushed past me with a straight-armed shove. I stumbled back, wincing at the pressure on my twisted ankle. Instead of storming off down the path back to her village, she veered off into the dense forest.

"Hey, where are you going?" I called out, limping after her.

"To save Gerald."

I caught her by the elbow and spun her around.

"Gwen, the ogre's got him. He's dead by now."

"Then…then I'll bring his body home. He sacrificed himself to save me. It's the least I can do." She shook loose my grip and disappeared into the thick foliage.

"What makes you think there's anything left to bring back?" I called out after her. Her only response was the loud rustling of bushes.

I tilted my head all the way back, straining my neck as I stared up through the tree branches at the clear sky. An exasperated huff left my lips. I rolled my head on my shoulders and looked in the direction Gwen had gone. Hands on my hips, I stared into the depths of the forest. Of course, I couldn't see anything except trees and underbrush. No a glimpse of a damsel to be seen.

"Ogre's probably already chewing on your bones. Bet he'll think you're a tasty dessert. Bite-sized." Rolling my eyes and muttering beneath my breath, I set out after her.

†

Tracking the ogre to his lair wasn't difficult. The moisture of the ground, coupled with the weight he carried, left deep impressions with every step he took. In the rockier terrain, Gwen's hunting skills saw us through. She led us right to the brush-hidden entrance of a cave set in the side of the hill.

A hand upon the rocky surface, Gwen bent low, peering inside. Drawing in a deep breath, she started to step inside. My hand upon her shoulder stopped her and she turned to questioningly look at me.

"Allow me," I said.

I unsheathed my sword and hefted its weight in my left hand. I breathed deeply, steeling myself as Gwen had, and ducked low inside the entrance. I felt Gwen following close, one of her hands gripping my tunic at the waist.

The cave was deeper than I'd initially thought, with a sloping path leading down. Somewhere below, a deep rumbling sound echoed. Luminescent rocks lined the cave walls, giving off enough light to guide our way. We gingerly picked our way along the path, being careful to not slip on the slimy surface of the slope.

The stench was awful. The air smelled of putrid decay, stagnant water, and defecation. I suppressed a shudder and tried not to think too much about what had made the slope so slippery.

The bottom of the path opened into a wide chamber. As with nearer the surface, luminescent rocks cast the chamber in an eerie, green glow. In one corner of the chamber, shone a small treasure pile of weapons, gold finery, trinkets, and glistening jewels.

That explains why the village saw so few travelers. No doubt, the ogre had made snacks out of them. Being an ogre, he had no need of their treasures and had left them in a discarded pile. In another section there were piles of bones, picked clean and glistening in the luminescent glow of the rocks.

The rumbling sound had been the ogre. He was asleep on a fur on the floor; his head tossed back, mouth open, and snoring loud enough to wake the dead. That brought to mind images of Gerald and I felt a pang of guilt. I imagined the ogre gorging himself on the lad's flesh and then picking his teeth clean with one of Gerald's bones.

"Bodhi?"

Gwen's whisper met my ears, followed by a tiny whimper. She tugged at my sleeve and I turned my head in her direction, never fully taking my eyes off the ogre. That is, until I saw what she was pointing at—or rather, who.

Facedown upon the dank, slimy cave floor was Gerald. He was curled nearly into a ball. His trousers were down about his knees, his bare backside raised high in the air. Something coated his back and rear and I grimaced as I realized it was ogre spunk.

Oh. Both my eyebrows shot up. *When I said the ogre was satisfying his carnal needs after a long winter, I never thought his needs were...* I grimaced again, trying to push the images of Gerald being ravished by the ogre from my mind. *Well, he did say he wanted a tender virgin.*

I felt something at my back and realized too late that it was Gwen tugging my spare sword from its sheath. Before I could stop her, she rushed across the cave. With a fearsome yell, she slammed the blade down across the ogre's face.

He yowled, arms flailing as he was brutally awoken

from his sated slumber. *Well, at least Gwen listened when I told her of the ogre's only vulnerabilities.* She'd gone for his eyes. Blinded and enraged, he lashed out, one of his tree-trunk sized arms connecting and sending Gwen flying.

I rushed forward as fast as my limp would allow. He was rolling over, trying to get up. I darted in, holding my sword in a two-handed grip. I lowered my blade, getting beneath the beast's neck. I lifted with a horizontal arc, my blade cutting deep into his exposed throat, sending blood spewing.

The monster fell and rolled over onto his back, his massive hands clutching at his throat. Blood was running down his face from his eyes and pouring from his throat. He choked, his blood gurgling in his throat. He tore one hand from his throat and blindly swung it around, as if he hoped to kill his attacker with a lucky strike.

Battered, bruised, and barely able to walk, Gwen made her way to my side. I reached out for her, but she pushed my intended embrace away. She stood over the ogre, breathing heavily, tears streaming down her filthy face. She lifted the sword and slammed it down into the ogre's groin and twisted the blade.

The ogre howled, his torso coming halfway up in reaction. Then, he fell backward, his head cracking against the stone floor. He took a last breath and then was still. The ogre was dead.

†

Haggard, bruised, and battered, we were sitting in a patch of grass a little ways from the entrance of the cave. The sun was bright overhead and it was warming up to be a beautiful day.

"So, where are you heading next?" Gwen asked.

I paused from sucking on a blade of grass and looked around before looking back at Gwen and shrugging.

"North, I guess. After I see about getting myself a new horse. You?"

"I hadn't really given it much thought. I never expected to survive past last night."

"You going home?" I asked.

"I don't think there's a home for me there, now." Her voice was low as she uttered that out loud for the first time since her ordeal began. She sniffed and wiped her hand across her nose. "If it wasn't for taking Gerald back, I wouldn't return at all."

We both looked at the magistrate's son. We'd dragged him up from the cave and dumped him on the ground. He was still in the same position we'd left him in, with his trousers about his knees, and his bare ass hanging out. He whimpered and sucked his thumb into his mouth.

"I'll help you drag him as far as the road. Someone will find him there and help him home. Once the shock wears off and he remembers where the ogre's cave and the treasure is, he'll get that respect he wanted." I saw no reason to mention that I intended to take my fair share for what I deemed services rendered.

She looked at me as if uncertain.

"He'll be fine," I insisted. "If you don't go back to the village, what will you do?"

"I don't know. I'm not sure what else I can do."

"Anything you set your mind to, I'd wager." I thought of the way she'd attacked the ogre and grinned. "Far as I know, this is the first time a maiden's ever killed an ogre; could be a future in that for you."

"Except I'm no longer a maiden, remember?"

Oh, I remembered. "Listen, I don't have anywhere I need to be. We can, you know, I don't want your first time being a disappointment."

"I'm not disappointed, Bodhi. All I wanted was to survive."

"Well, yes, but I don't want to leave you with a jaded impression. I'm naturally left-handed, you know. I don't think you had a fair sampling of my talents."

"I see. Your concern isn't about my pleasure, but about your own reputation." Her lips curved as she tried to disguise her smile.

"You do owe me for saving you from the ogre."

"As I remember it, Bodhi, I struck the killing blow."

"True, but it was my sword you used…"

Malodorous

Malodorous
Del Robertson
Affinity eBook Press NZ LTD

Malodorous

The Story Continues…

Chapter Six

My bottom has never ached so much in my life.

Not even during her sixth summer, when it seemed every time Gwendolyn turned around, she was in trouble for some reason or another. More often than not it was for, as her mother called it, *shirking her chores*. Whether it was washing clothes in the river, minding the stew that continuously warmed in the kettle over the hearth, or tending to her younger siblings, it was all women's work and that held no interest for Gwen.

Gwen was constantly dodging her mother in favor of tagging along behind her father. Hunting wild hare in the woods, mending the thatching on the cottage roof, and taking their pigs to market held so much more appeal to her than darning socks and stonewashing breechcloths. She was smart enough to know that helping her papa was chores, too, but they were fun chores.

The day she helped her papa wrangle two of their largest sows was seared into her memory. The local tavern had contracted their farm to deliver the pigs for the Midsummer Eve's festivities. Herding the obese swine from their sty to the village had seemed like the grandest adventure. That is, until Gwen grew bored waiting for her father to finish haggling with the tavern keeper. Boredom soon gave way to curiosity and she followed her nose and the smell of something delicious straight into the tavern's kitchen.

That's where her father had caught her with her mouth stuffed full of meat pastries and even more pushed down inside her blouse. Never mind that old maid Mavis had told him she'd baked far more than needed and it was better to feed a starving waif than a hungry hound. Her papa turned red in the face, grabbed her by the upper arm, and marched her straight out of there.

He dragged her halfway home without uttering a single word or even sparing a sideways glance at Gwen. When they reached the river, he finally released her. The only reason he'd turned her loose then was because he needed both hands to pull up one of the cattail reeds growing along the bank.

He took her across his lap to dole out her punishment. Gwen screamed and kicked and hit at him with her closed fists, to no avail. The heated flush on her face soon matched the stinging welts on her upturned bottom.

When he finished, he pushed her off his knee and uttered the only words he would speak to her for nearly a fortnight.

"No child of mine will be raised a thief, nor to accept charity. I only wish that whooping I gave you hurt you half as much as the pain you've caused me."

Gwen often wondered if her papa ever knew that it was the disappointment in his voice and the look in his eyes that hurt far worse than any spanking she'd ever had.

Not that the reed switch didn't hurt. It hurt so badly, I thought I might never sit again.

That spanking had been sharp, quick, and then over with. It in no way compared to the constant ache she was suffering now.

Gwen's grip on the reins tightened. She braced her feet, pressed down firmly on the stirrups, and raised her backside from the leather saddle. Immediately, the sensation of stinging nettles lanced through her thighs and calves.

I should have stopped candlemarks ago. I'd gladly stop now, if I could find shelter.

The sun was at its zenith, but ominous storm clouds were gathering, threatening to break, and promising to soak anything hapless enough to be caught beneath them. Right now, that included Gwen.

She couldn't remember the number of days gone by since she'd packed her saddlebags full and set out from her village. Nor was she certain how far she'd traveled since the last town. It seemed as though it'd been forever ago since she'd started out on this path. What had begun as a nice wide, flat road had gradually lessened in width and steadily increased its incline. Worse, there were now enough twists and turns that she thought perhaps a cow had been set loose to randomly map out the trail.

Poor cow and its owner probably died before they found their way to a village.

Gwen was, by her best guess, in the middle of nowhere. As far as the eye could see, there was nothing but rock-strewn, verdant hills all about. Not a thatched roof, a well, or even a lone sheep dotted the horizon. The only sign of civilization was the wagon wheel-rutted trail she was on.

She gingerly lowered herself down, wincing slightly as her tender backside connected with the hard leather. She'd been in the saddle far too long and wondered how she would ever steady herself enough to walk when she finally did dismount.

It's not that she'd never ridden a horse before. She had. Farmer Horace down the road from them used to have an old, swaybacked plow horse. When Gwen was little, he would lift her up and let her ride perched on the horse's bare back while he was sowing the rows of grain. As she grew older and bigger and the horse grew older and more swaybacked, the rides had ceased. It would be many more seasons before Gwen would have the chance to ride again.

Her growth spurt from child to maid continued, her body's changes becoming more pronounced. The straight, stick-like figure gave way to the flare of curved hips. Flatness developed into fully ripe breasts that strained at the thin fabric of her elder sister's hand-me-down blouses. The village lads, as well as many of the older men, had taken notice. On days that she went to market, she found no shortage of escorts willing to accompany her on the long road home.

It had been her sister, Cathryn, who had advised her not all those offers of rides actually came with horses. Not that Gwen had any intention of accepting *any* offers for a ride, nor for anything else. She'd seen firsthand what happened when a maiden gave up her virginity for a quick tumble in the hay. She didn't want to be her sister—a harlot scorned by the virtuous women of the village. Nor did she desire any of their men—their decent, upstanding men that propositioned the likes of Cathryn the instant their wives' backs were turned.

No, thank you.

Gwen got quite good at saying that. *No, thank you.* Those three words worked for any suggestion whether it was an innocent ride home or something more direct. No matter the offer, *No, thank you* was Gwen's standard rule.

Gerald had been the exception. Not because he was any more adept at hiding his desires than the other lads. He wasn't. What Gerald was, though, was exasperatingly persistent. He followed her like a puppy, always there whenever she turned around. He presented her with bouquets of blooming weeds he'd picked and bundled himself, his nose and eyes watering so much it pained her to look at him. He gave her honeycomb straight from the hive, the sticky sweetness still dripping onto his bee-stung swollen fingers and hand.

No, Gerald was far from skilled at hiding his intentions. He was painfully obvious, hopelessly awkward and, in Gwen's opinion, also completely harmless.

Perhaps that was why on one unbearably hot summer day, she finally accepted his offer of a ride. Chasteness was an admirable quality, but virtue alone wouldn't protect her from the heat. The only things walking had gained her so far were a set of well-defined calves and a severe case of chafing.

Besides, as the magistrate's son, Gerald did have his own horse. It was a beautiful, blonde-maned mare with a sweet disposition. At first, Gerald had wanted her to sit on Dusty behind him, her arms wrapped tight about his barebones, skinny waist. It didn't take her long to convince him to allow her to take the reins and ride alone.

Gwen felt a momentary pang of guilt for what she could now see might have been her taking advantage of him. She may have been a simple country maiden, but she was far from naïve. She'd known all along what Gerald wanted from her. Just as she also knew she never had any intention of letting him have so much as a kiss. Even a peck on the cheek would have been more than she was willing to give.

It was wrong of me to ever allow him to believe otherwise.

The horse's bulk abruptly shifted beneath her and Gwen let out a squawk of surprise minced with pain.

The incline had crested and they were now coming down the other side. It was a steep descent, made all the more terrifying by the added height of horse and saddle. Gwen reflexively tightened her grip on the reins. The mare whinnied, shaking her head in protest.

"Easy, Dusty."

Gwen forced herself to release her white-knuckle grip on the reins so she could reassuringly stroke her fingers through the horse's blonde mane.

"Good, girl." She kept her voice low, hoping her tone was calming. She relinquished her control and allowed Dusty to set the pace, trusting the mare to guide them safely down the slope.

Far below, she could see where the ground leveled out again. The base of the trail was surrounded on all sides by sharp rocks and boulders. The height and steepness were dizzying and Gwen felt a knot tighten in her stomach. She averted her gaze, trying to look anywhere except straight down.

She focused on the landscape beyond. The worn road stretched out far into the distance, twisting and turning, gradually descending and disappearing into a mist-shrouded valley. Rocks were scattered on the road and boulders were strewn about lush hillocks. It reminded Gwen of the area surrounding the ogre's lair.

That, in turn, brought back memories of Gerald.

Poor, sweet, bumbling Gerald. He didn't fully understand what he was doing. He thought he was trying to save me. Perhaps if I'd only ever shown him the tiniest bit of affection—

Gwen's distracting self-reflection was interrupted by the sound of a frightened whinny. She blinked and looked down, eyes widening at the sight of the soft earth giving way beneath the horse's weight. Hooves slid, leaving deep impressions in the ground. Dirt and grime flew up, getting in Gwen's eyes, and obscuring her view of the path.

Dusty lost her footing.

Gwen screamed, clenched both reins and mane in a tight grip, and hung on for dear life. She felt the horse seemingly going one direction as the saddle, and her along with it, went the opposite way. Then, Dusty was stumbling and Gwen was sent flying.

Her body sped toward the uneven ground. Eyes widened and she reflexively flung out both arms. She landed hard, the loose dirt not quite soft enough to cushion her fall. Her arms gave way and she collapsed, her temple striking against a stone.

†

A tiny cry for *help* echoed in Gwen's ears, urging her toward consciousness. One eye cracked open, the pupil rolling, her brow furrowing as first the distant sky and then the much nearer ground came into focus. Her other eye refused to open and she felt a surge of panic before realizing it was because she was lying facedown. The road felt rough beneath her, tiny pebbles scratching at her cheek, their pointed edges pricking at the sensitive flesh of her breasts, stomach, and thighs through her clothing.

Gwen planted her hands palms down, feeling pebbles and loose dirt sifting between her fingers, and pushed up. Pain lanced through her body, beginning in both wrists. There was a throbbing in her temple and a blinding ache when she tried to hold her left eye open.

Spirits, everything hurts. Gwen realized that the cry for *help* she thought she'd heard must have been hers.

She struggled into an upright position, her legs curled beneath her as she sat in the middle of the road. Gwen glanced from side to side, as if worried she might be ran over by a cart if she stayed there too long. Gwen's eyes locked on a red pattern spattered on a stone. The throbbing in her head echoed louder. She placed a hand to her temple, jerking her head back as her fingertips made contact. She looked down, numbly staring at her blood-coated fingers. Then, her muddled mind recalled exactly where she was, the desolate path she'd been traveling on, and precisely how she'd come to be sprawled out on the ground.

"Dusty? Dusty?" Panic rang in Gwen's voice. Her heart was pounding in her chest. Her breath was coming too fast.

A faint *whinny* was her answer.

Gwen felt a wave of calmness wash over her. She released a deep sigh and looked around. Gwen fully expected to see Dusty right side up, with all four hooves on the ground and grazing on a clump of grass the proper way a horse should be.

She was in no way prepared to see the mare on her side, pitifully making attempt after attempt, but failing in her efforts to get up. Her front leg was bent at an impossible angle, broken bone protruding from the flesh.

"Spirits, Dusty."

The mare lifted her head, looking in Gwen's direction. She held the position for only a scant heartbeat before her head lolled back again.

Gwen rolled onto her side, gritting her teeth against the pain, and pushed herself up. A grunt escaped her lips as she made her way to her feet.

On shaky legs, she staggered a drunkard's path to the fallen horse. Gwen more collapsed, than knelt, beside Dusty. She pressed her palm against the horse's coat, her fingers stroking through the blonde mane.

Dusty struggled, her front legs flailing, as she tried to rise. She collapsed almost immediately, her chest heaving, lather forming about the edges of her mouth.

"Shhh, Dusty. Be still, girl." Gwen tried to keep her tone low and steady, even as she stared wide-eyed at the grisly scene of bone sticking through mangled flesh.

"Let's get some of this weight off of you."

Her fingers felt as if they were far too uncoordinated to accomplish the simple task of undoing the fastenings about the saddle and saddlebags. At last, she managed to unlace all of them, leaving them dangling. She knew she lacked the strength to pull the cumbersome saddle free, but thought loosening the bindings might allow the horse to breathe somewhat easier.

She dragged the saddlebags and her gear off Dusty, letting everything fall in a heap on the ground beside them. Stiff fingers worked to untie the hemp knotted about the brown bundle of cloth that served as her cloak. Gwen spread the material out on the ground, unfolding the edges of the fabric. Nestled inside the drab brown cloth were a bow and a leather quiver containing half a dozen arrows.

Gwen took a deep breath and stood up. Her head was pounding. Her vision was blurred. She broke out in a clammy sweat. Knuckles clenched white about the grip of her bow as she fought down waves of nausea.

The sensation passed. Experienced fingers fixed the flax bowstring onto the horn nocks at each end of the bow. Gwen drew two arrows from the quiver.

Slow, determined steps had her standing in front of the downed animal. Gwen's eyes swept over the blood-soaked coat, the gaping wound, and the bone jutting from ruined flesh. Her gaze traveled past flaring nostrils and met big, brown eyes looking back at her.

"I know, girl. I know."

Gwen swallowed against the lump in her throat. She thrust the tip of one arrow into the ground, within easy reach. Fingertips smoothed the fletching of the other arrow as she fit the groove into place, nocking it on the bowstring. She raised the bow, her thumb touching her chin as she drew back, the goose-feathered fletching brushing against her cheek as she found her anchor position near her ear.

She watched the ragged rise and fall of Dusty's chest. Gwen swallowed hard. It would do no good to aim there. A horse's chest had too much flesh, muscle, and sinew. The arrow might not pierce deep enough to reach the heart. The last thing she wanted was to cause Dusty a slow, painful death.

Gwen blinked against her blurring vision. Lining up her sight, she stared down the birch shaft at the iron arrowhead. With the tip of the arrow and the horse in her view, she drew an imaginary line from one eye to the opposite ear and centered her aim at the midpoint.

Her arm shook. She shifted her foot on the grass to locate the arrow she'd thrust into the ground. Her buttercup leather boot brushed against the wood shaft. Gwen marked the position. If she missed, she needed to quickly grab the second arrow, string it, and fire again so as not to prolong Dusty's suffering.

Gwen drew in a shuddering breath and released the arrow.

†

Thunder rumbled and lengthening shadows fell across the ground. A cool breeze swept Gwen's hair about her face. Dirt-coated fingers brushed the errant strands away from her eyes and mouth.

She turned and looked down at the mound of stones. Spirits knew she wished she could have done more for Dusty. She was a good horse and deserved a proper burial. She certainly deserved better than Gwen was able to provide.

Unable to budge any of the large boulders, Gwen gathered as many of the smaller stones as she could from the surrounding area. She placed them around and over the fallen horse as best she could. Even as she placed stone after stone, she knew she'd never be able to completely cover Dusty's entire bulk. When she lacked the strength to tote a single stone more, she sat down on the ground, cradled her head in both hands, and cried.

Tears all cried out, Gwen looked up. Red-rimmed eyes scanned the sky for scavenger birds. She thought she saw the darker wingspan of one against the backdrop of the heavy storm clouds that blotted out the sun.

Even if it wasn't, they'll be here soon enough. Carrion eaters can smell death miles away. Most likely, they're waiting for me to leave…or die also.

Gwen turned her head, her gaze traveling the length of the slope, following the treacherous path they'd taken. Midway up the trail, she could see the deep furrows where Dusty had dug her hooves in, then the place where she had lost her footing completely, and had finally fallen.

We could have both been killed. Instead, only Dusty had died while Gwen hadn't suffered a single broken bone. She swallowed against the excess saliva pooling in her mouth. *What was I thinking coming out here? Believing I could do this?*

Gwen looked at the trail leading the opposite direction. From the top of the slope, she had seen numerous twists and turns on a desolate road that stretched out as far as the eye could see. She looked again at the slope behind her. Teeth chewed her bottom lip.

Spirits, help me.

Gwen looked toward the heavens. The first fat drop of rain fell, hitting her squarely between the eyes. She shook her head and blinked against the moisture. Her gaze fell on Dusty's makeshift grave.

I never should have taken her from Gerald. Poor Gerald. Gwen took a shuddering breath. *No. Despite any false hope he might have garnered from me…or outright encouragement he may have gotten from Bodhi…no one forced him to do anything he didn't wish to. Gerald chose his path.*

Just as you chose yours, Gwendolyn.

The rain was falling in earnest now. Gwen tied the worn leather straps of her quiver bag about the belt at her waist. The saddlebags, she slung over one shoulder. She donned her cloak, tucking her bow beneath the folds of material.

Besides, he'll heal. He's back at home, with his family about him.

Gwen thought back to the last time she'd seen the chubby-cheeked youth. He was sleeping, the edge of a quilt pulled all the way up to the light brown wisps of hair jutting from his chin. On the table beside his bed was an empty tankard that smelled of apple wine and six gold coins she'd left as payment for his horse. She left the way she'd come in, through the open window, without disturbing him.

Gwen lifted the hood of her cloak into place. She hunched her shoulders and ducked her head, focusing on each step on the trail.

I may not know what's on the path ahead, but I know there's no shelter on the trail behind me. Unlike Gerald, I can never go home again.

Chapter Seven

It was raining. Still. Not the normal summer cloudbursts that unexpectedly drench everything in sight before quickly moving off, leaving nothing but stifling heat in its wake. This was worse. It had been over a fortnight and still the rain lingered on, day and night.

It was a misting rain, the sort that took its sweet time covering everything in a fine layer of wet. Everything. It lazily rolled off the eaves of already saturated roofs, falling with steadily maddening *drip-drip-drips* into anything that might hold water. It slipped down into the chimneys and wall braziers, causing the fires to sputter and hiss. It crept beneath doorways and into nooks and crannies, soaking into rushes and sacks of grain with equal ease.

Even the city rats had come out of hiding, looking for higher, drier ground. It wasn't unusual for a shrill-pitched scream to pierce the air as a woman awoke to find the beady eyes of unexpected bedmates staring back at her. Wives were kicking their husbands from their beds in droves and inviting the cats in, hoping they would prove better mouse-catchers than their two-legged counterparts.

The unscuffed soles of shiny boots too new to have yet been broken in, despite countless candlemarks of marching, slid on slick cobblestone. The guard reflexively reached out, bracing his palm against the perimeter wall. Fuzzy lichen growing unimpeded on the stone was slimy to the touch. Ernest grimaced and jerked his hand back, briskly shaking it. He wiped his hand on his trousers, his lip curling in disgust at the stain it left behind.

Ernest turned and craned his neck, looking down the length of the wall to the recessed alcove of the guards' room. There was no outer door to the room, only the outline in the carved stone of where one might have once stood. A brazier mounted on the wall outside the doorway gave off just enough light to discern shadows in the tiny room.

There was the silhouette of a single chair and a small table pushed up against one wall. On the table was a round tray containing a pitcher and two mugs. The polished hilt of a sword in its scabbard dangled from a hook mounted on the interior wall.

The palm of a thick hand was braced against the same wall, the hand attached to a beefy length of arm that extended to a massive torso. The dark burgundy material of the guard's tunic appeared nearly black in the dim light, but the golden sergeant stripes on the sleeves were clearly visible. So was the scarf tied about the wench's red hair. The yellow cloth seemed to catch and reflect the glowing red hue cast by the coal-fed brazier. It looked as if the flames were dancing, mingling crimson and gold as the girl's head bobbed up and down, the sergeant's hand and arm going with the motion.

Ernest had seen the girl as she approached their post, carrying a tray in her hands, and recognized her as a serving wench from the tavern up the street. He'd also seen the look on the sergeant's face as his eyes raked over pitcher and maid with equal craving.

He'd known what that meant. Under the sergeant's vague order to patrol, he was all but shoved out of the guards' room. Indignant about not getting so much as a sip of ale, Ernest had turned to protest.

Eyes widened as he saw Sarge's bulk already pinning the girl against the table. He had a mug to his lips, ale running from his mouth and down his chin. His other hand was roughly mauling the girl's breast through her peasant blouse. She turned her head to the side as he attempted to plant a slobbering kiss on her mouth.

His appetite for drink firmly squashed by the spectacle, Ernest turned thought and effort to his duty. He paced up and down the stretch of wall, his stride carrying him quickly back and forth past the large gate for horse and cart use and the smaller Judas gate used for light foot traffic. He knew both gates were secure, but he still rubbed his lucky coin and intoned a word to any protective spirits that might be listening.

Neither sense of duty, propriety, nor even the pattering of the rain could drown out the unmistakable noises coming from the guards' room. Despite his best efforts, Ernest looked. Earlier, he'd been able to turn from the sight. Now, he stared, transfixed. There was a churning in his gut and a bitter taste in his mouth. Still, he couldn't turn away from the sight of the maid servicing the sergeant. His fingertips brushed against the lichen stain on his trousers, reinforcing the visual, and his stomach turned more.

"Hello?"

Ernest turned and squinted against the night, looking for whoever had called out. He spotted a cloaked figure, on the wrong side of the gate, outside the wall.

"What do you want?" Ernest called out.

"In." The voice that answered was distinctly feminine.

"Go away."

"Pardon?"

"Go away. Gate's closed." Ernest firmly grasped one wrought-iron bar and shook it to demonstrate the gate was, indeed, locked.

"Please, let me in."

The cloaked figure outside the gate lifted an arm, pushing back the material comprising the hood. The twin braziers mounted on each side of the gate gave off enough light to illuminate the stranger's features. The voice matched the face. She was most definitely female. Long, chestnut tresses framed her face. The misting rain quickly gathered on her unprotected skin, catching in her thick eyelashes. She blinked against the wet. Her big, brown eyes seemed to be silently imploring him.

Ernest's resolve faltered. There was a jangling sound as his fingers brushed against the ring of keys at his waist. Eyes still on the maid's face, his fingers sorted through each key, until he selected just one.

He took a step toward the locked gate.

The maid took a step back, as if to give him room.

He watched her face.

Her eyes were fixed on his every movement.

His hand shook beneath her gaze. The sound of metal on metal rang too loud in his ears as the key scratched against the surface of the lock. He got the key in.

Her lips bowed into a smile.

His wrist turned and he pushed against the iron bar. There was a soft *click* upon the air as the metal frame slid past the locking mechanism.

Something in Ernest clicked, also. He hadn't seen nor heard her approach. True, night and mist cut down visibility dramatically, making distant hills look dark and indistinct. However, the terrain between the hills and the city wall was uneven, yet clear. There was no looming forest, no ground cover to speak of. He should have seen her long before she reached the gate.

His fingers brushed over the lucky coin he carried. Eyes blinked and he shook his head from side to side to dispel the siren's hold. He slammed the gate shut and scrambled to turn the key.

Instantly, she was at the gate, fingers wrapped about the iron bars as she pressed herself against the metal. There was a burning intensity in her eyes.

"Please. Allow me in. I'll catch my death if you refuse me."

"I can't. I've orders."

"Let me in." Her tone was more insistent and her arm was stretching through the bars, her fingers reaching for him.

"No." With each step back he took, Ernest gave a resolute shake of his head.

As he slipped out of her reach, she closed both hands about the bars. Her knuckles clenched white as she gripped the metal. She gave the bars a savage shake, causing the frame to rattle.

Ernest's heart pounded in his chest. His heated breath shone in rapid puffs upon the damp night air. Despite the chill, he was suddenly sweating.

"Ah!" Ernest visibly jumped as he backed into something.

†

"What's with all the commotion, then?"

At the sound of the booming voice in his ear and the firm grip on his shoulder, Ernest turned around to discover that *something* he had backed into was the sergeant.

His sword was dangling in the leather scabbard loosely belted at his hip. His tunic was only half-laced, his thick chest hair further emphasized by the beefy arms folded over his stomach. A deep scowl creased his face.

"Some…someone at the gate." Ernest pointed.

Sarge looked past the guard to the maid.

"What'd ya want?"

"Shelter from the storm," she answered.

The sergeant nodded once and started forward.

Ernest reflexively reached out.

Sarge stopped, looking down at the hand upon his forearm and then slowly lifted his gaze until he was looking into Ernest's eyes.

Ernest swallowed loudly and removed his hand.

"Sarge, you can't—"

"I have coin. I'll pay," called out the woman.

"Let's see it." Sarge's lips curved. He took a step nearer the gate.

The maid opened her cloak. She was clad in a tunic, breeches, and boots. It was hardly standard attire for a young maiden, but certainly acceptable gear for a traveling merchant.

Guess it's safer for a woman alone if she can pass as a man, Ernest supposed. *She's certainly armed like a man.*

A dagger was at her waist, the hilt riding low in its sheath. She wore a quiver bag strapped to her thigh and Ernest counted the fletching of at least six arrows. He had a hunch that the bow those arrows belonged to was hidden somewhere in the folds of her cloak.

Spirits help me. I've never seen a man that looked like that, though. If it were, indeed, her intent to pass for a man traveling alone, she'd only fool someone from a distance.

Even dressed in male's clothes as she was, there was something about her that fairly screamed *all woman*. It was as if there was a force drawing Ernest to her, attracting him. He'd felt it as soon as she'd appeared at the gate. And, despite his lingering misgivings of this creature of the night, he felt compelled to let escape a low whistle of appreciation.

The maid's fingers were undoing the drawstring from a coin purse. She withdrew three gold coins from the bag and held them out for the sergeant's perusal.

Sarge's gaze was firmly locked on the maid's ample bosom straining against the confines of her tight tunic.

Ernest was equally mesmerized. He stood by as Sarge inserted the key into the lock, turned it, and then swung open the wrought-iron gate. Ernest's eyes widened as the apparition walked through the open Judas gate. She boldly sashayed past him and it was all he could do to blink.

It wasn't until she was well within the confines of the city walls and the sergeant was closing and relocking the gate that Ernest found his nerve. He reached out, once again grabbing Sarge by the arm.

This time, when the older man turned to glower at him, he didn't remove his hand. Ernest gritted his teeth, feeling his throat muscles tighten. When he spoke, his voice came out strained.

"Sarge, Commander Thorne's orders—"

Ernest's impression of the sergeant was that he was old, fat, and lazy. He'd never thought Sarge capable of moving so fast. Before he could fully comprehend what was happening, though, Sarge had shaken off his grip, spun him around, and shoved him back against the wall.

"I'm aware of Commander Thorne's orders, Corporal." There was a dangerous glint in the sergeant's eye and his nostrils were flaring. He emphasized each word with a pointed finger jab to Ernest's chest. "But if you think I'm leaving a fine piece like that out there, you're daft. Get in my way again…" The sergeant's hand went to the grip of his sword. He made a show of sliding it in and out of the scabbard. "…I'll cut you into small enough bits that they'll be able to use you for mutton stew. Is that clear?"

"Um…clear." Ernest bobbed his head vigorously up and down.

Sarge smirked. His sword dropped back into its scabbard with a rattle. He gave Ernest a double-handed shove backward. Then, he turned and sauntered after the maid.

Ernest pressed his palm flat over his heart. His entire chest ached from Sarge's repeated jabs. The cold damp of the bricks seeping through his clothes and into his bones only added to his physical discomfort. Still, given Sarge's threat, he didn't dare move away from the wall.

†

The maid's soft-soled boots made a scuffling sound on the wet cobblestone as she walked away. The sergeant openly stared at her backside. Even with that drab, formless cloak on, there was a truly distracting sway to her hips. Sarge licked his lips then rubbed his fingers across his mouth to wipe the excess moisture away.

He hitched up his belt and trousers and rushed after the maid, his military-issued boots sounding loudly as he gave chase. As he reached her, he slowed her to a stop by gripping her by the upper arm.

"Not so fast, my sweet. I let you in, but you still have to state your name and business. For the official record, you understand."

"Oh. Gwen. Gwendolyn." She gave a slight shrug. "As I said, I'm simply seeking shelter from the storm."

Sarge's eyes narrowed as he looked her up and down.

"Then, you have family in Fairhaven to provide lodging?"

"No, my nearest family lives in the farming village of Chatham. I thought perhaps I might seek comfort at a local tavern."

Sarge rubbed his hand over the stubble of growth on his chin and nodded his head. He gave a look back over his shoulder. That green recruit, Ernest, was still standing against the wall like an obedient pup. He glanced toward the alcove and caught sight of the serving wench in the guards' room, retrieving her blouse from the stone floor.

Out of the corner of his eye, he saw the current object of his desire begin to turn her head in the direction of the guards' room. He hastily grabbed her by both arms and spun her around so she was facing him, placing her back to the alcove. Over her shoulder, he watched as the serving wench adjusted the pleats of her peasant skirt.

"So, my sweet," he put on his most roguishly handsome smile, "I believe there was mention of payment?"

"I've already placed three gold coins in your palm."

"Monetary payment for coming in, of course. Allowing you to stay in, however, requires…a more personal type of payment."

A sharp gasp escaped the maid's lips, her eyes widened, and she looked suitably appalled.

Sarge wasn't fooled, though. No wench dressed like that was all so sweet, innocent, and pure. No, he'd wager that she'd bruised her knees behind the barn at home on more than one occasion. *Probably got caught at it. Why else would a piece like that be roaming about the countryside all by herself?*

He could see he'd caught her off guard. He took advantage, using his greater bulk to manhandle her, forcing her back, step by step, toward the shadowed alcove. Soon, he had her pinned against the outer wall of the guards' room.

The fingers of one of the wench's hands were clutched about the doorframe. She had her other hand up, palm pressed flat against Sarge's chest.

He pushed in with puckered lips.

She kicked at him.

He felt the toes of her leather boots ineffectively kicking against his shins. Amused by her girlish efforts, he heartily chuckled.

Her eyes flashed. She tore her fingers from the doorframe and let loose a curse.

He caught her wrist a heartbeat before her nails could scratch his face. He grinned. He liked it when they fought back. Sarge leaned in.

She turned her head and avoided his lips.

His tongue slid past to her neck. He thought she tasted like roasted apples and gave a deliberate lick to her flesh.

She tried to jerk away. Her eyes were wide, her breathing was coming quick.

Sarge could see her ample bosom rising and falling with each haggard breath and he was openly laughing at her.

"Come on, then. Give me a proper kiss." He made an exaggerated puckering of his lips.

"I'd sooner kiss your big, fat hairy backside."

Sarge's laughter abruptly died. The grin fell from his face. A beefy hand shot out, catching her chin, fingers clenching about her jaw, and squeezing hard. All joviality gone now, he looked her dead in the eyes and spoke in a lowered voice.

"Let me explain something to you, little maid. I guard the gates of Fairhaven. No one gets in or out unless it's through me. Now, seeing as how the next town is more than a fortnight's travel away by horse and considering you're on foot…it's either sharing warmth with me for the night or freezing to death outside the city walls. You understand?"

He felt her tender throat work beneath his fingers as she roughly swallowed. He could see her fear dancing in her eyes and she nodded.

His fingers lessened their grip on her jaw. He moved his hand so that his fingertips were caressing the softness of her cheek.

She trembled, but didn't try to evade his touch.

"Good girl. Now, what say we step into the guards' room and you show me exactly what you've got beneath that cloak of yours?"

"No, thank you."

"What?" Sarge's fingers abruptly stopped. He felt his anger flare. Spirits help her if she was toying with him—

"No, thank you," she repeated. "We needn't go to the guards' room or anywhere else. I can show you what I've got right here."

He released a heavy breath. Spirits knew he liked it when they fought, but something could also be said for the giving in, too. He'd had plenty surrender. *Spirits, they all surrendered.* Eventually. He'd never had one to be so brazen about it, though. Most of them pleaded for discretion. They wanted it to be in the shadows, in the dark, behind closed doors, or anywhere else that no one might see. All of them begged that their husband, betrothed, brother, father, or *fill in the relation* not know what they'd done. Here was this one, though, offering right out on the open street…

Sarge felt her hand upon his shoulder. Then, the palm that had been pressed firmly against his chest was traveling lower, down his belly, and onto his belt. He felt her hand between the press of both their bodies.

His eyes that had half-closed with desire suddenly flew open. He looked down and saw the glint of the dagger she gripped. The blade was pointed directly at his crotch, the tip pricking at the fabric of his trousers.

Sarge tried to take a step back, but felt her hand tighten its claw-like grip upon his shoulder. Her nails dug deeply into his flesh. His anger boiled as he looked up at her face and saw the slow smirk forming on her lips.

I'll wipe that smug smile right off her face. Let's see if she can smirk when her lips are wrapped around my—

"Sergeant."

Sarge stiffened at the sound of the crisp, clear voice behind him. He saw the maid looking past him. Then, her hand was suddenly off his shoulder. He felt a warning thrust from the knife, just enough to poke the tip of the blade through his trousers and prick his manhood.

"Sergeant," repeated the sharp voice. "Report."

Sarge performed the quick heel-click and about-face expected of one in his profession with flawless precision. All the while hoping that the maid wouldn't thrust her dagger deep into his back. He gave the standard fist-to-chest then straight-armed salute by rote, without any extraneous enthusiasm. He steeled his expression into one of perfect military impassiveness.

The commander was tall—at least a full head and shoulders taller than him. He had to tilt his head up at her and he resented her for it. He resented her for a great many reasons, her greater height and youth not the least of these.

She was no milksop maiden, but she was still a good fifteen winters younger than him. She wasn't what he'd term a pretty girl, either. There was beauty there, he supposed, but not the sort that appealed to many men. *Handsome,* he'd heard one of the tavern wenches describe her.

He saw a rawboned harshness to her face. Her cheeks were too well defined, her lips too thin for his liking. She wore her hair pulled back into a too-tight braid that ended between her shoulder blades. The color of it was as black as coal, except for a solid streak of white rooted at her left temple and grew the length of her braid. Her eyes were too bright of an emerald green, like a cat's that flicked back and forth, intently tracking every movement up until that heartbeat in which it pounced upon its unsuspecting prey.

Sarge could feel those eyes boring a hole into him now as Commander Thorne awaited his response.

"Perimeter remains secure with nothing amiss." Despite the sharpness of the blade pressed to his spine, Sarge kept his tone as dispassionate as his salute.

"On the contrary, Sergeant. There is something very much amiss," said the commander.

Sarge gave a quick look to the wall. The gates were closed. Ernest was at his post, standing at dutiful attention, having no doubt spotted the commander's approach. *Little rat might have warned me.* Sarge looked back into those cat's eyes, feeling very much like the commander's latest prey.

"Gates are locked tight. There's nothing out of the ordinary."

"Who's this, then?" The commander's gaze flicked to a point past the sergeant's shoulder.

Sarge felt the sharp prick at his spine, imagined he could feel the tip of the blade press between his vertebrae.

"I'd say she's very much far from *ordinary.*" He could see her cat's eyes sparkle and there was a feral smile upon the commander's thin lips.

Then, the blade was gone and the girl was stepping out from behind his back. She was smiling broadly, one hand extended to the commander in greeting even as the other surreptitiously tucked the blade once more into the folds of her cloak.

"I'm Gwen. I've just come—"

"—to bring us a pitcher from The Dirty Duck, Commander."

"You're from The Dirty Duck?" Commander Thorne's eyes narrowed as they flitted back and forth between Gwen and Sarge.

The maid gave a half shrug.

The commander seemed to take that as answer enough.

"Very well. I thank you for the thoughtfulness, but the evening grows late. I suggest you return to the safety of your proprietor's establishment as quickly as possible."

"Of course." The maid gave a quick bow and a smile at the commander before stepping just far enough inside the doorway of the guards' room to retrieve the pitcher, mugs, and serving tray.

Sarge bristled as the wench brushed past him, displaying a smirk that he was positive no one else was privy to but him.

Then, tucking the tray beneath her arm and carrying the pitcher and mugs so they clinked together with every step she took, she sauntered up the cobblestone street toward the city interior.

The commander stared after Gwen for long heartbeats before turning her level gaze back to the sergeant.

"Sergeant, I trust there will be no further…visitations…this eve."

Sarge rubbed the stubble of his chin. *Thorne must think me and the girl…* Sarge drew himself up straighter as he felt most of his bluster return.

"Well, now, Commander Thorne. I don't know how citizens behaved at your last command, but here in Fairhaven, folk know that the city guard, the gatekeepers in particular, are what keeps them safe in their homes. Or, their businesses, as the case may be. And, well, if some of them choose to show their…let's say, appreciation…by sending a pitcher of ale or such our way, well, who's to say we should refuse their generosity?"

"I'm to say. As commander, I say that every guard should perform their duty for a fair wage, with no expectation or coercion of receiving more."

"Aw, come on, Thorne. You can't tell me you've never once used your rank to…"

Sarge saw something flash in those emerald eyes. Then, he noticed the commander's hand resting on the pommel of the sword she wore at her hip. Long fingers flexed about the grip.

"Never." Her tone was like sharpened steel. "And, I fully expect that no one under my command shall, either. Is that clear?"

"Clear, Commander Thorne." Sarge was compelled to salute her; a proper salute this time.

Commander Thorne came to full attention and gave a crisp salute, her fist soundly connecting with her upper chest over her heart. Her boots sharply clicked together as she performed a perfunctory turn on her heel. Even her departure was one of perfect military precision.

Sarge rolled his eyes and let out a heated puff of air behind her back. Not that he was all that concerned about the commander.

Thorne may be just that, a sharp pain in his side, but it'd soon pass. It always did. Every time they got a new commander, there was a period of adjustment. This time was no different.

The commander was new and a hard-ass, to boot. But, she was still a she. Not a *she* that he was attracted to in any way, but still a woman, nevertheless. She'd give in to him, just like all the little tavern whores did. *Speaking of...*

Sarge fairly rubbed his hands together as he remembered the original serving wench from The Dirty Duck. He'd seen her dressing earlier, but then had lost sight of her during that whole mess with that other crazy wench. He hadn't seen her during the confrontation with the commander, either. But, he also hadn't seen her sneak out. With any luck, she might still be cowering in the shadows somewhere.

Sarge stepped foot into the small room.

"Oh, Sergeant?"

Sarge ducked his head back out. He had to fight to keep the scowl off his face when he saw the commander looking back at him.

"Yes, Commander?"

"Just so we're both perfectly clear...you and..." The commander looked at Ernest, still standing guard at his post, and then back to the sergeant "...the corporal will report for reassignment to the gaol at first light."

"Yes, Commander."

Sarge glared daggers at her back as she walked away, on an exact path to The Dirty Duck Tavern.

Sarge spat at the ground and turned before ducking back into the guards' room. He spied the yellow scarf upon the floor and bent to pick it up. His eyes quickly scanned the rest of the dim interior.

"Spirits be damned."

The room was empty.

He kicked at a chair, sending it skittering across the floor. He picked up the table and slammed it down with all his might, one of the legs splintering beneath his efforts. Fists closed, the yellow scarf tightening about his hands as he shouted out his rage.

Chapter Eight

As soon as Gwen closed the tavern door, she crinkled her nose and gave a wary sniff. Something foul wafted on the air at The Dirty Duck. Perhaps it was the thick smoke caused by the torches lining the wall and the fire burning in the great hearth. Perhaps it was the smell of burning fat as it dropped from the joints of roasting meat in great sizzling dollops onto the fire. Spying the clumps on the floor, Gwen also thought it might be caused by wet rushes that hadn't been swept out since spirits-knew-when.

Or, perhaps, the odor was just from the crush of too many bodies in one place. The Dirty Duck was packed to the point of being overcrowded. As far back into the tavern as Gwen could see, every seat at every table was taken. Even the warming stones in front of the great hearth were occupied. Those that weren't fortunate enough to have found seating were aimlessly milling about the common room.

Gwen was jostled from behind as a man dressed in merchant's clothes pushed past her with a tankard clutched in his fat fist. He elbowed his way through the crowd, slammed his empty mug down on the bar, and demanded more ale. A haggard-looking innkeeper took the mug and the merchant's coin and refilled the tankard from a barrel. Ale sloshing over the rim of the mug with each step, the merchant picked his way back through the crowd to his table.

Taking her lead from the merchant, Gwen elbowed her way to the bar. The innkeeper's back was to her as he refilled another mug. She placed the pitcher, mugs, and tray she'd carried from the guards' room on the bar. The innkeeper didn't even look up as he exchanged drink for coin with patron after patron.

"About time," he said, his gaze finally drifting to the wooden tray. "Get that loaded up with stew and ale and start serving."

"I'm not one of your serving maids."

"What?" The innkeeper turned and cocked his ear toward her.

"I'm not one of your wenches," Gwen shouted to be heard above the din.

The innkeeper refilled a mug and passed it to a patron by rote, all the while looking at Gwen as though she were daft. She could almost read his mind. After all, here she was, standing in front of him with pitcher and mugs on a tray sitting on the bar. Who else could she be but one of his serving maids? He looked her up and down and Gwen saw something akin to comprehension light in his eyes as they settled on her traveling cloak.

"Ale or cider?" he asked.

"What?"

"Ale or cider. I'm out of everything else. Which is it goin' to be?"

"Oh, um, neither. Just a room."

"I'm out of those, too."

"But, you've got upstairs." The second floor had been one of the first things Gwen had noticed from the tavern's exterior.

"Aye, and the rooms are all full up. These animals are sleeping two and three deep in most of 'em."

"I have coin. I'll pay extra." Gwen palmed five gold coins and passed them across the bar.

"Don't say that too loudly, girl. You'll only invite trouble. Why'd you wait so late to look for lodging, anyway? Everyone knows they need a place to stay come sunset."

It didn't escape Gwen's notice that despite his admonishment, the innkeeper didn't give her coins back. She waited a few heartbeats and he gave a long-winded sigh.

He made an overhead motion with his arm.

Gwen watched as a dark-haired maid in a mid-length patched peasant skirt and off-the-shoulder blouse wriggled her way through the crowd.

With just a short jerk of his head, the maid followed the innkeeper's cue and stepped behind the bar, smoothly taking his place. Another jerk of his head had Gwen following him down the length of the bar to a more secluded spot.

"Look, I might have something," he said. "If you'll work for it tonight."

"I've already said, I'm not one of your wenches. I won't whore for you or anyone else."

Gwen snatched her coins back from the innkeeper and turned on her heel. She had every intention of leaving the shelter of the tavern and, if need be, spending the night curled up on the cold, damp cobblestones with only her cloak for warmth. She'd scarcely taken two steps when there was a restraining hand at the crook of her elbow.

"Hold on, now. I don't pay wages for whoring." The innkeeper actually looked offended. "What the serving maids do or don't do to earn extra coin is their business, as long as it don't interfere with mine. All I'm asking is that you wait some tables. Do that and you can share a room with one of the girls."

"That's all?" Gwen eyed the innkeeper dubiously.

"That's all. Someone catches your eye and you get an itch, well, you let them scratch it for you after closing."

"Believe me, the only itch I have is to spend the night in a nice, warm bed." Gwen paused and then felt the need to add, "Alone."

"Then, we have an accord?" asked the innkeeper.

"We do." Gwen nodded her head and met the innkeeper's handclasp in agreement.

The innkeeper gave a shrill whistle that cut through the din and motioned for the girl at the bar. She nodded her head, passed a tray of tankards along to another maid, and edged her way down the bar to them.

"Rachel, this is…"

"Gwen."

"Gwen," agreed the innkeeper, as if he'd known all along. "Show her where she can store her gear and," his lip fairly curled as he looked Gwen up and down, "find her something more suitable to wear."

"Sure, Roe. Come on, Gwen."

Rachel pulled aside a quilt hanging across an open doorway that Gwen hadn't noticed earlier. Beyond, there was a long hallway, lit by a single flickering torch. There were a total of five doors, two lining each side and one at the very end of the hall.

Gwen started to follow Rachel down the dimly lit corridor.

"Oh, and I keep these." Roe snatched the coins from Gwen's hand.

She started to object, but the words died on her lips as Roe quickly returned to his position at the bar.

So, not only must I work for my keep, I'm expected to pay to work here, as well? That cobblestone bed is looking better and better by the heartbeat.

"Come along, luv," called out Rachel. "You can share with Beatrice, seeing as how she's gone off and left us with all the work."

With a resigned sigh and a slump of weary shoulders, Gwen trailed along behind the serving maid turned guide.

✝

Despite insisting that he did not promote whoring at his establishment, it was abundantly clear that Roe did nothing to actively discourage the trade either. How else to explain what he deemed *suitable attire* for working at The Dirty Duck?

The patched linen skirt ended just short of the knee, showing far more leg than a proper maiden should. If the skirt was immodest, the blouse was outright inappropriate. It was collarless, the front cut to a very deep V between the breasts. The material was light-colored and thin and gave more than a hint as to the maid's attributes beneath the fabric.

Gwen slid her empty tray onto the bar. She leaned heavily on the counter, trying to take some of the weight off her throbbing feet. She silently prayed that Roe would take his time filling the pitcher and mugs so she might have a heartbeat or two longer to rest.

Someone brushed against her. A hand stroked through her hair. Gwen stiffened as the overly familiar touch moved down the length of her back. She turned sharply, ready to lash out at yet another ill-mannered, drunken lout.

Gwen breathed a sigh of relief when she realized it was only Rachel. The serving maid placed her tray containing a large wooden bowl and several pitchers on the bar beside Gwen's and gave Roe the signal that she needed more ale.

"Rough night?" she asked.

"Following one of the roughest days I've ever had." Gwen grimaced as she clutched a hand to her lower back.

"Just think, luv." Rachel brushed Gwen's hand aside and replaced it with her fingers. "Three more candlemarks till closing."

"Unh." Gwen arched as Rachel's fingers dug into a knot of muscles. "I'll give you till then to stop what you're doing."

"Workload wouldn't be so bad if Beatrice would hurry back."

"I thought I was taking her place tonight."

"No offense, luv, but you're hardly an experienced serving wench, are you? Besides, we were already down one before tonight."

"Looks like we may be down another," said a third serving maid as she joined them at the counter.

This one was a cute, little thing. She was short, with a slender build, tawny hair, and big doe eyes. She couldn't have been more than eighteen or nineteen summers old. Rachel introduced her as Fauna and Gwen wondered if that was the girl's real name.

"Not Karyn?" asked Rachel.

"Karyn," confirmed Fauna. "Got grabbed going past one of your tables, Rachel. Mind you, it didn't look like she was trying all that hard to get away."

Roe slammed a pitcher down on Gwen's tray. Ale sloshed over the rim and he brusquely shook it off his hand.

"Hey, I'm not paying you lot to stand around and cluck like a bunch of hens."

"You're not paying me at all, remember?" Gwen asked.

"Come on, Roe, we're exhausted. With all the extra coin you've got coming in, you should close early tonight and treat us all to a hot soak in scented oils."

"Hush up, Rachel. Don't be putting foolish ideas into their heads." Roe wiped his hands on his tunic and looked at each of the girls in turn. "Dry roof over your head for the night should be payment enough."

"Sorry, Roe." Fauna ducked her head, averting her eyes from the innkeeper's hard gaze.

He must really intimidate her. Gwen noted that in her haste to get away, Fauna had exchanged her empty tray for Gwen's full one. She started to call out after the girl, but she was already halfway across the tavern, serving a table of four near the door.

Gwen flicked a glance back at the bar. Roe had a wooden chisel and mallet and was hunkered down, trying to tap a fresh keg of ale. She took advantage of the lull in work to keep a watchful eye on Fauna.

The girl moved with proficient ease from table to table, smoothly refilling mugs and taking coin in payment as she went. Some of her customers looked rather rough, but beyond what seemed to be some light flirting, none of them appeared to be bothering Fauna.

Spirits, she's an experienced tavern maid. She could probably handle all of them without any help from me.

Still, Gwen knew from the stories that her sister Cathryn told that the life of a serving maid was a hard one. There were long candlemarks, poor wages, worse tips, and sometimes no tips. Then, there was the pawing, pinching, and grabbing in general. And, that was just from the patrons. Spirits help the maids that worked for lusty tavern keepers.

Cursing drew Gwen's attention and she looked in Roe's direction. The innkeeper was sucking his thumb. He rapidly shook it and took up the mallet and resumed pounding on the keg in earnest.

Gwen idly wondered if Roe were the type to take advantage of his tavern maids. *Is that why Fauna's so skittish around him?* There was no doubt that Fauna was young and sweet-looking and most of the men in the tavern were attracted to her because of it. If she were wenching, though, she wouldn't keep that aura of innocence about her for long.

That drew Gwen's eye to Rachel. Rachel was attractive enough. Even in the smoke-filled haze and dim lighting, though, there were laugh lines clearly visible around the corners of her eyes and mouth. Gwen guessed she probably wasn't much past twenty-five, but deeply etched lines in her brow made her look at least ten summers older.

Roe loaded Rachel's tray with two pitchers of ale. Rachel looked at the tray, but appeared to be in no rush to be on her way.

"Come on, girl. The customers are thirsty," admonished Roe.

"Yeah, and don't I know it? Be easier to roll a whole barrel of ale across the room instead of taking it one pitcher at a time."

"Might consider it if they had enough coin to pay for it up front." Roe rubbed his chin, as though giving it serious thought.

"They? There's only the one, luv, and the coin is flowing as freely as the ale," said Rachel.

The tavern door blew open, allowing in a gust of chill air, sideways falling rain, and a tall figure in a hooded cloak. The braziers nearest the door flickered, but remained lit.

She pushed back her hood, revealing ebony hair with a distinctive white streak running through it. She used the heel of her boot to kick the door shut and stood on the threshold, keeping herself between the patrons and the exit.

She turned her head with her eyes doing a slow scan of the smoke-filled tavern. Her gaze fell across the bar and she paused, her eyes narrowing.

Gwen's breath hitched and she felt a surge of panic. *She's come to arrest me, or worse, toss me out the city gate.* Heart pounding loudly in her chest, she felt the overwhelming need to hide from the scrutiny of that unnerving gaze.

"Rachel, you want to switch? I'll take it for you."

"You sure? The back tables are the rowdiest. That's where all the bad boys and girls like to sit; think they can watch the entire room that way. As if they can even see, the way some of 'em have been putting it back."

The commander was standing with her head cocked to the side, her hand on the hilt of her sword.

Gwen felt the commander's dark eyes upon her. "Don't worry. I can handle myself."

"Right, luv. Stew goes to the back corner. Yell out if you need any help."

Gwen drew in a deep breath, braced herself, and lifted the tray. She nodded once at Rachel and then started off, trying her level best to keep the pitchers of ale balanced. She hunched her shoulders, kept her head down, and her face hidden behind the loaded tray. She thought she heard the commander call her name, but she scurried past without slowing.

÷

Commander Thorne idly rubbed her thumb over the emerald embedded in the pommel of her sword. Her eyes followed the serving maid as she hurried past carrying a tray laden down with food and drink. She'd called out her name, but the girl had gone past without so much as a hitch in her step.

Her clothes were different. Thorne had caught a glimpse of a tunic and breeches beneath her cloak earlier. Now, she was wearing a peasant blouse and skirt. Still, the commander was certain she was the same maid she'd spied in the alcove at the guards' room.

She hadn't for a heartbeat believed the sergeant when he'd said she was a serving wench at The Dirty Duck, despite the pitcher and tray she'd seen the woman carrying.

The commander might be newly assigned to this post, but she was far from naïve. She knew all too well how things worked in cities like Fairhaven. Crime was rampant, the guards were either inept or corrupt or both and the honest citizens either had their heads in the sand or were just too plain scared to take action.

Her gut said the sergeant was lying. There was more to this maid than met the eye. For one thing, as she walked away, Thorne could have sworn that she had something hidden beneath her cloak. She'd even thought it might have been the curve of a bow.

What was I to do? Chase her down and ask her about having a suspicious curve to go with that sway? She'd think me as lewd as the sergeant.

Thorne made her way to the bar.

"Ale or cider?" asked the tavern keeper.

"Neither, I'm on duty."

"Cider, then. Less of a kick than ale, but it'll warm the bones."

The tavern keeper placed a mug in front of Thorne and she looked at him askance.

"We here at The Dirty Duck know our civic responsibility. Don't let it be said we don't take care of the guard." Roe puffed out his chest as though proud of that fact and gave the commander a wink and a nod.

"Water." Thorne pushed the mug away and plunked down a bronze coin on the counter.

Roe shrugged and moved away. When he returned, he carried a mug so full that liquid sloshed over the side as he placed it on the bar.

Thorne used a fold of her cloak to wipe the rim of the mug and brought it to her nose, surreptitiously sniffing. She took a cautious sip and swished it around in her mouth before taking a deeper draw. Satisfied, she turned around and propped her elbows on the counter as she surveyed the tavern's dim interior. She spotted a flash of chestnut hair moving through the room.

Thorne was convinced. This was Gwen—the same Gwen she'd met near the gate. However, it would take more than a change of clothes to convince her that this maid was a common tavern whore.

Idly sipping her water, Thorne watched as Gwen made her way back to a table at the far corner of the room.

†

Gwen could feel eyes upon her. She was staring. She'd been staring ever since she'd come in the tavern. Gwen didn't know how the commander had done it, but it was like she'd picked her out of the crowd the instant she'd stepped foot inside.

She'd hated the lie when it'd first come out of that overbearing guard's mouth, but then the lie had turned into her means of escaping him. Yes, perhaps she should have spoken the truth when she'd had the chance, but she didn't know what to expect if she had. Certainly, the guards would have been in trouble, but she didn't know if she would be rescued, arrested, or turned out. Spirits knew she wouldn't last the night outside the shelter of the city's walls.

So, she'd taken advantage of the lie. Now, it seemed, she was forced to live it.

She'd hoped that once the commander had seen her, seen the way she was dressed, the tray she was carrying, and the tables she was serving, she'd be convinced. She'd thought that once the commander's curiosity was quenched, she'd leave. Instead, she'd sidled up to the bar and was having a drink.

Gwen sneaked a peek. The commander was standing with the sole of one boot propped against the bar behind her. Her arms were folded over her chest as she leaned back against the counter. There was a mug on the bar beside her elbow.

To her consternation, she found emerald green eyes looking back at her. Gwen hastily dropped her gaze and turned away, weaving her way through the mass of tables and chairs.

It's okay, Gwen. You can do this. Just keep your head down and your mind on your work.

Gwen didn't realize she'd reached the last table until she bumped right into it. She grimaced, knowing come morning, there'd be a bruise on her thigh.

True to her mantra, Gwen kept her head down. She placed the bowl of mutton stew on the table, managing to spill only the tiniest bit. She balanced the tray on one hip as she lifted a pitcher so she could fill an empty mug on the table. The ale had just started to come out in a steady stream when the slap came.

It was sharp, it hurt, and to Gwen's ears, it sounded as if it echoed loudly even over the raucous din in the noisy tavern. The momentum shoved her forward, the pitcher sloshed, the mug was overturned, and ale went spilling out all over the table.

Gwen spun about, cocked her arm back, and brought her open palm forward to deliver a resounding slap in turn. Her hand was seized in mid-swing. Fingers tightly gripped her wrist, turning the surrounding flesh white. Gwen's livid gaze traveled from clenching fingers to defined wrist veins and tanned arms. She looked at her assailant's broadly grinning face. There was a mass of blonde hair and bright blue eyes.

Oh, spirits. Gwen's gut clenched. *And, dimples.*

"Fair, Gwendolyn!" Bodhi chased her overturned mug, righted it, and raised it in salute. "Welcome to Fairhaven."

✝

She was a rake if ever Thorne had seen one.

100

She had a big smile and even bigger swords, their pommels riding high behind each shoulder in a double crisscross harness. Her hair was an untamed golden mane, the length of which fell over both shoulders of her tunic. Her sleeves were rolled up to her elbows, revealing arms corded with muscle.

At present, one of those arms was firmly clasped about the waist of a tavern whore perched upon her lap. The dark leather of the rogue's wrist cuff stood out in stark contrast against the white material of the peasant blouse as her hand cupped one of the wench's breasts.

Not that the serving wench seemed to mind. Her head was tossed back, her curly black hair bouncing with the motion as she wholeheartedly laughed at something being said by lips pressed to her ear.

Then, Gwen was there, her back to the warrior as she placed the bowl on the table and began pouring from a pitcher.

The warrior turned her head, blatantly looking the maid up and down.

Then came the slap to Gwen's backside.

Thorne slammed her mug down and pushed herself away from the bar, her boots disturbing the rushes on the floor. Her hand went to the hilt of her sword, her fingers tightening upon the grip as she inched the blade from its sheath. She felt the muscles in her arms and upper body tighten in anticipation of a fight. Mouth set in a fine line and jaw clenched, Thorne took a step forward.

She drew up short as a guardsman appeared directly in front of her. His cheeks were tinged rouge as if from windburn and his breathing was haggard. He gave a rapid hand-to-chest salute before pulling himself to attention.

"Commander, come quick." When she didn't immediately respond, he added between hastily drawn in breaths, "We've found another."

Thorne looked from the guardsman to Gwen and the ruffian that had just accosted her. With a displeased growl, she let loose the grip on her sword. The hilt jangled as the blade dropped back into the sheath.

"Problem, Commander?" asked Roe from the other side of the bar.

"No," was the ingrained response.

Thorne paused and turned, seeing the innkeeper pouring ale into a mug and the way the guardsman's eyes followed every move Roe made. She deliberately pulled a bronze coin from her purse and placed it on the counter, pushing it toward the innkeeper.

"For the water," she specified, loud enough for the guardsman to hear. "No more drinks for guards on duty. If any should ask, I expect you to report their names to me."

"Of course. Anything for the commander of the city guard." Roe smiled widely as he scooped up the extra coin.

Thorne frowned at the innkeeper, wondering as to the true meaning behind his words. Then, she gestured for the guardsman to lead the way. When he was a little too slow to leave, she gave him a shove, pushing him along ahead of her to the door.

†

Bodhi was drunk beyond measure. That much was clear. What was not was *what is she doing in Fairhaven?*

Besides the tavern whores, Gwen added that bitter thought as she eyed the trollop curled up on Bodhi's lap. One arm was draped about Bodhi's shoulders, her fingernails tracing an idle pattern upon the warrior's collarbone. The tip of her tongue moistened full, pouty lips. Brown eyes boldly gazed at Bodhi, openly teasing with professional promise.

"Karyn, I presume?" asked Gwen.

Before the tavern wench could respond, Bodhi answered for her. "Karyn, this is Gwendolyn."

Bodhi seemed stirred to make formal introductions by stretching out both arms as if she intended to envelop Gwen in a hug. Instead, she lifted one of the pitchers from Gwen's tray and drank straight from it. After several hearty swallows, Bodhi slammed the pitcher down on the table and wiped her mouth on her upper sleeve.

"Bodhi, what are you doing here?"

"I was about to ask the same of you, fair Gwen." Unfocused blue eyes looked her over from head to foot. "But, I see now."

Gwen followed her line of sight, taking in her manner of dress and the tray she had perched on the edge of the table. "Bodhi, it's not what you think—"

"Shush, it's fine, Gwen. I understand. Really, I do."

"You do?" Gwen felt both her eyebrows go up.

"Of course. It's not the first time it's happened." Bodhi waved her hand as if to dismiss the occurrence. "I have that effect on some women."

"Bodhi, what do you think this is?" Suspicion laded Gwen's tone.

Bodhi turned to look at Karyn, as though she felt the need to explain to the tavern wench rather than simply answer Gwen's question.

"One tumble and they can't get enough." She turned to look back at Gwen, boldly meeting her gaze. "I once had one follow me from Dorchester all the way to Whitley—"

"I'm not following—"

"—on foot."

"Bodhi, I am not following you."

"Of course not." Bodhi gave an exaggerated wink.

"Bodhi, who is she?" Karyn squirmed on Bodhi's lap. She skillfully arched her back so that her breasts were pressed more firmly against Bodhi. Her fingers moved from Bodhi's shoulder to possessively tangle in the warrior's hair.

Apparently the whore is worried she's got competition.

Bodhi swiveled her head to look at the wench perched on her lap. Her eyes narrowed to tiny slits as though irritated she had to explain again.

"Karyn, this is Gwendolyn, virgin sacrifice."

It seemed to Gwen as if with those two key words spoken aloud the clatter at the tables nearest them fell away. Gwen felt as if suddenly all eyes were on her. A heated flush rose to her cheeks and she dropped her face into her hands.

"Well, don't look. She's not anymore," said Bodhi.

Gwen prayed to all the spirits she knew that they'd instantly render her deaf. Or better yet, Bodhi mute.

"See, there was an ogre and we were chained to these pillars in the ruins of an ancient temple. He was coming for the virgin sacrifice and I couldn't free—"

"Sheep shit."

Gwen's head snapped up as the guttural voice interrupted Bodhi's drunken ramblings.

Bodhi's blue eyes were clear now, her steely gaze fixed on a man at the next table.

Even hunkered down over his bowl of stew as he was, there was no doubt that he was still a man of considerable size. His greasy, black hair was long all over, the length of it hiding his eyes and most of his face from view. His tunic was sleeveless, the material at the shoulders frayed and ragged as if the size of his muscles had been sufficient enough to rend the fabric in twain. His bare arms were lined with old scars, some of them very deep. A battered battle-ax rested on the table within easy reach. *Barbarian,* thought Gwen.

"What'd you say?"

Bodhi pushed Karyn off her lap. She placed both hands palms down on the table, emphasizing the stark delineation in her arms as she slowly pushed herself up. She wore dual swords at her back, a long knife sheathed at her waist, and a dagger belted at her thigh. There was a sense of danger about her, and the icy blue stare coupled with the slow smirk spreading over her lips caused a shiver to run down Gwen's spine.

"I said, sheep shit," drawled the barbarian.

The legs of the chair scraped the wooden floor as he climbed to his feet. It seemed as if it took him forever to unfold his body completely, but once he did, he was tall—taller than Bodhi. As he deliberately stood toe-to-toe with her, Bodhi was forced to crane her neck to look up at him. *Big, mean barbarian.* Gwen noted how much he dwarfed Bodhi. He folded his arms over his massive chest and looked down at Bodhi.

"No such things as ogres," His lip curled up into a sneer as he turned his head to look at Gwen. "Nor virgin tavern wh—"

The resounding *crack* of knuckles against jawbone echoed loudly in the tavern. Gwen blinked, not clearly recognizing until the sound had fully resonated that Bodhi had thrown the punch.

The barbarian's head violently snapped to the side. He just…stopped…for a heartbeat. Then, he stood up straight, placed a beefy hand to his jaw, and cracked his neck. He grinned widely, balled the front of Bodhi's tunic in his hand, and cocked his fist.

†

A full yellow moon peeked out from the cover of clouds and overhanging rooftops, offering more light than wall braziers alone could provide. Soles of boots splashed through water puddles lining the cobblestone. More than once, Thorne found her soft soles skidding on the rain-slicked streets as she rushed in her pursuit of the guardsman.

She trailed him through a myriad of tight, dimly lit alleyways through the city's poor district. They turned left, then right, and Thorne was certain she'd seen that same black cat staring at her from that door stoop twice already.

He was half a block distant when she lost sight of him. She gave chase, determined that she not become lost in the dark maze of narrow streets and back alleys. She thought she saw a flash of burgundy tunic rounding a distant corner and she ran full-out, taking the same corner and nearly toppled right over the waiting guardsman. She peered past him, into the darkness.

And, there she was. On her back, arms flung out to the side, legs curled at an awkward angle beneath her. Water poured in a steady stream from a gable, drenching her red hair, her upturned face, and the scarf knotted about her neck.

Chapter Nine

Gwen pushed aside the quilt hanging across the hall and stepped into the main room of the inn. The tavern was dimly lit, the wall braziers having burned low overnight. It was a dreary, gloomy midmorning with the incessant sound of rain pitter-pattering against the pane windows.

The main room appeared deserted. The smell of musty brushes, stale ale, and day-old mutton stew made the air smell foul. Gwen stepped behind the bar and poured herself a mug of cider in the hopes it would settle her queasy stomach. Crossing to the hearth, she used a poker to stir the ashes and sat down on the warming stone in front of the fire.

She sipped her cider and grimaced as the liquid stung. Gwen touched her bottom lip, feeling the split. Her fingers moved to her cheek, wincing as she felt the bruise there.

Gwen looked about the room, surveying the damage. She saw three overturned tables. Spirits only knew how many chairs had been broken in the brawl. There were too many disjointed legs and splintered backs to make an accurate count. One of the windows was busted out. Someone had rigged a blanket over the frame in an attempt to keep out the wind and rain.

Probably Roe. Gwen saw the burly innkeeper coming through the front door. He had a hammer and bucket of nails. The two men trailing along behind him were carrying planks of lumber between them.

"Morning." Roe nodded at Gwen as he marched past.

The man following closest behind Roe echoed the greeting with a clearing of his throat. The last one, more of a lad than a man, grinned at her and then shyly ducked his head. Gwen saw him turning his head and sneaking peeks back over his shoulder at her as he nearly ran up on his partner when he came to a stop at the far wall.

The two older men put the younger lad to work clearing out the mess of wooden chairs while they took care of the window. Gwen watched as they took down the blanket and knocked out the remaining bits of glass from the pane. Then, they placed lengths of lumber over the frame and started nailing them in place.

"Heck of a brawl, wasn't it, luv?"

Gwen looked up to see Rachel dragging a chair over to the hearth. She looked like she'd just rolled out of bed. Her hair was tousled, there were dark rings beneath her eyes, and her clothes were wrinkled. Rachel tenderly lowered herself onto the chair, grunting as she connected with the wood.

"Got kicked in the backside," Rachel said.

"Must've been one heck of a brawl," echoed Gwen, wincing as she took another sip from her mug.

"Ooh, that looks painful. First thing I should've told you…if a fight breaks out, duck and run for cover, luv." She reached out and cupped Gwen's chin, turning her head this way and that as she studied her face.

"Easier said than done, Rachel. You didn't see her get hit." Fauna emerged from behind the quilted curtain, yawning and rubbing sleep from her eyes. She shuffled to the bar and poured two mugs of cider.

"Oh, and I suppose you saw the whole thing, luv?" Rachel folded her arms over her bosom.

"I did. That beast of a barbarian hit Gwen and sent her crashing into that table of merchants." Fauna joined them. She handed one of the mugs to Rachel and then sat cross-legged on the floor in front of the hearth. "Do you remember anything after that, Gwen, or were you already unconscious?"

Gwen's fingers went to her face and she winced. She remembered seeing the barbarian making a fist. Nothing beyond that came to mind, though. She furrowed her brow and shook her head.

"After you went down and took all their drinks with you, those merchants and that woman warrior were all over the barbarian."

"Bodhi." *It just had to be Bodhi.*

"I think that's her name," said Rachel.

"What happened to her?" Gwen was surprised to hear herself ask.

"Last I saw, Karyn was leading her off to soak her swollen knuckles in some cool water."

The way she batted her eyes and the coy smile on Fauna's face suggested to Gwen that Karyn might have tended to more than merely Bodhi's knuckles.

"Anyone else, he would've let 'em haul off to gaol."

"Don't be that way, Rachel. She paid Roe, didn't she?"

"Bodhi paid the damages?" Gwen looked around the tavern, wondering how much coin that had taken.

"And then Karyn went off with her and left us to clean up the mess." Rachel took a drink from her mug and then made a face as though it wasn't the taste she'd been expecting. "Ugh. Cider, Fauna?"

"Cider's better for you. Besides, it was just some spilt stew and ale. It only took a few extra candlemarks to set everything right again. Well, except for the big repairs. But, Roe's handling that."

In spite of her current employment, Fauna seemed to be an innocent, able to find the good in any circumstance. Gwen wondered if she had ever truly been like that, even in her seemingly carefree days of youth. *Was it really so long ago?* This morning, it seemed as if Chatham was immeasurable miles and ages away.

Rachel seemed agitated, taking up the poker and jabbing at the logs in the fire, knocking the ash away.

"All I'm saying is, I don't think it's right that we got stuck with the cleanup while everyone else went off to bed."

That brought back fuzzy memories of waking up that morn. She'd been in bed, in the room that Rachel had shown her last eve. Her traveling clothes were still folded neatly in a nearby chair. Her bow and quiver of arrows were leaning against the corner exactly as she'd left them. Even her saddlebags appeared to be undisturbed. To her immense relief, when she pulled back the bedcovers, she discovered that she was still fully clothed as she'd been last night.

"Who put me to bed?" Gwen abruptly asked.

"That would've been Roe," Rachel said.

Gwen's eyes drifted to the tavern keeper. He wasn't an entirely unattractive man, she supposed. He was older, with lines etching his face and white in his beard. His stomach was beginning to develop a paunch, but otherwise, he seemed to be in pretty good shape. His arm muscles flexed as he hammered nails into the boards over the window at a steady pace.

"Don't worry, luv, Roe looks after all his girls."

"Oh. I'm not one of the girls. I mean, I'm not…I don't…this isn't what it seems. I'm not working here?" Even to Gwen's ears, she sounded so unsure.

"Right, luv. None of us are, are we, Fauna?"

Roe stopped his hammering long enough to fetch a hatchet from behind the counter. He passed it to the lad that was working with the broken furniture and instructed him on how to separate out the pieces of good wood from what would become kindling.

"Rest easy, girls. We'll be open by dusk," Roe called out to the women seated about the hearth.

Rachel lifted her mug in acknowledgment and took a healthy swig. As soon as Roe smiled and looked away, Rachel turned and spat the mouthful of cider into the fire.

"Hope you're ready for another rough night, luv."

"What? Why?" asked Gwen.

"You woke up alone, didn't you?"

Gwen, not quite certain what Rachel was getting at, nodded slowly.

"That was Beatrice's bed you were meant to be sharing. No telling where she spent the night or if she'll even be back this eve. And, as for Karyn, well if that big, blonde warrior's willing to spend the coin—"

"Don't expect me, either. This," Gwen gestured to encompass herself, the serving maid's outfit she was wearing, and the whole tavern in general, "was only for the one night. I've other plans."

"We've all had other plans, luv. Do you think any of us wanted to wake up here this morning or any morning? Plans have a way of changing."

"Perhaps, but I'm only passing through."

"That's what I told myself, too. I was only here long enough to earn the coin needed to open my own bakery. Every morning and every night for five summers straight, I told myself that. And after those five summers, all I got was smart enough to stop counting."

"Oh, Rachel, you'll still get that bakery one day. In the meantime, Roe lets you bake the bread trenchers and some treats, doesn't he?"

"Yes, Fauna. Yes, he does." A small smile formed on Rachel's lips.

Rachel's features seemed to soften as she looked down at Fauna sitting on the floor before her. She leaned forward and brushed her fingers through the girl's tawny hair. She seemed content, becoming momentarily distracted in the action. When she looked at Gwen again, her smile dropped away.

"We're all here for a reason. Beatrice came here looking to hide from an abusive husband. Elisabeth got pregnant by some randy traveling merchant and her father booted her out. Fauna ran away from home because her parents betrothed her to someone she doesn't love. And, she just knows she'll only marry for love." Rachel gave a derisive snort and looked at Fauna. "Believe me, kid, if it's true love you're waiting for, you'll die a spinster."

"I don't believe that. I won't believe that. Karyn married for love, didn't she?"

"Yes and look what that got her, luv."

Fauna downed her head. Her bottom lip quivered and for a heartbeat, Gwen thought the girl was going to cry. Then, she let loose a heavy sigh and looked up again. There was just a hint of moisture at the corner of her big brown eyes.

"It got her a home, Rachel. A real home that she goes to every night at closing."

"She still comes back to work here every day, though, doesn't she? How many times have I told you that love and marriage ain't all it's cracked up to be?"

The creak of hinges and the tinkling of the bell above the frame announced the opening of the tavern door. The smell of rain and a chill breeze accompanied the footfalls of boots into the room.

Gwen turned to look. Her mouth felt suddenly dry as she recognized the commander from the night before. Green eyes scanned the room. This time, Gwen couldn't hide in the shadows of a dimly lit smoke-filled tavern.

"We're not open," called out Roe.

Commander Thorne turned her head in the direction of Roe's voice. She held up her hand to motion for him. He jerked his head in greeting and met her at the bar.

"Ooooh, now I'd be willing to marry that one," cooed Fauna.

"That's great, luv, except you're confusing true love with lust."

"Whatever it is, I'd go for her in a heartbeat."

"Don't let her fool you, Gwen. Fauna's already got one admirer in the guard."

"Rachel." Fauna playfully slapped the other serving maid's knee. "Ernest is sweet, but he's just a lad. Commander Thorne, on the other hand, is a woman."

"Fully grown, I'd say, luv."

The chatter of their idle gossip faded away as Gwen continued to watch Commander Thorne and Roe. They were standing close together, speaking in low tones. Gwen couldn't make out what they were saying, but the grave looks on their faces indicated it was serious.

They both looked in the direction of the hearth. Emerald eyes met hers and Gwen felt her heartbeat quicken. She judged the distance from the hearth to the hall and the room where her weapons were. Her path would take her straight past the bar where Commander Thorne and Roe waited. *If I bolted for the door—*

The commander reached inside her tunic and pulled out a yellow scrap of cloth. Roe took it from her, unfolding it as he looked it over. A crimson stain marred the cloth.

The sound of a mug clattering on the floor drew Gwen's attention. Fauna pushed herself to her feet. Rachel reached out a hand for her, but Fauna pushed her off and ran across the room. She tore the material from Roe's grasp and sobbed.

"What's happened? What's going on?" Gwen turned to ask Rachel.

The tavern maid had gone deathly pale.

"That's Beatrice's scarf."

÷

The stairs were enchanted. They had to be. How else to explain that every time Bodhi tried to step down on one, it moved of its own accord?

Bodhi fastened a two-handed grip around the stair railing. She closed her eyes, immediately realized what a mistake that was, and opened them again. She took a steadying breath and stepped down, hoping that the double image she chose was the correct one. With the success of one stair, she gingerly picked her way down to the next.

Blessed mother, how much did I drink last eve?

Bodhi had woken sprawled across her bed, mostly dressed, and completely alone. The knuckles of her left hand were bruised, as were her ribs on her right side. A thorough search of her body revealed no significant cuts or gaping wounds, indicating it was a fistfight and not a duel she'd had. Other than that, she had no idea what events had transpired the night before.

Must've had a good time, for certain. Bodhi ground her teeth against the jarring motion caused by each step down she took. Her stomach was queasy. Her tongue and teeth felt as if they were lined with fur. Her vision was blurred as well as double. She had a pounding headache and—

"By the Spirits! What is that infernal caterwauling about?" Bodhi braced a hand to her head as piercing shrieks reverberated inside her skull.

With only one hand left on the rail, she managed to edge her way off the last step so that she was standing squarely on solid ground.

As squarely as I can. Bodhi felt the floor lurch beneath her, sending her stumbling against the wall. She braced herself and looked up to see several blurry people-sized shapes.

Standing in front of the hearth, was someone wearing the distinctive burgundy-hued tunic of the city guard. She recognized the innkeeper by his general build and the fact that he was standing behind the bar. The other shape hunched near the bar was a comingled mess with possibly two arms and six heads. It wasn't until she identified three heads and at least one peasant skirt that she was able to discern that it must be a gaggle of tavern maids.

Bodhi navigated her way on unsteady feet across the room. She leaned one elbow and most of her body against the bar and plunked down a bronze coin on the counter in exchange for a full mug. She cradled her pounding head in her hand and lifted the mug to her lips.

She choked, her body wracked with a coughing fit, and liquid spewed from her mouth.

"Gah. Cider."

Bodhi snatched up a bar rag and tried to wipe the cider remnants from her tongue, lips, and chin. She shot the innkeeper a glare until he reached beneath the bar and brought out another mug. She suspiciously eyed the contents and took a tentative sip until her taste buds confirmed that it was, indeed, ale and not something else even more vile than cider.

Satisfied this was more of the hair of the dog that bit her last eve, she turned up the mug and heartily drank. She drained the entire contents before righting the mug and slamming it down on the counter. The innkeeper was there with another. This one, Bodhi gingerly took a sip from and then placed back down.

She rubbed her eyes and looked up and across the bar. This time when she looked at him, she was able to clearly see every line in the innkeeper's grizzled face.

Bodhi braced herself and turned her head, ready to face her three-headed beast. Thankfully, it had morphed into three separate bodies. They were all huddled close together, with arms wrapped about each other the way young maids will do.

The middle one, that little slip of a tavern maid, had tears streaming from her eyes. Her teeth were leaving a white line against her bottom lip as if she were trying to bite back her tears. The one nearest her, with an arm wrapped protectively about her waist and a hand stroking through her hair, Bodhi recognized as Rachel. The one on the other side of her was—

"Gwen?!?"

"Bodhi."

"Gwen, what are you doing here?"

Eyes the same hue as that of warm honey blinked and the dark brows above them rose.

"You don't remember anything of last eve, then?" asked Gwen.

Bodhi's gaze swept over her, taking in the peasant skirt and blouse. She lingered over Gwen's bosom, her eyes caressing the curve of a breast. She saw the outline of a prominent nipple and gave a loud swallow. It was only when Gwen folded her arms protectively over her chest, thereby blocking her view that Bodhi's eyes drifted back to her face.

"Well, fair Gwen, if memory serves of our previous entanglements, I'd say last night must have been spectacular."

"If it was anything of the sort, it was only in your dreams, Bodhi," was Gwen's terse response.

There was a snigger and Bodhi turned to glare at the innkeeper. He took up his bar rag, turned his back, and proceeded to pick up and wipe out mug after mug. Bodhi could still see his shoulders shake with silent laughter.

She looked back at the tavern maids. Gwen's cheeks were tinged pink, there was a fire in her eyes, and a firm set to her mouth. Mirth was reflected in Rachel's eyes and there was a broad smile on her lips. The serving wench huddled between them was still trying to stifle her tears.

"What are you simpering about?" barked Bodhi.

At which point, the girl burst into heaving sobs. Rachel and Gwen both shot Bodhi dagger looks. Rachel wrapped a protective arm about the girl's shoulders and turned her away from Bodhi's stare.

"Come on, luv. Just ignore that…that…inconsiderate brute." Rachel steered the still-bawling girl toward a quilted curtain hanging across a doorway.

"What?" Bodhi shouted at their retreating backs. When they disappeared behind the curtain, she asked, "What is going on here?"

"We've discovered another body."

Bodhi stiffened. She'd forgotten about the blurred burgundy tunic in the room. *No wonder, the state I'm in this morn.* She turned and looked in the direction of the hearth. Eyes locked on the commander of the guard warming herself in front of the fire. Bodhi's hand went to her waist, her fingers caressing the hilt of her sheathed knife.

"Last eve…a maid from this tavern," the commander said as she stalked across the room to the bar.

She signaled the innkeeper and he poured a mug of water.

Bodhi watched her take a drink and felt herself grimace in response to the commander's swallow.

"I noticed you didn't ask." Thorne placed her mug on the counter.

"Who?"

"Does it matter?" Green eyes intently stared into hers.

"Yes, it does." Bodhi slammed her open palm down on the bar, causing the mugs to rattle.

"You said *another* body. How many have there been?" asked Gwen.

Bodhi ignored Gwen, continuing to glare at Thorne. It seemed the commander was also going to discount Gwen's question, as her eyes remained locked with hers.

"Who?" Bodhi clenched her jaw so tight her teeth ground together.

She felt a touch on her forearm and looked down to see Gwen's hand on the crook of her elbow. Her gaze traveled up, along Gwen's arm, over the delicate curve of her shoulder, and to her face. Brown eyes were looking back at her.

"Beatrice," Gwen said.

Bodhi released a sigh of relief. Then, hating herself for the feeling, she turned and lashed out at Thorne. "What are you doing here, warming yourself by the fire? You should be out there, doing something useful." Bodhi pointed toward the door and the streets that lay beyond.

"Rest assured, the city guard will bring the killer to justice."

"When? After half the city is murdered?"

"A handful of tavern wenches is hardly half the city."

"Is that why the guard isn't doing anything…because they're only tavern wenches?"

"I've doubled patrols in this sector. Don't insinuate I'm not doing my job."

"I'm not insinuating. I'm openly questioning your priorities. If they were merchants' daughters, would justice come swifter?"

Bodhi saw the twitching of Thorne's cheek muscle and flexed her fingers about her knife hilt in response. On the edge of her sightline, she saw the commander's hand steal to her waist and the knife she wore belted there.

"Bodhi."

She heard Gwen's low warning. Bodhi's eyes remained locked with Thorne's, refusing to give ground.

"Hey. No more fighting in my tavern." Roe pushed his way between them. "You want to behave like wild animals, take it outside."

Chapter Ten

With every fiber of her being, Thorne wanted to do just what Roe had said. She wanted to grab this rogue by her wild, unkempt blonde hair and drag her out into the streets and pummel her.

But, she was the leader of the guard. She was in control of this city. It fell to her to be disciplined, to maintain order, and uphold the law. She was the commander. She was the standard by which all others were to be measured.

"As much as I would enjoy teaching this braggart some manners, I haven't the time," she told Roe.

Thorne cast a disparaging look about the tavern. Upon news of the serving wench's death, Roe had dismissed his workers. They'd slunk past her and out the door, leaving a scattered array of tools, wood, and sawdust in their wake.

Given their reaction, I should check to see if there are outstanding charges against either of them.

"I expect all the repairs to be completed and the rushes swept out before you reopen." Thorne crinkled her nose and looked at Roe with an air of disdain. "It smells like a privy in here."

Roe opened his mouth as if to protest.

"Another disturbance such as the one that obviously occurred here last eve and I'll have you shut down."

"You," she pointedly jabbed Bodhi in the chest, "stay out of this. Interfere and I'll throw you into the deepest cell in the gaol."

Blue eyes flashed and white teeth were bared. Muscles strained as Roe held the warrior back.

Thorne smirked, amused by how easily she'd baited Bodhi. Knowing it would only rile her all the more, she deliberately turned her back on the warrior and stopped to speak with the remaining serving maid.

"Gwendolyn, my condolences on the loss of your companion."

"Thank you, but I didn't know Beatrice—"

"And, yet you work at the same tavern? Interesting. I think we very much need to speak further, Gwendolyn." She tilted her head at the brunette. "When next I return."

Thorne looked about. Gwen was pale and shaken. Bodhi was enraged. Roe was holding the warrior back, entreating her to be sensible. Was that fear she saw in his eyes and heard in his voice?

With slow, deliberate steps, she retrieved her cloak from beside the hearth. She donned it, feeling the weight and warmth of the material through her tunic. Thorne opened the door and cast a look up at the dark gray sky before stepping out into the misting rain.

†

No sooner had the door closed behind Commander Thorne than Bodhi brushed Roe off. She clasped Gwen's upper arms in her hands, squeezing hard, forcing her up onto her tiptoes.

Gwen looked up, staring into the cold depths of ice-blue eyes. "By the Spirits, girl, why are you here?"

There was a frostiness in Bodhi's tone that made Gwen shiver. When she was too slow to answer, Bodhi shook her. Gwen saw Roe take a step forward, as if he meant to intervene.

Bodhi must have seen him, too, as she flicked an eye in his direction. She released her grip and Gwen had both feet back flat on the floor again.

Roe looked from one to the other of them, then snatched up a broom from behind the counter. He stormed to the other side of the room and began furiously sweeping.

So much for taking care of all his girls. Gwen remembered Rachel's earlier words of praise for Roe. Free of Bodhi's grip, she paced the distance from the bar to the hearth. She stood before the fire, arms folded about her waist, as she stared into the dwindling flames.

It was only a matter of heartbeats later that she sensed Bodhi standing behind her. She felt a breath upon her neck and a hand clasp her shoulder.

"Damn it, Gwen. Answer me. What are you doing here?"

118

"I'm my own person, Bodhi. I don't answer to you or anyone else."

A stifled noise, something akin to a cross between a frustrated curse and a rumbling growl, met Gwen's ears.

"When I left Chatham, you were safely out of the clutches of both your fellow villagers and an ogre. You were free to go anywhere, to do anything, to be anyone you desired to be."

"And, that's precisely what I've done."

Both Bodhi's hands were on her shoulders, adding pressure. Not enough to hurt, only to turn her about. It unnerved Gwen to find Bodhi standing so close that there was scarcely a hairsbreadth between them. Bodhi gripped Gwen's jaw, the calluses of her fingers felt rough against her skin. Blue eyes darted about Gwen's face. Fingers reached up, caressing a cheekbone. Her thumb dragged across Gwen's swollen bottom lip.

Gwen licked her lips in reflex, wincing when her tongue grazed across the split.

"Not this," said Bodhi. "This isn't for you."

Gwen saw something reflected in Bodhi's eyes she'd never seen before. Then, she heard it in her voice and realized what it was. *Pity.*

"You…you…"

Gwen thrust both arms out, giving Bodhi a shove.

Apparently caught off guard by the sudden movement, Bodhi was sent stumbling back several paces. Her brow furrowed and she wore a dismayed expression on her face.

For some reason, Bodhi's apparent incomprehension only served to irk Gwen all the more. She balled both hands on her hips and glared daggers at the warrior.

"You feel sorry for me, don't you?" she accused.

"Well, I—"

"Oh, poor Gwen. She ended up just like her sister. Is that it, Bodhi? You think I'm some common tavern whore, don't you?" *It was what Bodhi thought of me the first time we met.* Gwen closed her hands into fists, her nails digging into her palms. She'd never been so angry. There were tears in her eyes and the fact that she was crying made her angrier.

She wanted Bodhi to hurt, too. Gwen gave her another vicious shove. This one sent Bodhi stumbling backward over a chair. She was on her feet instantly. Her eyes were flashing, her nostrils flared, and her jaw was clenched tight. Her hand was at her waist, her fingers tight about the hilt of her knife. Her thumb caressed over the cut sapphire embedded in the pommel of the knife.

Gwen saw Bodhi draw in a ragged breath as she slowly released her grip on her knife before dropping her hand by her side.

She let out a long exhale. Her icy gaze was unwavering. When she spoke, her tone was steel honed to a sharp edge. "If it's in a tavern and it's dressed like a tavern whore, it's probably a tav—"

The slap came so fast that Gwen didn't even realize she'd done it until she saw Bodhi's head snap to the side with the impact. Then, she felt the tingling numbness like that from a hundred stinging nettles against her reddening palm.

†

"Damn. Damn. Damn."

Bodhi's sword was drawn and she was ruthlessly hacking away. Bits and pieces flew up into the air, creating a miniature blizzard falling about the interior of the stable as she took her frustrations out on a hapless stack of straw. She swung and hacked and butchered the stack until it was reduced to nothing but scattered strands.

Her sword drooped, her arm heavy from exertion. She was breathing heavily, with her heart hammering, and her chest heaving. She sank to the floor, her back pressed up against the wall of the stall her horse was in. She sighed and drew in a deep breath, inadvertently inhaling bits of straw. It tickled her nostrils, causing her to snort.

"Damn," she said again. Sniffing, she breathed in the straw-filled dust she'd created. She sneezed. Again. Again. "Double damn."

She sat cross-legged on the floor, her arm tucked against her bruised ribs, and her sword cradled across her lap. Her eyes burned and her nose felt heavy. She looked around the stable, taking in the destruction she'd caused.

When was the last time I let this happen?

Some common, run-of-the-mill city guard had gotten the best of her. Thorne was goading her, and like some damned green recruit, Bodhi had let her. If it hadn't been for Roe restraining her, she'd be cooling her heels in the city gaol this very heartbeat.

Then, after Thorne had left, she'd approached Gwendolyn only to be rebuked. After the slap, Gwen had clenched her jaw and her fists, stomped her foot, and stormed off behind the quilted curtain.

Not that Bodhi couldn't have followed her, had she wanted. After all, it was only a quilt across an open doorway. And, it wasn't as if she didn't know what lay beyond the drapery.

It wouldn't be that difficult to find which room was Gwen's, even if all the doors were closed. Her strength was honed from a lifetime of being a warrior. It'd be a simple matter to kick open each door in turn, until she found what she desired.

To what end, though?

Bodhi's problem as of late was that she was finding more and more that not all of life's troubles could be solved at the end of a sword.

Not that she hadn't tried. She'd offered her services. Thorne had made it abundantly clear that her assistance would be neither appreciated nor tolerated. In truth, the commander had treated her more as suspect than professional colleague.

I suppose she doesn't consider us equals, professional or otherwise. Bodhi had seen the looks, felt the hostility rolling off Thorne in waves from their very first encounter. Their latest altercation at The Dirty Duck had only intensified the feelings of animosity.

Bodhi felt hot breath, followed by snuffling at her hair. She tilted her head back, looked up the length of a long nose to see two big eyes looking down at her. She climbed to her feet, sheathing her sword. Reaching up, she gently scratched behind the mare's ears. Each time she tried to stop, her horse nudged her with her nose.

At last, Bodhi retrieved a brush and began smoothing down the mare's coat. She soon became lost in the repetitive motion. With each stroke of the brush, a little more tension eased out of the warrior's body.

Time slipped away. Bodhi wasn't conscious of how long she'd been brushing the horse. She caught herself humming the words to a particularly ribald tavern song. Bodhi's lips curved into a smile. This was the most relaxed she'd been since arriving in Fairhaven.

There was a slight falter in the smooth stroke of the brush. Her grip tightened and then forcibly relaxed upon the wooden back. She followed through with the motion, careful not to let on that anything was amiss.

Someone's here.

Thought and action were seamless and she threw the weapon by reflex.

Bodhi looked up and saw a set of wide, brown eyes staring unblinkingly back at her.

Gwen.

Only, this was Gwen as she'd never seen her before. Oh, she'd made quite the first impression in her off-the-shoulder, virgin-sacrifice peasant garb. And, Bodhi doubted she'd ever forget the look of her in a filthy, bedraggled, torn, and blood-and-gore spattered bridal gown. Once she'd gotten past her anger, Bodhi had to admit, if only to herself, that Gwen made a very comely serving wench.

All of those Gwens paled in comparison to the woman that was standing before her now.

Her leather boots were short, coming up slightly past her ankle. Tucked into her boots, she wore a pair of tan breeches. They were tight, almost like a second skin, showing every curve of her legs. Like her breeches, her tunic was also tanned in color.

As well as tight fitting.

The tail of her tunic fell to mid-thigh and was belted at her trim waist. The front opening exposed more flesh than what was considered modestly acceptable, as evidenced by the delectable swell of a breast. The leather cording laced through the eyelets had no doubt come undone by the strain of her ample bosom pressed against the taut fabric.

A bag of quivers was belted at her waist and there was a bow hitched over one shoulder. She wore a drab brown cloak, the hood down, her chestnut tresses falling over her shoulders.

In one hand, she carried a set of saddlebags. With her other, she reached up over her shoulder and wrapped her fingers about the hilt of the dagger Bodhi had thrown.

†

With effort, Gwen pulled the blade free of the fabric from the support post her cloak was pinned to. She could feel the rampant beat of her heart in her chest and to her ears, her breathing sounded much too loud.

She walked deeper into the stables, pleased that although her legs might be wobbly, at least her knees weren't knocking together. Gwen turned the dagger around so that she was holding the blade and presented the hilted end to Bodhi.

"Nice farewell." Gwen kept her words short so that Bodhi might not hear how her voice trembled.

Bodhi arched a brow and took the dagger, but made no apology for throwing the weapon.

"What? It's not as if I actually hit you." A blonde brow furrowed. "Farewell?"

"It's a customary term of departure."

"You are? Leaving, I mean?"

"Just as quickly as I can. There's nothing tying me to this city."

"I'll assist you in saddling up. Which horse is yours?" Bodhi turned and looked around the stalls.

"I…um…don't…there isn't…"

"What?" Bodhi turned around again, facing Gwen. "Which one?"

"None of them. I don't have a horse, Bodhi."

"Come on, Gwen. You must. You didn't walk to Fairhaven, did you?"

Gwen felt the heat tingeing her cheeks.

"Gwen?"

She averted her gaze, looking at the rafters, a bucket of oats, and the straw-covered floor. Anywhere she could except for directly at those piercing blue eyes she just knew were boring into her. An exasperated sigh had a heated puff of air lifting the hair from Gwen's forehead.

"Dusty…died. I took her from Gerald and rode her out here. There was an…accident. She lost her footing and I had to put her down. I walked the remainder of the way here."

Out of Gwen's breathless narrative, Bodhi apparently took away, "You stole Gerald's horse?"

"I purchased her."

"From a lad that had his senses so addled that he couldn't pull up his breeches on his own?"

"I left six gold coins on his bedside table in exchange. It's not as if anyone else in Chatham would have willingly sold me a horse."

"No doubt. Still, to take the lad's horse on top of everything else he went through? Don't you feel just a little bit bad?"

"Of course I do. Just as I feel bad for slapping you earlier." Gwen waited for Bodhi to respond. She got nothing. Not even a blink. "Customarily, this would be when you say that you deserved it."

"I didn't, though. Unlike you, fair Gwen, I don't feel guilty for my actions. Everything that I've done is out of necessity and without remorse."

"Really, Bodhi, nothing? You don't regret anything? Not even this?"

Gwen's gesture encompassed her face—specifically, the split lip and the bruised cheek. This time, she did get a reaction from Bodhi. However, she wasn't entirely certain that it was the response she desired.

Bodhi put down the bristled brush and stepped closer, so close the toes of their boots were nearly touching.

She could feel the brush of Bodhi's tunic against hers as she lifted her arms and cupped her face. Callused fingers that had seemed so rough in the tavern now felt soft as lamb's wool upon her cheeks. Blue eyes stared into hers.

"I struck you?"

She doesn't know?

"You dodged." Gwen's tone was indignant.

"I what?"

"You," she poked Bodhi in the chest, "dodged."

"I'm not certain what that means."

"You don't recall picking a fight with that barbarian?"

Bodhi's guileless look convinced Gwen.

"You hit him. He swung at you. You…dodged."

Bodhi's brow furrowed and she looked down at her hand where dark bruises had formed on her knuckles. She pursed her lips and raised her eyes to meet Gwen's.

"So, in actuality, I never struck you."

Oh! What were you expecting, Gwen? An apology, an admission of guilt, mayhap a kiss to make it better? Don't hold your breath, girl.

"No. No, Bodhi, you didn't." At Bodhi's smug look, Gwen's temper flared. "But, you might at least have the decency to have some culpability since you threw the first punch. You don't recall anything of last eve, do you?"

"Rest assured, fair Gwen, there were some parts that I found quite memorable." Bodhi gave a brazen wink.

"I've already told you, Bodhi, none of those memories were made with me. Spirits be, you can't even remember a tavern brawl, much less which wench was perched on your lap. You're a warrior, Bodhi. How could you allow yourself to get that drunk?"

"Don't judge me, Gwen."

"The way you didn't judge me when you called me a tavern whore?"

Bodhi drug a hand through her hair and clenched her fingers at the base of her neck. She released a deep sigh. "My apologies if I made an untrue assumption."

Gwen was certain both her eyebrows had crept up onto her forehead. Her mouth dropped open in surprise at Bodhi's apology. *Well, as near an apology as Bodhi is apt to give.*

"Look, I'm no common drunk. It's only that there's nothing else to do here during the day other than sleep and the only things worth doing at night are drinking and wenching. Fortunately, The Dirty Duck has some of the comeliest tavern maids in Fairhaven."

"All the more reason for me to leave today."

After she'd calmed down from her altercation with Bodhi, Gwen went to Roe and he'd told her about the recent murders in Fairhaven. Specifically, that Beatrice was the fourth victim. Like her, all the murdered women had been serving maids. Two of them had been from other taverns, while the last two had been from The Dirty Duck.

"As soon as I can purchase a horse, I'll be on my way," said Gwen.

"Easier said than done, I'm afraid. There are no horses available in Fairhaven."

"Bodhi, you jest." Gwen looked around at the stalls. "The stable is full of horses."

"Which the livery master refuses to part with."

Gwen felt something clench in her gut. "Let me guess, part of Commander Thorne's efforts?"

"That's right. No one gets in or out of Fairhaven without her direct permission."

That *something* in Gwen's gut twisted like a knife that had been turned. Bodhi must have noticed, for she gave Gwen an odd look.

"Earlier, in the tavern, when Thorne said she'd speak with you later, you went deathly pale. You did the same just now when I mentioned her name. Is there something going on between the two of you?"

"What? No." Even to Gwen's ears, her answer sounded too quick, too defensive. "I've hardly met her. Why?"

"Well, she's certainly no rose, I'll give you that. But, that's no reason for you to be so skittish around her."

"Bodhi, I've only just escaped being a virgin sacrifice. Pardon me if I don't relish hanging about a town where women are being hunted down."

Gwen turned her back on Bodhi, unable to look her in the eye. She felt like she was a roiling mess of emotions. Her thoughts were all over the place. To distract herself, she reached out a hand, patting the horse in the stall in front of her.

Bodhi cupped her shoulder. Fingers brushed against the strands of her hair. Bodhi was so close that Gwen could feel her breasts against her back. She felt something hard press at her backside and she stiffened before realizing it was only the knife that Bodhi wore belted at her waist.

A hand reached about her, fingers grazing her stomach before moving to the door of the stall. Bodhi flicked open a latch. Moving back, she swung the door open and took up the horse's reins. She passed them to Gwen.

"What are you doing?" Gwen was annoyed at how breathless she sounded.

"I'm putting you on my horse and you're riding out of here."

"I'm not taking your horse." Gwen thrust the reins back at Bodhi.

"You are." Bodhi caught Gwen by the wrist, applying pressure so that her hand opened enough. She placed the reins in Gwen's palm with a slap.

"I've already told you, Bodhi. I go where I want, as I please." Gwen let the reins drop.

"Not in Fairhaven, you don't."

Bodhi drew some coins from the pouch tied at her waist and placed them in Gwen's palm along with the reins. This time, she folded Gwen's fingers so that they closed about the objects and didn't let loose of Gwen's hand.

"Watch the guards at the gates. You're a smart maid. You should be able to figure out which ones can be bribed. This should be enough to give one to let you pass," Bodhi said.

"I have money of my own, same as you. Besides, if it's that simple, why haven't you left?"

"I can't."

"Why? Because of some ridiculous competition between you and the commander to see who wields the bigger sword?"

"Look out there." Bodhi moved to the doorway, but stood to one side of the frame as if she didn't wish to be seen from outside.

Gwen did the same, coming to stand directly across from Bodhi, on the opposite side of the doorway. Fingers curled about the doorframe, she peered out.

"Across the way. See there, in the shadows of that alley?"

Gwen followed Bodhi's line of sight. She spotted a man wearing a burgundy tunic leaning with his shoulder against the wall. He was picking his fingernails with the tip of a dagger and watching the stable.

"One guard?" Both Gwen's eyebrows rose. "Come on, Bodhi. I know you. If you really wanted out, you'd find a way even if you had to fight your way through the gates. What's really holding you in Fairhaven?"

"Let's just say I was specifically asked not to leave. You've seen the countryside. It's plain and flat. I'd scarcely make it twenty paces before I'd find an arrow in my back."

Gwen fell silent as she studied Bodhi. There was something the warrior wasn't telling her. *For Spirits' sake, the woman took on my entire village as well as an ogre without batting an eye. Does she really expect me to believe that she wouldn't go up against a few city guards?*

"Come on. Let's get you mounted up." Bodhi turned away from Gwen and walked back to the stall. She lifted a saddle from a rail and flung it across the horse's back.

"I won't take your horse and leave you stranded here."

"I'm touched you care." Bodhi continued to cinch the saddle.

"Don't be. I don't. I simply wish to make it on my own, without being indebted to anyone."

"Then pay me the same amount you gave Gerald for his horse."

"No."

Bodhi crossed her arms over her chest and rolled her eyes.

"Fine. Then, take her as a gift."

"Why are you in such a hurry to see me out of Fairhaven?" asked Gwen.

"The same reason you said. There's a beast going about killing women. I didn't save you from an ogre just so you could be murdered in some back alley."

"As I recall, I had a hand in saving myself. I don't need to rely on you or your horse."

"There's nothing wrong with accepting help, especially when it's freely offered."

"Sometimes, there is."

"I'm offering you my horse, Gwen, nothing more. I'm only asking you use her to ride straight out of Fairhaven."

"When I leave, it'll be on my terms, not yours. Until then, I'm staying." Gwen stepped to the other side of the horse and began to undo the saddle.

"Stubborn wench. You'll get your throat slashed."

"Then you'll be able to say *I told you so* to my corpse, won't you?"

Bodhi gave an exasperated huff, but nevertheless stepped back.

Gwen twisted, pulled, and tugged at the saddle. She frowned. It had taken Bodhi considerably less effort to put it on. She tried again, straining from the exertion. Above the noise of her own grunting, she heard the unmistakable sounds of stifled laughter.

"I'd offer to lend a hand, but I know you want to do for yourself, without being indebted to anyone else." Bodhi's face was flushed from suppressing her laughter. Her smile was wide, her dimples deeply pronounced. Merriment twinkled in her blue eyes.

Gwen tried once more to lift the saddle. Her grip slipped off the leather and she nearly fell backward.

"Oh! It's your horse." Gwen pushed past a still chuckling Bodhi on her way out of the stall. "You unsaddle her."

"Fine." Bodhi stepped up beside the horse and softly whispered something in her ear. Using both hands, she lifted the saddle off. "After I brush her down again, I'll be ready for my morning meal. Hen eggs will do nicely, I think. Oh, and you can haul in the water for my bath. Seeing as how you're staying and all."

"You…you…" Gwen gritted her teeth and balled her fists at her sides. "You can haul your own water, Bodhi. I'm seeking other lodging besides The Dirty Duck."

"You'd best hurry. Once evening comes, rooms tend to fill up fast."

Gwen waited for a snide comment to be added, something to the effect of whom she might find herself sharing a bed with. To her surprise, Bodhi didn't say another word, merely took up the bristle brush and began stroking it through her horse's coat. Gwen stared at her for several long heartbeats before turning on her heel and walking away.

"Oh, Gwen?"

Gwen paused at the doorway and looked back at a smirking Bodhi.

"My sword *is* bigger than Thorne's. And, I've got two of them."

Chapter Eleven

Bodhi was right. Dusk fell in Fairhaven before Gwen was able to secure better lodgings. She also arrived too late at The Dirty Duck and was forced to renew her arrangement with Roe. Payment of five gold coins and serving drinks and stew in the main room in exchange for bunking in one of the serving maid's rooms. Fortunately, her arrangement from the night before still held and she had Beatrice's room to herself.

She changed quickly from her traveling clothes into the serving maid's outfit. She stood at the end of the bed, fastening the skirt about her waist, doing her level best to not think about how she was wearing a dead woman's clothes, how she'd slept in a dead woman's bed, or that she'd be sleeping there again this eve. Her saving grace was that she'd never met Beatrice. If she had, she doubted she'd be able to stay in the room, no matter the necessity. *It's only an empty bed and empty clothes,* Gwen told herself again.

She folded her traveling clothes and tucked them beneath the bed frame with her saddlebags and bow. The rooms were supposed to be secure, but there was no sense in tempting a thief by leaving her belongings out in plain view.

Gwen stepped into the hall, still tucking the end of her blouse into the waistband of her skirt. She gave one last glance about the room before pulling the door to. She walked to the end of the corridor and slipped past the quilt separating the staff quarters from the common room.

The tavern was crowded. People were scared and the only thing to keep their minds off their fear was to get lost in the crowd, spending their night wildly cavorting, drinking, feasting, and gambling.

It seemed for all her claims of heroism that Bodhi had resigned herself to the same. She was holding court at the same table as she'd been last eve, telling wild tales and placing bets on a dicing game. Karyn was perched upon her lap, fawning over her, and keeping Bodhi's mug full.

When she saw Karyn actually dip a spoonful of mutton stew out of a bowl and bring it to Bodhi's lips, Gwen turned away. As she did, she bumped against someone standing near the hearth. Ale sloshed from the pitcher she carried on her tray.

"Oh, so sorry." Gwen briskly brushed a rag over the shoulder and sleeve of the tunic she'd spilled ale on.

It wasn't the first spill she'd had that eve. Spirits knew it probably wouldn't be her last, either. *Spill once, luv, apologize twice* had been Rachel's advice to disarm the situation. She wiped dry the burgundy material as best she could. Then she looked up, ready to apologize yet again to the tunic's owner.

"I didn't see you—"

"You." The guard's mouth formed an O and his eyes went wide as he pointed a finger at Gwen. "You're—"

"Incredibly clumsy, but still help. These days, bad help is better than no help at all. Hello, Ernest." Fauna wrapped an arm about the guard's waist and leaned into him, giving him a little squeeze.

"Hello, Fauna." The guard ducked his head, a shy smile forming on his lips.

"Ernest here's a corporal in the city guard." Fauna brushed her fingers over the stripe on his sleeve, as if to draw attention to his rank.

If it was possible, Ernest ducked his head even more. Even in the smoky, dim lighting of the tavern, Gwen could see the flame-red blush on his cheeks.

"A corporal?" She looked to Fauna, a teasing smile on her lips. "Very impressive."

The look that Fauna sent her way suggested that she already owed the tavern maid for stepping in. No reason to further indebt herself by mentioning that the guardsman that was sweet on her was also one of the guards she'd encountered at the gate last eve.

Someone brushed by Gwen, cutting in between her, Fauna, and the guardsman. As she was pushed aside, Gwen's entire range of vision was filled with a mass of ebony hair and a serving wench's full bosom. Gwen immediately recognized her as the tavern whore that had been all over Bodhi. *What was her name? Carrie? Kara? Oh, that's right...Karyn.*

Karyn knelt on the warming stone in front of the great hearth. She picked up a large wooden spoon and leaned in closer to the fire. Using the spoon to stir the congealed skim at the top of the cooking pot, she dipped deep into the boiling gruel. The scent of scorched meat wafted on the air and Karyn wrinkled her nose.

"Ugh. If I have to ladle out one more bowl of mutton stew this eve..."

"Could be worse, Karyn. Barbarians swill that stuff like ale," said Fauna.

"I'd gladly take a table full of barbarians over that warrior. All hands, that one."

"Lips and teeth, too, I'd say."

At Fauna's tease, Ernest choked on his ale. Fauna gave him a hearty slap on the back and steered him away from the food cooking on the hearth.

Gwen gave Karyn a closer look. Fauna's words may have been meant in jest, but there were numerous love bites visible about Karyn's neck and upper chest. Gwen knelt beside Karyn on the warming stone. She took up a poker and knocked off ash gathering on the logs.

"If you don't desire Bodhi's touch," Gwen's voice was a near whisper as she leaned in close to Karyn's ear, "perhaps you shouldn't warm her lap with your backside."

The wooden spoon slipped from Karyn's fingers, landing with a splash in the cooking pot. It floated upon the thick surface for a heartbeat before plummeting like a stone into the murky depths of mutton stew.

Karyn turned her head sharply, giving Gwen a harsh look. "Ah, I remember you. Gwendolyn, the virgin sacrifice, isn't it?"

"You know any virgin serving wenches?" countered Gwen.

"Not in this day and age. At least not with that warrior anywhere nearby."

Gwen flushed hotly. She knew Bodhi had loved women. Many women, by Bodhi's own admission. *But to suggest that she would deliberately—*

Her thoughts were cut off as Karyn reached out and grasped her by the wrist. She looked Gwen squarely in the eye. When she spoke, her voice was low and dangerous.

"I know you're new, so I'll give you fair warning. Don't come between another maid and her purse."

"Purse?"

"That's right. That warrior has a purse full of coins and I'm apt to see she spends a fair amount of them on me. So, you just make sure you don't come between me and them."

Karyn added a twist before releasing Gwen's wrist.

As she went to stand up, Gwen reached out and grabbed her by arm. "Bodhi's not the sort you should tease."

"She's a big girl. I think she can stand a little teasing, don't you?" Karyn gave a broad grin, a bold wink, and shook off Gwen's touch.

Gwen stared as Karyn expertly weaved her way through the crowded room, her serving tray held above one shoulder. Gwen knew the extra sway to her hips was added for her benefit. As was the way she sat on Bodhi's lap with equal flourish. She looked directly at Gwen, as if to make certain she had an audience, before grabbing Bodhi by the back of the neck and pulling her in for an open-mouthed kiss.

†

Bodhi had just rolled another pair and was scooping up her winnings when she once more found herself with a handful and mouthful of tavern wench. Hands were cupping her face, then fingers were tangling in her hair. A hand roamed down her side, inching too close to her belted knife. She caught Karyn's wandering hands in her grasp and leaned back, effectively ending the kiss.

Bodhi studied Karyn's face, looking for any hint of duplicity. Karyn's expression was heated. Her eyes were half-lidded, her look sultry. Her face and bosom were slightly flushed with the heat of rising desire. She licked her lips, moistening them with the tip of her tongue.

Bodhi relaxed a bit, believing that Karyn's wandering fingers nearly touching the weapon at her waist had been purely unintentional. When Karyn leaned in again, Bodhi allowed this kiss to progress to its natural conclusion.

There was good-natured ribbing and laughter from the five men seated at the table. A man with a blonde mustache seated to Bodhi's left picked up the carved bone dice and shook them in his hand.

"Spirits, girl." Bodhi's voice was husky. "Kiss me like that again and I'll concede now so that I might have you in my bed quicker."

"I accept," chuckled a bearded warrior seated across the table from Bodhi.

"No, no. Don't concede on my account." Karyn leaned forward, pushing a stack of Bodhi's coins into the center of the table. "There's still candlemarks before closing and the game has hardly begun."

Bodhi caught Karyn looking off in the distance, toward the direction of the hearth. She followed the look, but found her gaze averted by a skillfully placed fingertip beneath her chin. Her head turned and she once again found her lips engulfed by Karyn's.

†

Gwen stood with both hands on her hips and rolled her eyes. She couldn't believe the spectacle Bodhi was making of herself. *For Spirits' sake, half the tavern could see her with a tongue halfway down her throat and her hand beneath that...that...tavern whore's skirt.*

She'd tried to ignore them, telling herself that Karyn was only doing it to rile her. It'd been easier while she'd been working the crowd, serving ale and cider. Now, though, that all the mugs appeared to be full and she had a brief respite at the bar along with Fauna and her doting guardsman, she couldn't help but stare at the spectacle they were making.

"Don't mind her, Gwen. Karyn's not generally mean-spirited. Some of the girls just tend to get territorial."

"Territorial?" Gwen looked askance at Fauna.

"Mm-hm. You should have seen the row Rachel and Beatrice had last winter over a purse. Come spring thaw, though, he was gone and they were friends again."

It was the second time that eve that she'd heard someone being referred to as a *purse* instead of a *customer*. It was another aspect of tavern work that Gwen found she didn't care for. Another in an ever growing list, it seemed. Thinking of her sister, now she could better understand how Cathryn had become so jaded. *Still, it beats being out on the streets with a killer.*

"Aww, no."

Gwen turned to see what had caused the thus far shy-beyond-words Ernest to voice complaint. Commander Thorne was shaking the rain from her cloak before hanging it on a hook beside the door. A moan of similar discontent escaped Gwen's lips.

"It's fine, Ernest. You're on break." Fauna patted Ernest's arm in a reassuring manner.

He must have seen the puzzled look on Gwen's face. "Part of Commander Thorne's new edicts. Tavern maids are no longer allowed to bring us food after dark. Her plan to keep them off the streets, I think."

"Sensible." Gwen nodded. "Still, though, she'd have to realize the evening guardsmen would need meals, too."

"I know, but I'm only supposed to pick up dinner and bring it back. I don't want her to think I'm a shirker."

"Look. See, your fears are unfounded. She's speaking with Roe."

Gwen and Ernest both followed Fauna's line of sight. The commander was, indeed, in what appeared to be deep conversation with the tavern keeper. They were standing directly between the bar and the entrance and Gwen saw that as a problem for Ernest and her, too. There was no way either could slip past without being spotted.

Gwen stared. Despite the lateness of the candlemark and the weather outside, Commander Thorne looked very smart. Her hair was pulled back and braided so not a strand was out of place. Her tunic was pressed smooth and neatly tucked into her belted waistband. The gold hilt of her sword glimmered in the tavern torchlight. Her breeches were pleated and tucked into her boots.

The only thing amiss was the layer of crusted grime about the edging of her soles.

It was unfortunate, but couldn't be helped. There had been so much drizzling rain in Fairhaven that dirt from the streets and ash from the wall braziers had mingled together to form an oily surface on the cobblestones. If it would only rain harder, there would be enough force behind the water to wash the streets clean. As it was, the perpetual mist only provided the paste that held the mess together, adhering to any surface it came in contact with—the tail end of cloaks, the hem of skirts, footwear—all was fair game.

It was something Gwen had discovered firsthand upon her return from the stables. She'd spent nearly a candlemark scraping the grime from the sides and soles of her boots. The same residue clung to the commander's boots. It was understandable, yes, but unfortunate in that it detracted from the crispness of her military persona.

"Ernest, what do you know of Thorne?" she turned and asked the guardsman.

"The new commander? Um, she's strict but fair. Sarge told me Fairhaven's her third assignment in as many seasons."

"Trouble at her postings?"

"No, I don't think so. She seems like a good officer; disciplined, diligent, and professional. No one really knows anything about her personal life. Rumor has it that she was off duty and coming out of a tavern in Lower Duxford when some bandits ambushed her. They split her head open and left her to die in a back alley. They say that's how she got that white streak in her hair...it grew in like that afterward."

Gwen's gaze drifted back to the commander. She was still with Roe. They were holding a parchment between them, their heads bowed together as they looked at it. Gwen wondered what business they were discussing.

"Story goes that after she healed up, she tracked every last one of those bandits down and paid them back in kind."

"How many?" asked Gwen, without taking her eyes off Thorne.

"Three. Four. Seven. More?" Ernest shrugged. "Number varies from telling to telling. Only part of the story that doesn't change is that none of them survived."

"Hm. Seems the commander has a wild streak, after all," mused Gwen.

Inexplicably, Commander Thorne looked up from the parchment. Intense green eyes caught her gaze and held it. Gwen wanted to, but was unable to break the stare. She felt herself shiver beneath Thorne's scrutiny.

✝

Without breaking her stare, Thorne rolled the parchment and passed it to the tavern keeper by slapping him in the chest with it. There was a muffled grunt of protest that she paid no mind. Her feet were already moving, carrying her deeper into the tavern, to the bar and the maid that had caught her eye.

"Commander Thorne."

She was aware of the fast salute, the crack of a fist striking against a chest, and the guardsman's uniform on the edges of her peripheral vision. The rest of her sight was captivated by a set of eyes the same shade as honey fresh from the hive on a warm summer's day.

"I'm only picking up supper. I'm returning to my post now."

She dismissively waved her hand in the air. She heard the click of his military-issued boots signaling he was turning to go.

"Guardsman, wait." Thorne blinked, dispelling the enthrallment. She reached inside her tunic, withdrawing two sheets of parchment and passing them to the waiting corporal. "Take these. Post one at The Red Fox Inn and the other in the main square on your way."

"Yes, Commander." Ernest offered another salute for Thorne and a shy smile for the girl standing beside him.

It was a smile that didn't go unnoticed by Thorne and she turned to appraise the young woman. She was petite, with tawny hair, and brown eyes. And, she was oh, so young. *Too young to be wearing the immodest outfit of a tavern wench.*

"I'm off, too," said the girl. "I've been too long on break as it is."

The other serving maid looked as if she was ready to bolt, too. Thorne effectively stopped her by stepping closer, hemming her into the bar, and cutting off her escape route. Thorne saw what appeared to be a flash of fear momentarily reflected in her eyes.

"I must be back to work, as well," said Gwen, attempting to ease her way past.

Thorne reached out and caught her by the wrist, effectively halting her.

"That won't be necessary. I spoke to the proprietor. He's agreed to allow you off the rest of the evening." Thorne's grip moved from Gwen's wrist to the crook of her arm. "Come. It's time we had that talk."

Thorne guided Gwen to an empty table located near enough the hearth that she could feel the warmth from the fire. After being out in the damp air and feeling the cold rattle in every breath she took, she welcomed the heat.

She discreetly kept her hand tucked into the crook of Gwen's elbow even as she pulled out a chair from the table. With stiff movements, Gwen sat. Thorne pushed the chair back in and settled into a chair beside her. *Best to be two steps closer in case she tries to run.*

"I'll get right to it." Thorne leaned her elbows on the table, steepled her fingers, and looked Gwen in the eye. "Exactly who are you and what is your business in Fairhaven?"

"We've already been introduced and you can plainly see my business." Gwen made a vague gesture that encompassed the tavern and herself.

"With the exception of the sergeant at the gate, not a single person I've spoken with will attest to having seen you before last eve. Not the livery owner, the shopkeepers, or even any of the gossipmongers that hold court in the main square. That alone is enough to raise doubt as to the veracity of the sergeant's claims."

"Perhaps a common tavern maid is beneath their notice," countered Gwen.

"Perhaps. Then again, they all seem to have noticed an encounter that took place between a certain tavern maid and a swordswoman earlier today."

"That might have been any tavern maid."

"They described you quite accurately. Now," Thorne held up her hand to signal for a tavern wench, "as I've yet to eat today, I'm going to order dinner. And, I expect that before my meal is over, the truth will have parted your lips."

†

Bodhi's luck had turned as sour as the ale churning in her gut. It'd been well over a dozen turns since her last win. Now, the dice were being passed to her yet again. She took them up by rote and rattled them in her hand.

She studied the table, her eyes raking over the growing pot in the center and the dwindling pile of coins in front of her. It irked her that a great many of her coins were now stacked in front of a red-bearded furrier. What irked her more was the way he kept stacking and restacking them into varying heights and metals.

He looked up, his gaze meeting Bodhi's across the table. He must have sensed her growing irritation, for he flashed her a big, gapped-tooth smile. His fingers were bent like talons over three coins, with more lined up in his palm. He let them slip through his grasp coin by coin, each one making a clinking sound as it was added to the growing stack. As he dropped the last coin, he repeated the process over and over again. His beady, little eyes drifted to Bodhi's left hand and the pair of dice she held, as if in anticipation of her making a bad roll.

Bodhi tossed a single copper coin into the center. She saw the clear look of disappointment in the furrier's eyes. She wanted to laugh in his face for being so drunk that his greed was transparent. *Then again, for all I know, that may be how he plays sober, also.*

She blew into her closed fist and shook the dice. She paused for a heartbeat as Karyn leaned forward, the wench's heavy bosom brushing against her forearm with the motion. Bodhi watched as the serving wench indiscriminately picked up four more coins from her stash and randomly tossed them atop the pot.

Bodhi threw. The carved bone rattled as the dice rolled end over end. Her lip curved up as one die stopped right side up. The other teetered, then turned over, landing the wrong way. Bodhi scowled. Picking up the dice, she passed them to the blonde-mustached warrior seated beside her.

Without a heartbeat's hesitation, he threw in two pieces of silver and tossed the dice. Like Bodhi's, they ended the wrong way up. He didn't bat an eye as he scooped up the dice and passed them to the next player.

Bodhi watched the game with waning interest. Karyn was perched atop her lap, one arm draped over her shoulders. Her arm was about the serving wench's waist, her hand cupping the curve of a womanly hip.

Then, Karyn was pressing the rim of her mug to her lips. Bodhi's lips parted beneath the pressure. The taste of lukewarm ale washed over her tongue and down her throat and Bodhi thought she could actually feel it traveling down her gullet and sloshing about in her stomach.

Bodhi swallowed against the excess saliva forming in her mouth. A trickle of sweat was running down her brow. She felt Karyn's fingernails against one side of her face. Then, there were nibbling kisses at her earlobe, working along the line of her jaw. Bodhi slammed her eyes shut.

She concentrated on taking in slow breaths. In through the nose and out through the mouth. Again. When she at last felt like she wouldn't heave all over the table, she opened her eyes and cautiously looked about. No one seemed to notice her condition. The game was continuing on, albeit two players further along than when she'd drank the ale. *Too much ale.* Bodhi figured that was why everything now appeared fuzzy around the edges.

She leaned forward, stretching so she could reach her stew bowl. She frowned, surprised to find it empty. "More." She crooked two fingers onto the edge of the bowl in order to pass it to the serving maid.

Karyn's lips left Bodhi's jaw. She looked about the table and then down at the bowl Bodhi was nudging her with.

"It's nearly our turn," said Karyn.

"More." Bodhi thrust the bowl into Karyn's hand. She picked up a bronze coin and dropped it down the front of the serving maid's low-cut blouse.

Karyn did a slow slide off her lap. Her gaze still upon the game, she took a few hesitant steps away.

"Now." Bodhi added a sharp slap to her backside as added incentive.

Bodhi saw the hitch in Karyn's step and heard the laughter of the men at the table. She turned her attention back to the table. She was still fuzzy-minded, but she clearly saw the furrier place his wager of six coppers.

†

Their conversation momentarily broke off as Rachel appeared at the table, carrying a tray laden down with a large bowl and two mugs. She placed the bowl and a mug of water in front of the commander. Gwen's gaze dropped to her hands folded in her lap.

She already felt bad about not being a good enough server to carry a complete section by herself. Given her difficulty in balancing a full tray, she'd been banned from serving stew, as Rachel feared her spilling something hot on some poor, unsuspecting soul. So, Rachel was not only serving her customers, she'd also been bringing food to Gwen's tables, as well. *Now, here I am, sitting down for a rest while she does all my work too.*

She felt Rachel brush her arm as she placed a mug of cider in front of her. Gwen's gaze drifted and her line of sight was filled with the patched material of Rachel's skirt. Gwen felt so guilty she couldn't bear to lift her gaze to look Rachel in the eye. A few heartbeats later, she saw the serving maid's skirt move away.

"In truth, I knew there was something amiss as soon as I saw you."

Gwen looked up and across the table. The commander was staring at her and idly stirring her spoon. Wisps of steam drifted above the dark liquid in the serving bowl.

"What I don't understand, though, is why you didn't simply tell me last eve at the guards' room?"

"I…I'm not certain. I'd only just arrived and I'd heard the guards arguing about the commander's orders and the sergeant threatened to put me back outside the gate. Then, you were there and I thought…"

Gwen chewed her bottom lip. She'd finally confessed the truth of her arrival to the commander of Fairhaven. She hadn't wanted to, but there was something about this woman, being in her presence, that Gwen felt compelled to tell her all.

Well, most all. There were still some details that she hadn't parted with, the fact that she wasn't an experienced tavern maid being one of them. Knowing little about this city and its commander, Gwen thought perhaps a bit of discretion regarding who she was and where she was from might be prudent. *For all I know, she might have some law about once a virgin sacrifice, always a virgin sacrifice.*

"Gwen, do you fear me more than the gate sergeant?"

Do I? Even knowing what it was that the sergeant wanted? Gwen's brow knitted as she fully considered Thorne's question. Her encounter with him had certainly influenced her decision about how much she revealed to Thorne.

Gwen felt a weight upon her hand. She looked and saw Thorne's hand resting atop hers on the table. She glanced up, seeing green eyes intently watching her, awaiting an answer.

"I think a person might fear you for a great many reasons," said Gwen.

Thorne showed no outward reaction, merely looked at her with those emerald eyes that reminded Gwen of a cat's. It was more than just the color. It was the way she watched. Not only her, although she'd been staring at her unblinkingly for the longest time now. It was as if she could observe the entire room with the slightest flick of her eye.

"Such as?" An ebony brow arched over an emerald pupil flecked with hints of gold.

"Your lockdown."

"My lockdown?"

"I've heard no one enters or leaves Fairhaven without your approval."

"Half-truth. It's not my lockdown. It was issued by the magistrate's office. I merely enforce the city's mandates."

"Yet, you and you alone decides who may come and go," countered Gwen.

"It was my recommendation to the magistrate's office, yes. You must understand, Gwen, I'm after a monster." She must have thought Gwen gave her a puzzled look, for she explained, "What else would you call something that cuts women open, slashing their throats, strewing their blood and innards out on the cobblestone, but a monster? At each of my three previous posts it managed to elude me, fleeing before I could make an arrest. With the lockdown, it won't be able to get out of Fairhaven."

†

Bodhi deliberately brought her booted foot up and crossed her ankle over her opposite knee. Bracing her elbow against the arm of the chair, she propped her chin on her closed fist. There was a thrumming inside her head and pressure behind her eyes. She steadfastly pushed the ache aside and focused on the game.

They'd already gone once around the table again, each of them wagering, tossing, and missing. The trader seated next to red-beard had just rolled and passed the dice to the next man over. It would be Bodhi's turn soon. She gave her wager careful consideration. She could hold steady, not betting anything more substantial than the previous player, or she could drop out of the round and concede the pot. They'd all held the bidding low, until Karyn had indiscriminately tossed that handful of mixed coins into the pile. Each successive player had followed her lead, adding more and more to the pot, driving the stakes higher.

Bodhi's stomach grumbled. She looked across the tavern, checking to see where Karyn was. She spotted her kneeling in front of the hearth, ladling stew out of the pot and into her bowl. The wench kept sending furtive looks her direction.

It hadn't escaped Bodhi's notice how familiar Karyn had become, nor how freely she'd taken to spending her coin. *Our turn,* she had said, just before Bodhi sent her off to fetch more stew. Even then, she'd only gone once Bodhi had dropped a coin down her cleavage. Blue eyes drifted to Karyn's bosom, her mind attempting to calculate over the course of her stay in Fairhaven, exactly how many coins had found their way down the serving wench's blouse.

As well as other places, thought Bodhi. Not that she'd minded at the time. After all, she felt she owed Karyn something. And, if there was one thing that could be said for Bodhi, it was that she always paid her debts.

Karyn flashed a smile and Bodhi looked away. She was in no mood to flirt, no matter how willing the maid. *Speaking of...*

Gwen was seated at a table near the hearth. There were two mugs and a bowl on the table. Thorne was seated beside her, in a chair that had been scooted much closer than needed to share a meal. Her hand was atop Gwen's and the maid was ardently looking at that…that…city guard.

An elbow nudged Bodhi and she looked down to see a hand holding out the set of dice in offering. She snatched them up, giving them a vicious shake. A hammering sound echoed in her ears. Her jaw tightened as she tried to decide on her wager. The pounding persisted. Her ire grew in direct proportion to the rapid hammering.

Bodhi slammed the dice down. Out of the corner of her eye, she saw blonde mustache hurriedly snatch them up.

"What is all that about?" She turned her full fury on the tavern keeper.

He was standing in front of a support post, his back to her. At Bodhi's outburst, he turned around. There were two nails clenched between his teeth. His fingers were wrapped about the handle of a hammer poised to strike a nail sticking a quarter ways into a sheet of parchment and the wooden post.

"What?" Roe's words were garbled around the nails in his mouth.

"What is that infernal hammering about?" repeated Bodhi.

"New edict from the magistrate's office." Roe turned around and read aloud the lettering on the parchment for all to hear. "Henceforth, the citizens of Fairhaven are under mandatory curfew from dusk till dawn. Anyone caught on the streets without proper documentation will be detained and taken to the gaol."

Bodhi glared imaginary daggers at Commander Thorne.

⁜

She's been tracking the killer since her three previous posts, Gwen thought. *By the Spirits, how many murders has there been?*

"Don't fret, Gwen. What's done is done. I won't penalize you for violating the lockdown by *entering* Fairhaven. Try to leave, however, and I'll be forced to arrest you."

Gwen felt her stomach clench and she swallowed convulsively.

Thorne lifted a spoonful from her bowl and, pursing her lips, blew on a large chunk of floating mutton. She lifted her spoon to her lips. She chewed, grimaced, and swallowed. Gingerly, she placed the spoon back in the bowl and dabbed at the corners of her mouth with a napkin.

"Oh, that's foul." Thorne chased the stew with a large draw of water.

Gwen knew precisely what Thorne meant. After a full day and evening yesterday, then another full day cooking over the hearth today, the mutton had lost much of its appeal.

To most everyone, it seems, except Bodhi. Gwen stole a look at the warrior. She'd seen Karyn at the hearth earlier, refilling yet another stew bowl. Sure enough, she was perched atop Bodhi's lap, spoon-feeding her. Gwen looked away, as the sight was enough to make her ill.

"I should arrest whoever cooked that." Thorne moved her mug away, revealing a tiny smile she'd been hiding behind the rim.

"You were jesting?" asked Gwen.

"About having you arrested? Yes. About the stew, perhaps not."

There was a mirthful cast to Thorne's green eyes. Somehow, it didn't make Gwen feel better. Their look reminded her too much of how a cat's eyes danced with glee as it tormented a trapped mouse.

"Gwen, relax. I'm not the uptight, do-it-my-way-or-die despot that you've been led to believe. Besides, you're living proof that

146

my word isn't law. Despite *my* lockdown, you managed your way into Fairhaven just fine."

Living proof. Those words brought Ernest's tale to mind.

"The rumors about you being attacked by bandits." Inexplicably, of their own accord, Gwen's fingers touched a white strand hanging against Thorne's left temple. "Are those half-truths, as well?"

"That depends on which truths you've been listening to." All traces of good humor left Thorne's face.

Thorne reached up, catching Gwen by the wrist. She lowered both their hands to the table, placing hers atop Gwen's. Gwen got the impression that it wasn't so much an act of intimacy as it was to divert her touch. She was silent for so long that Gwen thought she wouldn't tell. Then, she looked off into the fire, as if she could see events from days gone by rekindled in the flames. When she spoke, her voice was low and smoky.

"I was off duty, drinking with some friends in front of an open-aired tavern. A maid appeared in the town square and waved at us. I remember thinking she was the most beautiful woman I'd ever seen. Or, perhaps, it was the mead that made it seem so. I waved back and she came over." The commander's voice was low and smooth and Gwen found herself leaning in closer.

"Of course, I knew she'd go with one of my friends. They were both big, strapping fellows and had quite a reputation for wenching. I could tell by the grins on their faces that they knew it too. I went back to my drink, not wishing to begrudge either of them their good fortune.

"I think we were all surprised when she came up behind me, wrapped her arms around my neck and shoulders and whispered low, breathy promises into my ear. She invited me back to her room and I followed on eager, drunken legs, stumbling after her through the twists and turns of back alleys.

"She said we were almost there, just a little further. It may have occurred to me then that she was a professional. I didn't care. At that point, I would have followed her anywhere. She led me around the next corner with her hands cupping my face and her lips pressed to mine.

"The first blow was a kick to the back of my knees to bring me down. A boot to my ribs ensured I wasn't going to make it to my feet. A stomp on my hand made sure I couldn't draw my sword.

"A big, grubby hand reached for my waist. I felt him jerking at my belt. Then, I saw him pull a knife. There was a sawing motion and I saw him come up with my coin purse, the strings frayed from where he had cut through them.

"He was laughing. It was high-pitched and even through the haze of pain, it grated my nerves. Then, he was running off, his cronies on his heels. All except one. I saw his boots, coming closer, as he walked over to where I was curled in a ball on the cobblestones. He reached down, grabbing me by the hair and pulled me halfway up off the ground. The last thing I saw was him pulling his arm back and swinging his mace…"

Thorne blinked and abruptly shook her head, as if to dispel painful memories. She lifted her mug to her lips, taking long, deep swallows. When she placed the mug back on the table, the contents had been drained dry.

"Did you…did you really kill them all?" Gwen was surprised by how raspy her voice sounded as she asked the question aloud.

"What do you think?" Those intense eyes stared unblinkingly into hers.

Gwen pulled her hand out from beneath Thorne's. It trembled as she picked up her mug of cider. She averted her gaze, staring off into the fire. As she watched the flames lick at the logs, the details of Thorne's tale burned deeply in her thoughts.

Chapter Twelve

"I don't give an ogre's left nut."

Gwen winced at the obscene vernacular, Bodhi's unmistakable voice drawing her out of her reverie.

The main room was considerably less crowded than earlier. *No doubt, due to the curfew,* thought Gwen. She'd heard Roe read the new edict aloud.

Her suspicions were confirmed when she noticed two armed guards standing near the door, ushering people either out of the tavern or up the stairs to their rooms. Roe was behind the bar, wiping out and putting away empty mugs. Rachel and Fauna were clearing tables and taking care of those customers that still lingered. As usual, Karyn was stuck to Bodhi like manure, although for once, she wasn't settled upon the warrior's lap.

The only reason, no doubt, because Bodhi wasn't seated. She was on her feet, her face beet red. Her arms were locked, palms pressing down upon a tabletop. She was staring down a little, red-bearded man bedecked in assorted furs. His head was down and he was scooping coins by the handful into a burlap bag.

"No one wins that much and walks away without giving the rest of us a fair chance to make our coin back," said Bodhi. "Right?"

Bodhi looked around the table at the other four players. None of them said a word. Two of them outright ducked their heads, as if that could prevent Bodhi's eyes staring holes into them.

A mustached man met Bodhi's gaze. He must have decided he'd be better off if he couldn't answer because his mouth was full, for he suddenly reached for a bowl sitting on the table. Karyn intercepted it, pulling it toward her, and snatching it up off the table.

"I…I must. The curfew—"

"Is a convenient excuse for you to weasel your way out of here," accused Bodhi.

"N…no. My wife. She'll be waiting."

"Little man, you are an unwashed furrier. I doubt you have a wife, unless it's the donkey you brought your pelts in on."

The red-bearded man glanced furtively about, as if looking for help. He latched onto Commander Thorne as she approached the group at the table.

"I do. I have a wife," he insisted, grabbing onto the commander's sleeve.

Thorne efficiently brushed the clinging man off her uniform and flashed a signal at one of the door guards. He rushed over, giving a brisk salute as he drew to a halt in front of the commander.

"The guard will gladly escort you home to your wife." There was a rush of relief visible on the furrier's face, until Thorne added, "Or, to gaol if, in fact, you have neither home nor wife in Fairhaven."

The furrier paled. His eyes went wide and his mouth slackened. He looked as if he were going to protest when the guard took him by the arm.

Gwen watched as the guard half-walked, half-dragged the little man to the door. They went outside, the guard closing the door behind them. They walked past the window Roe had repaired, crossing the narrow cobblestone street.

To Gwen they appeared as little more than silhouettes set against the backdrop of night and mist. A fog was rolling in, covering their feet and ankles, making it appear as if they were gliding rather than walking. The little man drew something out of the bag he carried and offered it to the guard. It didn't require perfect vision to see that it was a bribe.

The sound of a heated argument drew Gwen's attention from the exchange outside. She turned to see Bodhi and Thorne, standing toe to toe, hands on their respective hips, each trying to stare the other down.

"It was a private matter and none of your concern," boomed Bodhi's voice.

"When it comes to what goes on in Fairhaven, everything is my concern," countered Thorne.

"Your *concern* just cost all of us," Bodhi gestured to include everyone at her table, "more coin than you'll see in a lifetime as a guard. Unless, of course, you're as corrupt as the rest of the officers under your command."

Gwen heard the conversation in the tavern abruptly cease and saw Thorne's flaring nostrils. Her arms had dropped to her sides and her fists were clenching and unclenching. Bodhi was staring her dead in the eye, her cheek muscles were twitching, and her jaw was set tight. The men seated beneath the women towering over them all looked as if they wanted to slide beneath the table.

Fauna dropped a mug, effectively shattering the silence.

"Oops," she said.

"If you or anyone else desires to levy a complaint against any city official, you may do so at the magistrate's office. I assure you, a prompt and complete investigation will be conducted." Thorne's voice was level, but her tone sounded dangerous.

"I'm sure it'll be handled just as quickly and unbiased as the one into the tavern maid murders has been."

Oh, Blessed Mother. Is she trying to get herself arrested?

Gwen had been transfixed by the confrontation between Bodhi and Thorne. Now, though, seeing that Bodhi had poked the proverbial hive with a stick, she felt herself spurred into action. She leapt up from her chair, striding briskly across the room, determined to pull Bodhi away before she was stung.

It seemed that she wasn't the only one concerned for Bodhi. Gwen was within a few steps when she saw Karyn reach out and place a hand upon the warrior's arm.

"Come on, Bodhi. Continue the game. There's still plenty of candlemarks left for you to recoup your losses," said Karyn.

Bodhi looked at the hand on her arm, then at the serving wench, and finally at the table.

Karyn gave Bodhi's hand a tug.

Bodhi went with the motion, allowing Karyn to guide her into her chair.

Gwen's step faltered. She hesitated, uncertain whether or not she should continue on her current course.

"I've mandated a citywide curfew in an effort to close the net on the beast."

Thorne was still standing beside Bodhi's chair and seemed unready to let the confrontation go.

"How effective do you think a curfew's going to be? Half-stoned and blind drunk, I could still elude your guards."

Even though Bodhi seemed just as unwilling to give in, she didn't have the same air of animosity about her as she did only heartbeats before. As a matter of fact, she seemed quite content, with Karyn curled up on her lap, stroking her fingers through her hair, and spoon-feeding her more of that damned awful stew.

Karyn leaned forward, across the table, retrieving the set of carved bone dice. She pursed her lips, blowing on them, and passed them to Bodhi. As Bodhi took the dice and eagerly shook them, Karyn motioned as if she were encouraging the remaining players to rejoin the game.

Karyn balanced the bowl of stew on her lap and placed her hand in a pocket of her skirt. Gwen watched as she withdrew her closed hand, held it over the bowl of stew, and crumbled something up. It fell into the stew as Karyn surreptitiously stirred it in.

"What was that?" asked Gwen, rushing forward.

"It's nothing. It's handled," answered Thorne, as if believing Gwen was referring to her altercation with Bodhi. "However, I do need something sweet to rid my mouth of the bitter taste of that awful stew."

"Um." Gwen blinked. "I'll see if Roe has something for dessert."

Thorne nodded at Gwen.

"You," Thorne said, poking a finger against Bodhi's nose. "I'm keeping an eye on you. One step out of line and I'll have you in chains."

⁜

"What was that?" Gwen asked the heartbeat the commander was gone.

"What?" Karyn asked, looking up and at the woman who had a firm grasp upon her wrist.

"I saw you. You put something into Bodhi's bowl."

152

Bodhi slowed her chewing before stopping altogether. She suspiciously eyed the bowl of mutton stew. Placing the bowl on the table, she used two fingers to deliberately push it away.

All eyes at the table turned to stare at Karyn. She reached into a pouch at the front of her skirt and drew out a partially crushed green sprig.

"It's nothing; an herb to add flavor." Karyn tore off a piece and popped it in her mouth. She made a showing of chewing and swallowing, opening her mouth so they could all see the sprig was gone.

"See, it's harmless." She took a long draw from Bodhi's mug, washing down the aftertaste.

"See, Gwen, perfectly harmless," echoed Bodhi.

Seemingly satisfied, the next player rolled and the dicing game continued.

Karyn hid her smile behind her hand. Bodhi's voice sounded far too mellow, there was a lazy smile upon her lips, and a slightly glazed cast to her eyes. Gwen, Bodhi's so-called virgin tavern maid, was frowning, no doubt wondering precisely how drunk her hero was.

"Karyn wouldn't try to poison me, Gwen." Bodhi reached across the table and drew her bowl back again. She scooped up a heaping spoonful of stew, chewed, and swallowed. She tilted her head to the side and looked askance at Gwen. "If it's my attention you desire, though, you needn't make up elaborate ruses. I know how it is for you virgins. Once your thighs have been pried apart, you can't seem to close them again, unless someone locks your knees together. I remember I once had one follow me all the way from Dorchester to Bellestone—"

"I thought it was Whitley," interrupted the mustached warrior.

"Ah, so you know her, too." Bodhi burst into raucous laughter.

The players at the table joined in, making ribald jokes. Bodhi continued to stare up at Gwen with a dopey expression on her face. It suddenly occurred to Karyn that from where Bodhi was sitting and the way she was tilting her head, Bodhi was at a perfect angle to ogle Gwen's breasts.

Gwen must have realized it in the same instant, as an indignant look flashed across her face and she took a step back. Bodhi's eyes followed and Gwen folded her arms over her bosom in a protective manner.

"Come on, Gwen." Bodhi patted her thigh, as if indicating Gwen should sit upon her lap.

"No, thank you. It seems your hands are already full." Gwen pointedly eyed Bodhi's palm curved about Karyn's hip.

"Got one free." Bodhi held up her left hand for Gwen's perusal and waggled her fingers. A lascivious grin spread her lips. "Come on, Karyn doesn't mind."

Karyn felt as if every eye at the table was upon her. She could hear the speculative murmurs from the men. She tried to convey to Gwen with just a look that she most certainly did mind.

"I mind." Gwen's voice was even, her tone icy. "If you'll excuse me, the commander's awaiting her dessert."

Oooh, thought Karyn, *that was a poor choice of words if ever I've heard one.*

She'd been around men, especially drunken men, long enough to know where their minds resided more often than not. Poor Gwen was clearly out of her element. Karyn almost felt sorry for her. Almost.

Sure enough, there was a new round of lewd comments around the table.

Bodhi turned her head, looking off in the distance. Karyn followed her line of sight.

Commander Thorne was sitting beside the hearth, staring into the fire. If she'd noticed Bodhi watching her, or overheard any of the ribald laughter, she gave no indication.

Karyn hooked her finger beneath Bodhi's chin and redirected her gaze. She'd meant to turn Bodhi's attention upon herself, but to her consternation, those baby blue eyes stopped upon Gwen instead.

"Gwen, you're not going off with her are you?" Bodhi sounded very much like a petulant child.

Why should she care? She's got me, doesn't she? Karyn felt heat suffuse her cheeks. In spite of all her efforts, it seemed as if that little milksop virgin sacrifice had some sort of hold upon Bodhi. Her eyes narrowed as she studied Gwen.

Gwen's brow was furrowed and her face was bright red. White teeth were biting down on her bottom lip. Her entire body was trembling, as if with barely constrained rage. Then, she seemed to get control of herself. Her jaw was set with a stubborn tilt to her chin. She smoothed down her skirt and with an air of dignity about her despite the circumstances, she turned on her heel and stalked away. Karyn grinned.

†

"Here." Gwen slammed the bowl of custard down in front of Thorne.

It was an almond milk pudding, topped with berries and frosted rose petals. The dessert was one of Rachel's recipes. Gwen had to admit that the tavern maid must, indeed, be a skilled baker to create such a delicacy.

Thorne immediately dipped the tip of her finger into the pudding. She brought it to her mouth, her tongue flicking out, giving it a lick. Her lips curved into a bow and she slid the rest of her pudding-covered finger into her mouth. Her eyes slowly closed.

"Mmm."

It was a soft moan, accompanied by a whispery exhalation. To Gwen's eyes and ears, Thorne looked and sounded very much like a woman on the edge of arousal. Unbidden, her memory brought back echoes of the suggestions some of Bodhi's companions had made as she'd walked away.

"Something troubling you, Gwen?"

Gwen looked up to see deep green eyes intently watching her. Her gaze drifted over Thorne's face, to her lips, and down to her hand, specifically to that still-moist finger. Gwen felt decidedly warm.

"Gwen?"

She had to think quickly. She couldn't very well tell the commander where her thoughts had really been. *There must be some safe topic of conversation.*

"Um, the curfew," came tumbling from her lips.

"What of it?" An ebony brow arched.

"It's harsh."

"It's also necessary."

"I mean, it's interfering with the natural business of the city."

"Personally, I can't think of any legal business transactions that need to be conducted on the streets after dark. Can you?"

"The taverns."

"May still operate, so long as their customers are in the door before dusk and don't leave before morning," reasoned Thorne.

Gwen fell silent. She had no further argument. Besides, if what Thorne had said was true, and she had no reason to doubt that it was, the killer had managed to elude authorities in three other towns. *Thorne. It eluded Thorne.* Perhaps a mandatory curfew was the only feasible way of keeping the citizenry of Fairhaven safe.

"You aren't thinking of breaking the curfew, are you, Gwen?"

"Wh…What? No."

"Good. I'd hate to have to throw such a beautiful maid in gaol."

"I have no intention of going anywhere, except my bed."

Thorne's brow rose.

Gwen's heart beat rapidly in her chest as she realized what she'd just intimated.

"I mean—"

"I think I should accompany you to be certain." There was a twinkling cast to Thorne's eyes and Gwen thought perhaps she was only teasing.

"Don't you need to be out on patrol?"

"First night of the curfew will be spent informing and educating the citizens. The guards will be lenient, for the most part. We don't want to lock up the entire city, you know." Thorne smiled. "So, I have a few candlemarks yet before I'm truly needed."

Gwen's breath caught. *Not much of a tease, after all.*

Thorne paused from where she'd been rimming the edge of the pudding bowl with her finger. She held out her arm across the table, extending her hand and the digit covered in white custard.

"Taste," she commanded, placing her finger against Gwen's lips.

Gwen tentatively extended her tongue, touching just the tip of Thorne's finger. *Rich.*

Thorne leaned back in her chair. Slowly, deliberately, she brought that same finger to her mouth and sucked the remaining treat off.

Gwen exhaled raggedly and glanced away. Her gaze fell upon the table of gamblers. Everyone seemed to be intent on their dicing. Except for Bodhi. Ice-blue eyes were staring directly at her.

"Come with me." Thorne's voice was husky and it drew Gwen's attention back to her.

Bodhi's words *'You're not going off with her, are you?'* whispered hotly in Gwen's ear.

"Don't you wish to finish your dessert?" she asked.

"I'm craving something sweeter." Thorne stood and extended her hand, palm up.

✝

Oh, Blessed Mother and all the Spirits.

Hands were closed about her upper arms, fingers digging in deep enough that Gwen knew, come morning, there would be bruises. No less bruising were the lips crushed against hers.

What am I doing?

Gwen tried to pull back, to put some distance between them. She had nowhere to go. She was already pressed up against the closed door inside her room.

Thorne's mouth fell upon hers, hungry and insistent. Gwen's forearms and hands were trapped between their upper bodies. Thorne pressed in closer, increasing the pressure upon her upper arms.

Gwen gave an audible gasp and Thorne's tongue thrust inside.

What was I think—

Gwen's mind splintered as she felt her feet kicked apart. A thigh pressed between her parted legs.

"Once a virgin's had her legs opened..." Not exactly what Bodhi had said, but those words, in Bodhi's raspy voice, echoed inside Gwen's head.

Bodhi. She'd been hurt and confused by Bodhi's actions. Even though the warrior was arrogant, rude, and jaded, she was still supposed to be Gwen's hero. *How could she treat me like that? Drinking. She was drinking...*

Lips were at her neck, teeth nipping at her throat. A hand was mauling her breast through the fabric of her blouse. Fingers closed upon a nipple and roughly pinched.

...and I'm a fool. Did I think this would pay her back in kind?

Thorne's thigh pressed in and up.

A harsh gasp was wrenched from Gwen's lips.

In order to hurt Bodhi, she would first have to feel something...

Gwen worked her hands free and clutched at Thorne's shoulders, her fingers digging into the maroon fabric of her uniform.

"I didn't fall head over heels for you at first sight and you weren't looking for anything beyond a quick tumble. Neither of us is in love." Gwen's own words, spoken to Bodhi in perhaps what had been the most honest statement she'd ever made, came back to her.

"No." Gwen pushed with all her might against Thorne's shoulders.

Clearly caught off guard, Thorne was sent three paces back.

"No?" Thorne was breathing heavily, her chest heaving.

"I...I can't. I thought this was something that I wanted, but it's not. You're not. I'm sorry, but I can't."

There was hurt reflected in Thorne's eyes and Gwen felt shame for being the cause of that pain. But, she couldn't. It would be untrue to herself. She'd had everything she cared about in this world ripped away from her—her father, her family, and her home. Her *self* was the only thing she still possessed of value. She couldn't lose that too.

Thorne took several shaky steps backward. She exhaled raggedly. Her jaw was clenched and there was a hard cast to her eyes.

"I can't," Gwen repeated, her voice sounding tiny.

"That story I told you earlier?" Thorne's eyes narrowed. "I didn't finish telling you."

Gwen, worried that Thorne was only prolonging matters, started to protest. Her back was still pressed against the door. Her hand stole down to the latch.

Thorne rushed forward, grabbing her by the arms, and spinning her around. Now, Thorne stood with her back to the door, her arms folded over her chest. Her steely eyes bored into Gwen.

"When I finally regained consciousness, I was in a small tavern room, in the tavern maid's bed. I'd been beaten so badly, I couldn't even sit up on my own. She took care of me, nursing me back to health. I relied on her for everything. To feed me, bathe me, and even to use the chamber pot.

"I remember thinking how fortunate I was, to be so close to death, and to have someone with such a kind heart to tend to me. I needed her. I trusted her. I think I may have even loved her.

"It was her guilt that finally made her confess. She was a pretty lure. You know, the sort of bait a fisherman might use to bring in a big fish. It was her task to find a purse. That's the term they use, you know, a purse.

"She told me she picked me because I wasn't as big as my two companions. She thought I wouldn't put up a fight. She was supposed to lure me along, into a blind alley, and after her friends robbed me, she was to meet up with them later to split the pickings."

Gwen's heart lurched. She reached out a hand toward Thorne.

Thorne evaded her. She raked a hand through her mussed hair and straightened her disheveled tunic—Thorne came to attention with her back straight. She was looking at some point past Gwen.

Her military persona is in command now, thought Gwen.

"Congratulations, Gwen." Thorne's voice was clipped. "Seems you did a pretty fair job of picking your purse, too."

Gwen's mouth dropped open.

Thorne reached into her coin pouch. She withdrew a single copper coin and threw it down.

Gwen's gaze followed the coin, watching as it rolled across the floor until it struck the far wall and bounced back, coming to a rest, and falling flat.

She heard the door slam and looked up.

Thorne was gone.

Chapter Thirteen

The flax string was extended to full draw. She looked past the goose-feathered fletching, down the bolt of the arrow, and over the iron tip. Her arm quivered beneath the strain. With an exasperated sigh, Gwen lowered her bow.

Usually, when something was bothering her or she couldn't sleep, she would target practice or go hunting. Tracking wild quail was a favored pastime to ease her mind. Gwen relaxed the tension on the string, eased the arrow off, and unhooked the bowstring. She slid her quiver and bow beneath the bed once more.

Can't target practice in here, she thought, looking about the sparse room. *Can't very well hunt and kill anything, either. Besides the curfew, I'm certain Fairhaven is bound to have a law against it.* Gwen added that annoying tidbit to her growing list of things she didn't like about city life.

Gwen paced the length of the room. It was only a distance of twelve paces, heel-to-toe lengthwise and ten the opposite direction. She was surprised she hadn't already worn a hole clean through the floor.

A yawn stopped Gwen in her tracks. She looked wistfully at the bed and the tangled covers. She stifled another yawn. She was tired, no doubt, but sleep was elusive. Every time her head hit the pillow, her eyes flew open. Even when she forced her eyes closed again, her mind ran rampant, troubling thoughts keeping her from oblivion.

It's because you feel guilty about Thorne. There was an attraction there. Gwen could feel it whenever the tall, dark, and handsome commander was anywhere near. She was intelligent, professional, and eloquent. And, when she looked at Gwen with those incredible eyes and spoke to her in that voice… She really hadn't meant to lead Thorne on.

Stop it. Don't lie. You weren't thinking about Thorne, at all. You were thinking about your own hurt feelings and you saw her attraction as a means of feeling better about yourself.

Gwen resumed her pacing, trying to think of how she could make amends to the commander of the city guard. She wasn't certain she could. *How do you say,* I'm sorry for not giving you a tumble, *to someone?*

Of course, not being an unattractive maiden, she'd had her fair share of offers, almost all the time up until the villagers decided she was to be a sacrifice. Difference was, they'd all come from the local lads. She'd never been attracted to any of them and she'd never had any qualms about discouraging their efforts. Certainly none of them had ever made it as far as Thorne.

Thus far, the only person she'd ever…with…was—*Bodhi.*

Gwen drew up short as images of blonde hair, blue eyes, and dimples filled her mind. It seemed to Gwen that everything about this night kept coming back to Bodhi. It seemed no matter what she did, she couldn't escape the bold, conceited, and arrogant warrior. Oh, how she hated that. Everything about Bodhi was just so…so…

Gwen let loose a long-suffering sigh. Determined not to spend the rest of the night climbing the walls and walking the floor, she decided a stiff mug of ale might be just the thing she needed to put her to sleep.

On stealthy feet, Gwen left her room, gently pulling the door to behind her. She tightened her cloak about her to guard against the evening chill in the dimly lit hall. Her fingers curled about the quilt hanging across the doorway.

Eyes widened. Mouth unhinged in shock.

They were silhouettes in front of the fire. From the lighting and the angle, Gwen could see nothing and everything.

I'll never eat at that table again.

Karyn's fingers were gripping the edge of the table she was sitting upon. Her head had fallen back, exposing her throat, and her curly, ebony hair was hanging down her back. She had one leg drawn up, her foot braced on the table edge. Her other foot was flat on the seat of a chair.

Bodhi was standing snugly between Karyn's open legs. Her hand was beneath Karyn's skirt, her hand and arm draped all the way to her elbow in the material. From the way Bodhi's arm was moving, it wasn't difficult to guess what she was doing beneath the tavern wench's skirt.

Karyn's mouth fell open and she moaned.

Gwen could empathize. After all, she too knew what it felt like to have Bodhi's hand between her legs. Even though she was a virgin sacrifice and thought she was in imminent danger of being eaten, or worse, by an ogre, she had still been aroused by Bodhi.

Now, she was watching Bodhi doing *that* with someone else. She wanted to turn, to leave, to flee back to her room. It seemed as if no matter how much her brain insisted she do just that, her legs and feet refused to move.

I should go. I need to go. This is private. I shouldn't be seeing this, listening to this.

Bodhi had claimed she wanted another go with Gwen, that she was much more proficient with her left hand. From the way Karyn was writhing and moaning and begging for more, Gwen could only presume that was true. She hadn't been terribly overwhelmed her first time with Bodhi, but then again, she was chained to a pillar as a sacrificial offering at the time.

A long, keening wail was drawn out from between Karyn's parted lips. Her bosom heaved as she drew in great, ragged breaths. One hand braced on the table, she leaned forward. She placed her other hand between her legs, stilling the movement of Bodhi's arm.

Her fingers clutched the back of Bodhi's neck, pulling her down for a kiss. The kiss ended and she wrapped both arms about Bodhi's waist. With her chin resting on Bodhi's shoulder, she looked dead-on at the hanging quilt.

Gwen swiftly released her hold upon the quilt and ducked completely behind it. *Did Karyn see me?* Gwen thought only her fingertips and eyes had been exposed, but couldn't be sure. Her heart was pounding a rapid beat in her chest and she hurried on shaky legs down the hall and into her room, closing the door behind her and breathlessly leaning against it.

†

Bodhi's eyes searched the dimness of the tavern. She thought she'd seen movement. She could have sworn she saw the quilt hanging across the doorway flutter.

She stayed very still, feeling the air about her. There was no breeze. Sharp hearing picked up a sound and she turned to find Karyn standing in front of the fire, straightening her skirt, and slipping her shoes back on.

"Stay." Bodhi reached out, taking Karyn's hand in hers.

"I can't. You've kept me far too long as it is."

With the skill of one born to the profession, Karyn easily slipped out of Bodhi's grasp. She picked her cloak up off the floor, dusted it off, and settled it about her shoulders.

"Then, allow me to escort you."

"The curfew is in effect and the guard is already watching you. Don't give Thorne an excuse to arrest you."

"You think I'm afraid of the city guards?"

Even as she was fastening her cloak at her neck, Karyn had been walking toward the front door. At Bodhi's question, she stopped and turned and looked at her, as if she were giving it serious thought.

"Bodhi, please. You can't go home with me."

There was something about the way Karyn said it that gave Bodhi pause. It was as if she truly regretted refusing the warrior.

I understand her reasoning. It's not as if my feelings are hurt.

"Take this." Bodhi's fingers closed about the knife belted at her waist and placed it in Karyn's hand.

"What's this for?"

"Protection. Take it with you. Keep it close."

"I can't take this. It's yours." Karyn's eyes were fixed upon the hilt, her thumb caressing over the sapphire embedded in the pommel. "Besides, I don't think I'd know how to use it."

She attempted to return the knife to Bodhi, but the warrior stopped her with a well-placed hand.

"It's just like using a carving knife. Pretend you're cutting a big, fat pig with it." She looked as if she were about to argue, so

Bodhi cut her off with a timely kiss followed by a command of, "Return it tomorrow."

✝

A full, yellow moon climbed above the eaves of the buildings overhanging the narrow streets. It glistened on the brackish water standing in the runnels between the cobblestones. The steady *drip-drip-drip* of water pinging against a brass pot echoed in maddening symphony with the *click-click-click* of a lone pair of shoes on wet pavement.

Moisture seeping into a brazier hanging on the corner of a building caused the fire to sputter and then go out completely, casting the adjoining alley into impenetrable darkness. The lone footfalls abruptly stilled.

Karyn cast a look up at the drifting clouds that further blocked the light of the moon. She bit her bottom lip and dubiously eyed the pitch-blackness that loomed deeper in the alley. She suppressed a shiver, gripped her cloak tighter about herself and continued on her way.

It was foolish of me to linger so long in Bodhi's arms. The deeper Karyn walked into the shadowed alley, the more she felt the hairs at the base of her neck and on her arms stand on end. *It was even more foolish to allow her to have me yet again in the common room.*

A tender ache echoed between her legs with every step she took. The fabric of her blouse rubbed coarsely against her oversensitive nipples, causing them to tighten and stiffen. Even now, blocks away from the site of her last seduction, Karyn felt tendrils of arousal creeping warmly through her body.

A wicked smile etched across Karyn's lips. It had been reckless to ingest the endive. Given the end results, it had also been *oh, so worth it...*

She'd hadn't known exactly what she'd needed when she stepped through the door of the tiny shoppe scrunched between two taller, dilapidated buildings on a desolate side street on the west end of the city. The crone that ran the herbalist shoppe had taken one look at her, though, and told Karyn she had precisely the thing for her.

She'd led her through cramped aisles to the back of the shoppe and reaching onto a shelf above her head, pulled down a vial so heavily laden with dust that it was black in color. With great difficulty, the old woman uncorked the container and shook out a handful of sprigs so green and vibrant that they appeared as if they'd been freshly cut from a lush, spring meadow.

Endive was a natural aphrodisiac, according to the crone. *A pinch in your intended's food will increase their appetite for more,* the elderly woman had assured Karyn with a wink.

Not that Bodhi needed too much encouragement. A smile was forming on her lips at the memory of the warrior's hands, lips, and tongue on her body.

Karyn had told the crone she wanted something that wasn't harmful to the user. After all, she bore Bodhi no ill will and did not intend malice of any kind. Mostly, she needed the aphrodisiac to make Bodhi more manageable and ensure that her head was turned in the proper direction. Specifically, toward her. Spirits knew she was getting older and couldn't fairly compete with some of those young tarts.

With the endive, that was no longer a concern. As long as she dosed Bodhi's meals enough, the warrior's time and coin appeared to be spent solely on her. *Sneaky? Yes. Underhanded? Again, yes. Immoral? Probably.* But, Karyn had more than one mouth to feed and she'd do whatever was necessary to provide for her family.

Karyn came to the end of the alley and paused, looking left, then right, and then left again. She started off to her right, then changed her mind, and went the opposite direction. It'd been a long time since she'd had difficulty finding her way home. She'd lived in the same hovel all her life and had often joked that she could find her way home blindfolded in the dark.

Hesitant footsteps slowed to a stop. Karyn's brow furrowed and she brought a hand to her head, fingers rubbing in circles at her temple. She leaned against the side of a building, feeling the dampness seep through the thin material of her threadbare cloak.

I had no intention of ingesting the endive. But, what else could I do? Thanks to Bodhi's sacrificial whore, I had to prove I hadn't poisoned the mutton stew.

Teeth biting against her bottom lip, Karyn looked up and down the street. The buildings seemed to sway and the street lurched beneath her feet with every unsteady step she took.

That was the side effect of endive. It made the user disoriented, fuzzy-minded, and forgetful. *Very much like coming off a three-day drunk.*

She'd heard that Bodhi hadn't remembered a thing of the drunken brawl she'd been engaged in. Rachel's loose lips had also told her that Gwen was rather miffed that Bodhi didn't seem to recall her from the night before, either.

Don't think I'll have that problem. Karyn felt herself clench as she took another step, a poignant reminder of Bodhi's fingers forcefully thrusting into her. Her knees trembled and a fresh wave of arousal soaked her breechcloth.

Karyn was shaken from her lust-filled, endive haze by a scritching sound. She turned and looked over her shoulder. Out of the corner of her eye, she saw a darker shadow moving against the gray walls lining the alley.

Her fingers closed tightly about the hilt of the knife she carried. The pommel was weighted, making the weapon feel heavy in her hand. Fingers flexed, seeking a more reassuring grip.

A chill wind blew in, sending misting rain falling diagonally into her face and against her cheeks. She blinked against the stinging moisture in her eyes. As her vision cleared, she saw the fluttering of the edges of a cloak in the distance.

Karyn ran. She sprinted around the corner and down the end of a side street before rounding another corner. Heart hammering in her chest, she pressed herself flat against a wall. She drew in short, shallow breaths and willed her heartbeat to calm.

After long moments, she leaned forward and cautiously peered around the edge of the corner. Standing in the light from a brazier mounted on a post at the four corners of a cross street, was the cloaked figure. The hood was pulled up, making the person unrecognizable, but the folds of the cloak fluttered open, revealing a dark tunic and a belted sword riding low on a hip.

Karyn pulled her head back in and stood stock-still. She didn't know precisely how long she waited, not daring to move a muscle. She waited so long, though, that the dampness from the wall soaked through to her back, causing her to uncontrollably shiver.

At last, she heard the telltale sound of boots on cobblestone. She held her breath, silently praying to any spirits that might be watching over frightened, fallen women huddled in dark alleys in the dead of night.

See me through this and I'll mend my ways. I'll start going to church again. I'll make my family go. I promise. To her relief, the echoing sound of walking boots faded into the distance.

Karyn risked a look around the corner. Sure enough, the streets were empty and she was once again alone. A heartfelt sigh escaped her lips. Now that the danger was past, she was cocky in thinking that Bodhi was right. *City guards are simple to elude.* Especially for someone like her that knew the streets of Fairhaven the way she did.

She boldly stepped away from the wall and out into the middle of the street. Karyn stood there, turning this way and that, looking up and down as she tried to figure out in which direction was home.

†

Gwen had raced back to her room, slamming the door behind her, and bracing her weight against it. She'd been standing there so long, her chest mightily heaving with each breath, until she thought perhaps she was safe after all.

Then, the latch had been pressed down and only Gwen's quick reaction had prevented the door from being immediately opened. Next came the calling of her name and the repetitive sounds of a palm being slapped against the door and then a shoulder and upper arm being slammed against the wood. The door bumped against her back, threatening to send Gwen lurching forward with each repetitive thrust.

At last, the door was hit with enough force that it flew open, sending Gwen stumbling across the room and landing sprawled out upon the floor. She braced her palm flat on the floor and brought herself up into a half-sitting position so that she could glare imaginary daggers at the intruder.

Her hair was a wild mane of blonde that fell over broad shoulders. The collar was cut from the neck of her cornflower blue tunic, exposing an expanse of tanned flesh. The blue material fell over the soft curve of womanly breasts. The tunic was belted at the waist by a strip of dark leather and ended mid-thigh. Sleeves were rolled up to her elbows, revealing forearms thickly corded with muscle. Powerful hands were clenching and unclenching at her sides.

Gwen looked up into hardened chips of blue ice that were unblinkingly looking right back at her. Unnerved by the intimidating stare, Gwen found herself on the defensive.

"What do you want, Bodhi?" Her words came out sounding much more clipped than she imagined they would.

"You," Bodhi boldly declared, looking Gwen directly in the eye.

There was a fire in Bodhi's eyes and the heat of her gaze could be felt the entire distance of the room. Her eyes roamed freely, seemingly caressing Gwen's every curve with longing desire.

Gwen's heart was hammering wildly in her chest, its erratic beat echoing in her ears. Her mouth was immediately dry. Between her thighs was instantly wet. She thought she might actually fall over, if she weren't already sprawled out on the floor at Bodhi's feet.

"I saw you spying from the shadows."

"I don't know what you're talking about."

"Your body can't lie to me. You're so aroused, I can smell you."

"Oh, Spirits," whispered Gwen.

In three quick strides, Bodhi was across the room and picking Gwen up in her arms.

Then, Gwen was on the bed, her top gone, her upper body exposed to the chill night air. Heated palms covered her cold flesh. Her breasts were cupped and lifted, thumbs worked over her thick, erect nipples. Gwen gasped aloud as her nipples were pinched.

"Bodhi."

Bodhi lowered her head. She licked at and then sucked the underside of Gwen's breast. She pointed her tongue, running the tip about the nipple before fully popping it into her mouth and sucking hard.

Gwen's head snapped back, her eyes slammed shut as Bodhi heartily feasted at her breast. Hands trembling with need came up, fingers twining in Bodhi's hair. Fingers guided Bodhi's mouth to her other breast.

"Oh, Bodhi," Gwen hissed as Bodhi's teeth closed about her nipple.

Gwen's eyes opened to see Bodhi sitting back on her heels, looking down at her with a cool expression.

"Tell me you want me," Bodhi said.

Despite the steely look, Gwen couldn't help the tremor that coursed down her spine and settled between her legs. Bodhi's voice was naturally raspy, its timbre enough to make Gwen weak in the knees under ordinary circumstances. When laced with the detectable huskiness of arousal, the effect upon her was devastating.

"Bodhi."

"Tell me."

A hand insinuated itself between their bodies, feather-light touches kissing across her ribs and over her stomach. Her hips instinctively took up a rocking motion as Bodhi's hand traveled beneath her skirt and up the outside of her thigh.

"Tell me," that voice insisted.

Gwen's lips would form only one word. She tasted it upon her tongue, felt it rumble in the strained muscles of her vocal chords.

"Bodhi. Bodhi. Bodhi…"

Gwen's eyes flew open. Her heart was thumping, her breathing was heavy, and a fine sheen of perspiration coated her flesh. Her gaze flitted about the room and to the closed door.

She sat up, bracing her arms on her knees. She was in her room, in her bed, and she was most definitely alone.

What she thought was her calling out Bodhi's name was in actuality someone else's voice. Gwen stumbled from her bed, quickly dressed, and stepped into the hall.

She followed the sound of heated voices to the third room down the hall. She edged her way past Roe and two city guards and rushed fully into the room before freezing in her tracks.

Bodhi was naked, her stiff nipples a pale pink in the early morning light. She was sitting up in bed, sheets pooled about her waist. Rachel and Fauna were on either side of her, also naked, an indecent amount of their flesh exposed. All three had sleep-tousled hair.

It didn't take any stretch of the imagination to figure out exactly how Bodhi had been caught off guard. A pitcher and empty mugs were scattered about the nightstand and floor. The air reeked of stale ale, sweat, and sex.

Bodhi's dual shoulder harness was hanging from the bedpost, her swords out of reach.

Thorne appeared to not be taking any chances, though. She was standing off to the side of the bed, also well out of Bodhi's reach. The tip of her sword was inches from Bodhi's throat. Her voice was harsh as she barked out her commands.

"Get up. Get dressed. You're under arrest for murder."

Chapter Fourteen

If gaols were meant to be depressing, unpleasant, inhumane places, Fairhaven's could rival the dungeon of any castle Bodhi had seen. The entire cell was nothing more than a single, spacious room comprised of rough-hewn stone walls. Midway up one wall, there was a solitary window no wider than the length of an arrow slit. It was barely enough to allow in a meager supply of light and air.

There's not a window large enough to allow in the fresh air needed to rid this place of the stench.

To say the gaol was filthy was an understatement. Bodhi couldn't begin to guess how long it had been since someone had brought in fresh rushes. The straw on the floor was dark, damp, and visibly moving from an infestation of all sorts of creepy-crawlies. The stone walls were stained with streaks of slime and moss from being used as a privy.

For as many people as Bodhi saw in the cell, it was strangely quiet. They all seemed determined to keep to themselves, their heads lowered, and in most cases, stringy, greasy hair falling about their faces, hiding their features from view. What Bodhi could see of them revealed them to be in varying stages of filth, ragged clothes, and malnourishment. No doubt an equal part of the stench could be attributed to both the *privy-walls* and the unwashed bodies of the prisoners.

Bodhi figured she was luckier than some. She saw a great many prisoners with chains about their wrists or ankles holding them to the wall. Bodhi's hands were chained in front of her, but she wasn't fettered to the wall. Her legs were unshackled, too, permitting her to walk about the cell as she pleased.

It wasn't because any of the guards had been particularly lenient, especially considering the crimes she was being accused of. It was more because she was fighting them tooth and nail and, after making the initial arrest, their commander had abandoned them to the task of getting her to the gaol. It had taken four of them to get her wrists shackled and to drag her kicking and screaming to the cell.

They hadn't been particularly gentle about it, either. Inside the door was a platform no larger than two feet wide. Five carved steps descended down into the main body of the cell. The guards hadn't bothered with the stairs. They'd simply shoved her through the door and off the platform to land as best she could on the rushes and stone floor five feet below.

Bodhi cast a disdainful look at the oak door. It loomed tall and wide, reinforced with thick iron hinges. In the center of the door was a cutout square, just large enough to slide a tray of food through. Not that the guards were in the habit of using it for that purpose.

Twice now, she'd seen two guards open the door and step onto the platform carrying buckets filled with gruel. They stepped to the edge, yelled to the prisoners to *Come and get it*, and tossed the buckets off the platform. She'd noticed that one of them, a skinny fellow, at least tried to gently toss the bucket so it might land right side up. The other, a big oaf of a man called Sarge, seemed to take great glee in throwing the bucket so that it turned over, spilling gruel out over the bug-infested rushes. He seemed to take even greater pleasure in watching the starving prisoners scrambling on all fours, fighting each other in an effort to reach the food first.

Bodhi wondered how long she could last. She'd been amongst them for a full day and a half. Thus far, she'd been able to distance herself from the spectacle. But, her hunger and thirst were palpable. Her stomach rumbled as if there were a whole dragon inside waiting to be expelled out and her guts were so tight they ached.

On trembling legs, Bodhi climbed the five stairs leading to the platform. She ducked her head and slowly, cautiously peeked through the tray slot. It was a dangerous thing to do. In her lifetime, she'd seen more than one careless guard lose an eye to the wrong end of a spoon thrust or a finger gouge. She was certain the same treatment could be applied to a curious prisoner.

Caution flew right out the window…or the tray slot…the instant she spotted Gwendolyn. Bodhi crouched down lower, pressing her face fully against the door, both eyes peering out the opening for a better look.

She was walking past the door, down the corridor Bodhi remembered being dragged through a day and a half prior. Walking beside her, with her fingers gripping Gwen's elbow, was Commander Thorne.

"Guh—" Bodhi's voice came out as nothing louder than a hoarse croak. "Gwen."

To Bodhi's consternation, Gwen didn't seem to hear her. She continued down the corridor beside the commander.

Bodhi saw something flicker and had the wherewithal to pull her face back from the tray slot. A sword blade was thrust through the opening and Bodhi dodged to avoid it. The movement had her backing up, sending her foot over the edge of the platform and into the pit below.

She fell—hard. Her body slammed into rush-covered stones. She felt the impact in her cheekbone, her shoulders, and chest. She saw someone scrambling toward her on all fours, his chain dragging through the rushes. Then, her vision blackened.

†

"Bodhi didn't do it."

Gwen was standing in the commander's office, her arms locked as she pressed down on the surface of Thorne's desk, and leaned in so close they were nearly nose to nose.

Thorne steepled her fingers and leaned back in her chair. Her expression was one of pure impassiveness.

"I know she did."

"The night she was murdered, I saw Bodhi at The Dirty Duck with Karyn." At Thorne's look of incomprehension, she elaborated, "I mean, I saw her *with* Karyn. Believe me, killing her looked to be the last thing on Bodhi's mind. And, when you came to arrest her, you saw her *with* Rachel and Fauna. Honestly, when would she have had the time?"

"The body was stiff, the blood around the wound sticky. She'd been dead for candlemarks before we found her. Bodhi could have followed her from the tavern, killed her in the dark of night, and crept into those tavern whores' bed before the light of dawn."

"To what end?"

"In the hopes of establishing an alibi, perhaps?" Thorne shrugged. "It's not the first time she's been linked to a body, you know."

Gwen looked sharply at the commander.

"Oh, you didn't know, then? I found her kneeling over the body of Fairhaven's first victim. She had an alibi for that one, too. Ironically enough, provided by the very same tavern whore that was murdered the other night. At the time, I suspected she was only covering for Bodhi, but I couldn't prove it."

"I don't care what you say. I know Bodhi. She didn't do this."

She watched as Thorne got up from her chair and paced to the window. She stood with her hands clasped behind her back, looking down on the streets of Fairhaven.

"You think you know her?" Thorne's reflection gave a bemused smirk. "You really think you know the first thing about her?"

"Yes, I do." Even as Gwen said it, she felt a churning in her gut. "You think I don't?"

Hands still clasped behind her back, Thorne turned from the window. She cocked her head to the side, looking at Gwen askance, as if taking her measure.

"Tell me something you know. Anything at all," Thorne challenged.

"She's…she's guard." Gwen shrugged, thinking of Bodhi's weapons, her skills, her arrogance, and swagger.

"So, you were fooled by the uniform, too."

Gwen's face fell. She remembered back in Chatham when she'd first met the beautiful warrior. She'd initially been misled by Bodhi's appearance, until she'd noticed the epaulets and stripes missing from her tunic.

"People see what they expect, not necessarily what's real. I'm sure you can see now the difference in our uniforms."

"Your tunic is burgundy and Bodhi's is light blue." Gwen's answer was clipped.

Thorne looked like the cat that had snuck into the dovecote and had her fill of bird. Quite frankly, it was a look that Gwen didn't appreciate.

"Faded blue, actually, and her rank is missing. Only the King's guards wear royal blue. You've heard the saying *once a guard, always a guard*? That's because there's only three ways out of service to the King. Retire with meritorious valor, be crippled in battle, or die. She looks far too young to have been decommissioned and I didn't notice any debilitating disfigurement, did you?"

"What are you saying; Bodhi's…" Gwen's face scrunched up "…some sort of deserter?"

"Either that or she killed the real guardsman and stole his belongings. The knife that was found protruding from the tavern whore's throat has a sapphire embedded in the pommel. As you know, sapphires are very rare jewels. Only the King's honor guards are issued those, as a sign of the Crown's appreciation of their sacrifice and service. The only evidence more damning than that would be if Karyn had named her own killer with her dying breath."

Gwen felt her knees go weak and blindly reached behind her for a chair.

✝

A deluge of water was splashed in Bodhi's face. She came up off the floor, spitting and sputtering. She brought her hands up to her face, her wrist chains clinking, and wiped the wet hair from her eyes. She used her palms to drag the excess moisture off her cheeks and down to her parched lips.

"Wake up, killer."

Bodhi glared daggers at the sergeant. He was standing at the top of the flight of stairs, beyond Bodhi's reach. An empty bucket was clutched in his beefy fist.

"On your feet," he ordered. "You've got company."

Bodhi made her way to her knees, feeling the dampness of wet rushes soaking through her britches. She braced her manacled hands on the stone floor and grunting with the effort it took, pushed her way to a standing position.

She looked past the barrel-shaped guardsman to the open cell door. Torchlight and a sigh of fresher air drifted through the opening and around the sergeant's massive bulk. She saw two silhouetted figures move beyond the doorway, into the room, and stop at the top of the stairs.

"Gwen," Bodhi gasped aloud.

At the sight of her, Bodhi immediately moved toward the maid. Eyes fixed on Gwen, she scarcely noticed when the sole of her left boot connected with the bottom step.

"Bodhi." Gwen took one step down.

Bodhi made it another step up before her path was barred. She blinked, looking down at the long shaft of the spear thrust across the width of the staircase. She looked up at the guardsman holding the weapon with a tight, double-handed grip.

"Don't get any nearer," said the commander. "She's dangerous."

Thorne was standing on the top step. She took Gwen by the elbow and guided her back up until they were standing side by side. It didn't escape Bodhi's notice that Thorne didn't remove her hand from Gwen's person.

"Bodhi? What happened?" Gwen's eyes were darting all about Bodhi's body. "By the Spirits, is that a bite mark?"

Bodhi's chains rattled as she lifted her forearm and turned it for a better look. The bite had been vicious and deep. Fresh blood continued to flow from the puncture wounds. Dirt and bits of filthy straw clung to the area surrounding the bite.

"Someone must've thought I was supper."

Driven mad by starvation, trained that their meal was always tossed to them from the height of the platform, Bodhi wasn't surprised that one of the prisoners thought she was food. In truth, she was stunned that more of them hadn't rushed her. Perhaps it was because they saw the first poor bastard get kicked in the teeth and decided they didn't want a meal that fought back.

"Commander Thorne, these conditions are appalling," said Gwen.

"It's gaol. It's not supposed to be pleasant."

"Still, there's no reason it should be inhumane."

"These are the scum of Fairhaven. This cell houses rogues, thieves, whores, and killers." Thorne's gaze pierced Bodhi as she said it. "They can hardly be considered human."

"They shouldn't be treated like animals, left to wallow in their own filth."

"I granted your request for a visit, not an inspection. We're here. Go on, ask her." Thorne jerked her head in Bodhi's direction.

Gwen stayed quiet. Her eyes dropped to her feet, as if she suddenly found something very fascinating about the stitch-work of her boots.

"Gwen? Ask me what?" Bodhi felt her brow furrow.

Hazel eyes slowly looked up, barely meeting Bodhi's gaze. When Gwen spoke, her voice sounded tiny in the massive cell.

"Bodhi, are you…were you…really one of the King's guards?"

"What?" *Why would she possibly ask me that?*

"It's the difference between a military tribunal and a magistrate's court. When we first met, your appearance suggested you were, but we never established—"

"Tell me, Gwen, was your appearance that of a virgin as pure as the driven snow or was it the image of a debauched maiden?" Bodhi's eyes narrowed until she saw Gwen's horrified look only through tiny slits. "Tell me, as I seem to have trouble recalling which Gwen I first met."

"Do you see now, Gwen?" Thorne pointed an accusing finger at Bodhi. "She's like them. No better than wild animals, the lot of them."

Hands on her hips, Gwen looked out over Bodhi's head, her gaze flitting about the interior of the dark, dank cell. Bodhi didn't have to turn to look to know what Gwen was seeing. They were pitiful creatures. Chained like dogs, their clothing rotting off their bones, open sores on their exposed flesh from living in the putrid filth of their own stench.

"Now that you know, it's time we leave. I have an appointment with the magistrate."

Looks of disdain, shock, and pity rolled across Gwen's features. All three were quickly followed by the firm set of a stubborn jaw and a defiant tilt of a chin in gestures that Bodhi was all too familiar with. Despite the hand gripping her elbow, attempting to guide her away, Gwen held fast her ground.

Thorne rolled her eyes and let out an exasperated huff. With an irritated expression, she turned to the sergeant holding the door open.

"Shovel those rushes out and put fresh straw down on the floor."

"Yes, Commander." Sarge gave Thorne a sharp salute and Gwen a hard stare. He stepped into the corridor beyond the open door, already shouting his own commands at his subordinates.

It wasn't until a guardsman appeared at the door with buckets and shovels that Gwen permitted Thorne to escort her from the cell.

✝

He was sweating. He hated sweating.

Here, in the depths of the gaol cell, the air was stale, the heat stifling. Salt ringed white on his tunic, staining the material covering his chest, his back, and beneath his arms. The only part of the burgundy material not darkened with sweat was the expanse of cloth hanging beneath the width of his belt.

Sarge dumped another shovelful into the bucket that Ernest was holding at arm's length. The guardsman's nose was crinkled and he wore a look of utter disgust on his face. On the next shovelful, Sarge deliberately brushed the corporal's knuckles.

Ernest leapt back and shrieked so much like a high-pitched girl that Sarge burst out laughing. That is, until he noticed Ernest's dropped bucket had landed on its side, its contents spilling back out onto the floor.

Sarge clutched a hand to his aching back and stood fully upright, the vertebra in his back giving a satisfying crack. He planted his shovel firmly in a crack in the stone floor and looked about. It had taken candlemarks and an entire squad to haul the buckets up the steps and out of the gaol, but they were nearly finished.

Finally.

His gaze fell upon the new prisoner, the one they'd arrested for those murders. She was standing in the shadow of the stairs, the sole of one boot planted firmly on the stone as she leaned against the wall. Her arms were folded over her chest, the length of chain comprising her manacles dangling from her wrists. Ice-blue eyes were staring dead at him.

The other animals were cowed into corners of the cell, huddled together like frightened beasts. *Why isn't she?* It irked Sarge that she wasn't.

"What're you looking at?" he snapped.

Bodhi slowly lowered her foot to the floor. She coolly unfolded her arms and pushed her long frame off the wall. She came to stand no more than a few feet from him. Her head cocked to the side. Eyes raked up and down his body and Sarge felt himself grow uncomfortable beneath her gaze.

"Looks to me like a pile of shit," she drawled, "shoveling more shit into a bucket."

Sarge spat and sputtered.

Ernest laughed.

Sarge gave him a look, then a kick to the chest that sent him and his bucket tumbling over backward. In three short strides, he was standing in front of that blonde wench. To his consternation, she stood a head and a half taller than him. And, she didn't look the slightest bit intimidated by him.

If I can't scare her one way...

"That little whore that visited you earlier? I hear she comes from a farming village." Sarge was leaning in closer now, so close he knew she could smell the raw onion on his heated breath. "First chance I get, I'm going to plow her like one of her father's fields."

Nostrils flared. Blue eyes flashed. She lunged for him, but he evaded her reaching grasp.

"Her father was a pig farmer, you daft bastard."

Sarge hit her open-handed across the face. She rode out most of it, but the impact caused her to take an unsteady step back. Her hair fell across her face and she had to flick it away as she raised her head to look at him. Her cheek was flared red from the strike and blood ran down her chin from a split lip.

"Tell me, does your whore squeal like a little pig when she's rutting? Or, is she more like one of those big, fat sows that just wallows about? Better yet, don't tell me. I'll find out for myself."

Bodhi spat. It landed upon the floor between Sarge's boots. She smiled at him, blood coating her teeth red. Her smile was too rigid, too dangerous, and far too confident.

Sarge paled. His hand reached for the hilt of his sword. He jerked at the grip, but his blade wouldn't come free of the scabbard. He looked down at the sword, cursing himself for not taking better care to keep the leather oiled. He felt a trickle of cold sweat roll down his spine and into the crack of his backside.

Mouth dry, heart in his throat, he looked at the prisoner.

Bodhi shot forward, raising her arms above her head as she rushed Sarge. She slipped her arms about his neck, looping the chain attached to her manacles as she went. Then, she was behind him, using leverage to pull him back.

Sarge couldn't breathe. He felt like his eyes were bulging out of their sockets. His fingers were clawing at Bodhi's arms, at the chain cutting into the flesh of his neck, and at anything he could reach. He saw Ernest scrambling toward him. Above the roar of blood in his ears, he thought he heard the far-off tramp of many pairs of boots rushing to him.

They were on her. They were on him. There was a myriad of punches and kicks and it crossed Sarge's mind that some of the men that had rushed to his aid with such zeal were using it as a chance to mask getting in their licks on him.

Gasping for breath, he was desperately clutching at one of the prisoner's forearms, but she wouldn't give. Her grip tightened, the iron links embedding deeper into his flesh.

She brought her face in right next to Sarge's. Her voice was low, but clear enough that every word was seared into his memory.

"You don't talk like that about Gwen. Not ever. Is that clear?"

Sarge tried to answer, but couldn't force out the words.

"Is that clear?"

Sarge frantically nodded, despite the chain chafing against his skin with every movement.

Bodhi released her grip.

Sarge, unmindful of the filthy mess he was lying in, fell back on the floor and took in heaping great gasps of fetid air. His head lolled to the side and he watched with dispassionate interest as Bodhi rolled into a ball, arms covering her head in an attempt to protect herself as his fellow guardsmen rained down brutal retaliation upon her.

Chapter Fifteen

It was dark. The street was poorly lit, the coal-fed braziers too sparse and too ineffectual to cut through the dense fog. Visibility was minimal; half a block at best.

In the distance, she could hear running footsteps upon cobblestone. Bodhi moved toward the sound, uncertain if someone was moving toward or away from her. She called out. The footsteps hesitated, but no one gave answer. When they started moving again, Bodhi was certain that the footsteps were now running away.

Bodhi ran in the same direction. Through the thick fog, she spied the dark shadows of a fluttering cloak and running legs. Bodhi gave chase.

Sweat was beginning to form on her brow, stinging as it dripped into her eyes. Her breathing was becoming heavier. The combined pounding of her heartbeat and her footfalls echoed between her ears. Still, she continued to run, spurred on by an occasional glimpse of the cloaked figure in the distance.

Her quarry ducked around a corner. Bodhi dug deep, increasing her stride. As she reached the corner, she reached out a hand, catching the side of the building, using it to help her make the turn. She went three steps deeper into a darkened alley before tripping over something.

Her hand blindly reached out, groping for something to brace herself on. Bodhi pushed herself up to her knees. Her brow furrowed as she looked down at her hand. Her fingers were closed about the grip of her knife, the blade embedded to the hilt in a woman's neck.

Bodhi came up with a start. Her heart was rapidly beating. Her chest was quickly rising and falling. She was dripping wet with sweat. She frantically looked about, only able to clearly see out of one eye.

Just a dream. She reassured herself before recognizing the now familiar surroundings of the gaol cell. *More or less.*

She hitched herself up into a better position, sitting with her back and side braced against the support of solid stone. Two walls formed a corner at the bottom of the stairs and she'd claimed the landing as hers. The strategic position offered protection on two sides and the vantage point of being able to view the entire cell, in case one of the other prisoners grew either too brave or stupid enough to come near. After the incident with the biter she learned that a scowl and a well-timed growl was sufficient to send any creepers scurrying back to their hidey-holes.

The landing was wide enough that she could sit with her legs drawn up to her chest. Bodhi looped her arms over her knees. The length of her chain had been shortened to prevent her from wrapping it around someone else's neck. It hampered her movements, making the position uncomfortable, but not impossible.

She propped her chin on her kneecaps and focused on the opposite wall, her eyes wandering up pockmarked stonework to the arrow-slit sized window. *Eye.* One was swollen shut, courtesy of a guard's boot during the fight. *Beating.* Fight implied fairness. There was nothing fair about six-to-one odds. *Seven-to-one.* Once he'd gotten his legs beneath his massive bulk and found his way to his feet, Sarge had zestfully stomped the soles of his boots on her ribcage.

As a matter of fact, all the guards seemed to derive great pleasure from beating her. *Except for that skinny one. Ernest.* The sergeant had bellowed his name but Ernest held back, pulling his punches, despite his superior's commands of *Harder. Harder.*

One lone eye stared skyward, trying to determine the time. It was daytime, as evidenced by the lighter gray framed by the window. *What candlemark, though? For that matter, which day?*

How long had she been in gaol? How long since the beating? Bodhi tried staying awake, but fatigue and unconsciousness had a habit of sneaking up on her. Time slipped away from her, turning candledrips into candlemarks and blending day into night.

The grate of a key in a lock drew her attention. The turning of the iron ring on the door had her sitting forward in anticipation.

Two people stepped into the open doorway, their figures silhouetted by the light in the corridor behind them. By the curves, one of them was most definitely female.

They came down the stairs together. Bodhi drew back. Since the incident with the chain, none of the guards came downstairs. Her eye adjusted to the filtering light and she recognized the male as Ernest. He stopped on the third step.

The woman advanced. Her foot left the last step and she knelt on the landing scant inches in front of Bodhi. Bodhi's good eye darted about, taking in the familiar brunette tresses and the light-hued eyes.

She tried to say the name, but was unable to form the word around her cracked lips. It finally came out as a low croak that burned her throat. "Gwen." Hands were on her shoulders, then her face. Fingers were brushing her hair back. Fingertips were tracing the swell of her black eye and her split cheek. Gwen's fingers were cool upon her flesh and Bodhi shivered beneath her touch.

"Bodhi, hold still."

Gwen pulled a vial from inside her tunic. She uncorked it, dabbing some liquid on a scrap of cloth before placing it against Bodhi's face. It stung like blazes, but Bodhi didn't shrink away. She held fast as Gwen applied it to her cut cheek and the bite on her arm.

Slender fingers corked the vial and tucked it once more into the folds of her tunic. She withdrew something else, something tiny, and placed her fingertips to Bodhi's lips.

"Open," she commanded in a low voice.

Bodhi obeyed. She felt the moisture against her lips, then on her tongue and inside her mouth as Gwen pushed the berry in. She slowly chewed, feeling juice squirting between her teeth. She swallowed, the coolness of the fruit soothing her raw throat.

"Where?" Bodhi managed to rasp out.

"The berries are from The Dirty Duck's kitchen. As for the medicine, Rachel gave me directions to a shoppe she knows. Bodhi, you should see it. I think the old woman there has an herb for everything."

"Don't think I'll be shopping there anytime soon," Bodhi said around another berry Gwen popped into her open mouth. She held up her hands, shaking her wrists, making the length of chain clink for emphasis.

Gwen's smile fell and she went quiet. She sat back on her heels, staring down at her berry-stained hands. When she looked up again, melancholy was reflected in her eyes.

"Bodhi, I wanted to ask you something." Gwen looked down again and began picking at the stains on her fingers with her nails. "Did you do it?"

Bodhi felt both her brows go up. Her last visit, Gwen had surprised and angered her with her questions about being in the guard. It paled in comparison to being asked if she were a murderer.

"What do you think?"

"No. I saw you with Karyn, in the main room of the tavern. There's talk, though, Bodhi. They're saying you killed Karyn and then used Rachel and Fauna as alibis."

"Is this *they* your Commander Thorne?" Since she'd been talking to Gwen, her voice was becoming steadily stronger. Now, she was beginning to sound, and feel, more like herself.

"Bodhi, what were you doing during the time between Karyn and the other girls? If you tell me, I can present it to Thorne as proof of your innocence."

"Blast it, girl, I was drunk. With the exception of three things that stand out clear in my mind, most of that night is a blank. I remember losing big at dicing, seeing you and Thorne sucking off each other's fingers." Bodhi saw crimson coloring Gwen's cheeks at her vivid depiction of events. It didn't deter her in the slightest. "And waking up in bed between two serving wenches with a sword pointed at my heart."

"That's my point, Bodhi. The night before, you didn't recall groping me or being in a brawl. Even falling down drunk, you should remember more than you claim to."

"Are you calling me a liar as well as a killer?"

"No, of course not. The old crone at the shoppe, she tried to sell me more than a simple vial of medicine. She thought I was there for the same herbs as another tavern maid. Bodhi, she described Karyn."

"Rachel probably told Karyn about the same herbalist. Lots of people use herbs, Gwen. What are you getting at?" Bodhi asked, wariness edging its way into her voice.

"Damn it, Bodhi. Are you deliberately trying to be obstinate?" Gwen's eyes flashed. "Fine. You want me to ask? I'll flat-out ask. How well do you…did you…know Karyn?"

"You think Karyn's some dirty, little tavern whore? She's the widowed wife of one of the King's guards. The only reason she's working the tavern is because he fell in battle. He died, leaving Karyn alone to care for her elderly mother and two small children."

"Oh, Bodhi. Is that what she told you? Don't you know that's one of the ruses they use to trick soldiers to part with their coin?"

Bodhi heard Ernest awkwardly shift his stance on the stairs behind Gwen.

"She didn't have to tell me. I served with her husband." She saw Gwen's eyes widen in surprise. "Do you know how much a guard's life is worth? Six copper coins paid at the time of his death. That's how much the king values his soldiers."

"Bodhi, I didn't know." Gwen's words were tinged with regret.

"No, you didn't, did you."

They both fell silent.

Gwen looked away, her sight fixed on the wall at some point past Bodhi's head.

Bodhi released a ragged sigh and looked down, staring at her chained wrists. She heard the far-off stomp of boots. There was the sharp slap of fists to chests in salute. It could only be an officer coming. It was either Thorne or Sarge. Bodhi looked past Gwen to Ernest. His expression indicated that he wasn't certain which. Sarge's vile threats came whispering back in Bodhi's ear. *She can't be here.*

"You have to leave."

Gwen's head shot up.

"No, not yet. Not now, not like this." Gwen reached out a hand to touch Bodhi's cheek.

The footsteps grew louder. A frantic look from Ernest indicated that the officer was drawing nearer.

"Don't touch me. I saw the sideways looks, the little sneers you gave Karyn, the way you looked down your nose at her." Bodhi pulled as far away from Gwen's tender touch as her sitting position would allow.

Gwen's eyes were shiny with moisture and Bodhi knew the girl was on the verge of tears. Still, she made no move to leave.

Damn it. She's got to go.

"You think the girls that work the tavern are tawdry whores like your sister? You think you're better than them? You're nothing more than a virgin sacrifice that got off lucky." Bodhi hardened her voice, forced her lips to form a derisive sneer. "You don't know them. You don't know me. Get out, Gwen. Get out and don't come back."

Gwen was on her feet, a scowl marring her features. Her arms were at her sides, her hands balled into fists so tight her knuckles were clenched white.

Good, thought Bodhi. *Get angry.*

"Take her away," Bodhi called out to Ernest. "I don't want to see her again."

✝

Sarge did a double take on his way into the cell. Ernest was coming up the stairs, a wench on his arm beside him. She looked like that whore from the other day, but her face was blotched red and her eyes were bloodshot. She was covering her nose and mouth with her hand and avoided his gaze as she rushed past.

Sarge wanted to stop them both and question them as to precisely what they were doing in the cell. He couldn't, though. They were already halfway down the corridor and he had a prisoner on his arm.

He was big. Big and greasy the way all barbarians are. His arms bulged with massive biceps and his legs resembled tree trunks. It had taken four guards to bring him down and three more to get the manacles on him. They hadn't stopped with one set, either. They'd gone for double wrist and ankle shackles with short lengths of chain in case he got any cute ideas.

Sarge stood on the platform just inside the doorway and looked down at the pit below. No way would he be able to shove the barbarian off the edge the way he liked to do with prisoners. *Probably take me and anyone else that tried with him.*

Sarge turned the barbarian toward the stairs. His stiff fingertips nudged the barbarian's shoulder, indicating he should move. The barbarian took one step and stopped. The sergeant was getting ready to take his life into his own hands and berate the barbarian when he saw what had caught the big, greasy brute's attention.

That damn bitch warrior was sitting on the landing at the bottom of the stairs. As she saw their approach, she started to get up.

The barbarian growled low in his throat and started down another step.

Sarge smiled. He placed both palms flat on the barbarian's back and gave a forceful shove.

The barbarian was sent flying down the steps. Slamming into the wall abruptly stopped his forward momentum. He crashed to the floor, landing atop Bodhi. A hand upon the stair, a bicep bulging, the barbarian pushed his way to his knees and then his feet. He glared at the sergeant, as if he were about to charge up the stairs.

Then, Bodhi groaned. She slowly climbed to her feet, using the wall to help herself rise.

The barbarian turned and caught Bodhi by the front of her tunic. His hand balled into the material, he lifted her up the wall until his arm was fully extended. Bodhi's feet dangled above the floor.

"Ogre-slayer," came the barbarian's guttural grunt.

"I take it…" Bodhi gasped, "…we've met?"

Bodhi's arms were raised, both of her hands wrapped about the barbarian's arm that was pinning her to the wall. Her fingernails were digging into the flesh of his arm. Her boots were kicking at his shins.

The barbarian apparently didn't seem to notice or care.

"Enjoy," Sarge called down to them.

Sarge backed his way out the door. He closed it, turning the key and locking it. He walked away, jauntily swinging the iron key ring on one finger, his belly-laughter drowning out the rising screams coming from the cell's interior.

†

Hands gesticulating wildly, Gwen paced the guard commander's office. Her voice was raised and her words were poured forth in rapid succession. Her long strides quickly ate up the length of the floor.

She was acutely aware of Thorne's eyes upon her, watching her every step, coolly appraising her. It irked her. It irked her even more that the commander was sitting in her chair, a nonchalant expression on her face as Gwen passionately pleaded Bodhi's case.

"Go to the herbal shoppe. Ask the old woman what she sold Karyn. I'm convinced she was drugging Bodhi."

"Doesn't mean Bodhi didn't kill her. Gives her all the more reason, if she found out." Thorne's voice was as cool and impassive as her expression.

"You've arrested the wrong person."

"Gwen, I've tracked this monster for a long time. I think, of all people, I would know the beast once I've caught it. The magistrate believes it, too."

Gwen's gaze stole across the parchment on Thorne's desk. It bore the wax seal of the Office of the Magistrate and was spread out for anyone to read. Which, Gwen supposed, was exactly what Thorne wanted.

"I went to see her." Gwen caught Thorne's disapproving look, saw she was about to scold her, and promptly cut her off before she could utter a word. "Did you know they beat her?"

"I have a written report from the sergeant on duty that there was an escape attempt. Disciplinary action had to be taken."

"To within an inch of her life, apparently. Does the magistrate's office condone excessive measures?"

"That's a very serious accusation."

"Mistreatment of prisoners is a very serious thing," countered Gwen. "Don't forget, I've seen firsthand the conditions of your gaol."

"You also saw me take corrective measures when we were there together."

"Having fresh rushes put down on the floor is simple. Starvation, dehydration, and physical abuse aren't so easily cleaned up. Allow the abuse to continue and your prize prisoner won't be fit to stand public trial."

Thorne sat forward, leaning an elbow on her desk. She cupped her chin in her hand and with what seemed like an air of indifference, looked across the desk at Gwen.

"It's not about how many women were murdered, is it? It's not about justice for them, either. It's something else." Gwen placed her hands palm down on Thorne's desk, bearing down with all her weight as she stared down the commander. "It's about your record. For you, it's about your command, the commendation the magistrate is rewarding you, and the adulation of the crowd."

"Ridiculous." Thorne leaned back in her chair in an obvious attempt to put distance between herself and Gwen.

"Is it? I've been talking for over a candlemark and you haven't batted an eye at anything I've said. This is the most honest reaction you've had this entire conversation."

"As long as we're speaking of honesty, Gwen, tell me why you're truly fighting so hard for a murdering animal."

"Because she's innocent," Gwen said quickly.

"I don't believe, in all my seasons as a commander, that I've ever heard of a prisoner demanding a visitor be taken away." Thorne snorted.

Gwen paled. She didn't know the commander had heard about that. *If she knew that, she also already knew I'd been to visit Bodhi without her consent.*

"Are you in love with her?" Thorne unexpectedly asked.

"What? No." That's when it dawned on Gwen. "Is this because of what happened between you and me the other night?"

"Don't you mean what *didn't* happen?"

"I thought we'd moved past this. I was truthful in my apology to you, Thorne." Gwen lowered her voice, trying to convey her sincerity. "But just because I wasn't with you, don't think I'm in love with someone else, least of all Bodhi."

"What nearly happened was a momentary lapse of judgment on my part. Never fear, it won't occur again. But that's not the only reason I ask."

"I don't know what you mean."

Thorne got up from her chair and moved around the desk. She gripped Gwen by the shoulders, turning her around. Green eyes darted about her face, as though searching for something.

She moved in closer and Gwen thought Thorne intended to kiss her until she leaned past her lips to her ear. When she spoke, her voice was so low that it seemed like little more than a whisper.

"There's something there, between the two of you. It's palpable. It can feel it. I can smell it." Thorne drew back until she was looking Gwen in the eyes. "I see it in the way you look at her, as if there's nothing you wouldn't do for her. It's almost as if you feel that you owe her something."

Thorne's look was too intense. Her words hit too close to home. Gwen felt the irrepressible need to lighten the mood between them.

"Well, she did save me from being an ogre's sacrifice, didn't she?"

"Yes, and can you honestly say your virginity is all that it cost you?"

✝

Thorne paused at the doorway, giving her eyes time to adjust to the dimmer lighting of the cell. As the room came into acute clarity, she stepped inside and turned to the guard three paces behind her. A curt nod had him saluting and taking up a position inside the door.

Hands clasped behind her back, she stood on the platform, her gaze sweeping over the pit. The rushes scattered on the floor were newer than those she'd seen the last time she was there. However, there were already clumps and mounds piled here and there, primarily against the walls. These had started turning from a golden straw color to mottled hues of greens, browns, and blacks.

Per her orders, a newly constructed water trough had been installed in the cell. It started at the top of the platform she stood on and ran through the middle of the room. In theory, the guards were to periodically add buckets of fresh water to the trough to prevent prisoner dehydration. In reality, the trough was three-quarters empty and the water that was in it had gone stagnant.

The air still smelled fetid. The prisoners looked worse than they smelled. Their filthy clothes, those that hadn't rotted off, were hanging loosely on their thin frames. She could count the ribs on several of them and saw that their pants were being held up by nothing but their jutting hip bones.

One prisoner was lying on the floor so still that Thorne thought he was dead. A mouse emerged from the waist of his raggedy trousers, scurrying up his chest, over his face, and into his long, straggly hair. Then, she saw him fast as lightning reach up and grab the mouse in his hand, tugging it from his hair. She turned away before she could see what he intended to do with the loudly shrieking rodent.

Well, it is still a gaol and not a royal room at the castle, thought Thorne.

Gwen had made some valid points and Thorne had to admit that there should be something done against the inhumane treatment of prisoners.

For the most part, anyway.

Thorne still believed that every one of the prisoners in her gaol were guilty and deserved to be locked up until they died. *Or, at least until the day of their execution.*

Her gaze landed on Bodhi. She was at the bottom of the stairs. One knee was drawn up, her other leg was curled beneath her. Her shackled hands rested limply between her legs. She was more leaning than sitting, her left side, shoulder, and cheek pressed into the corner of the stairwell wall. Her eyes were closed and she was very still.

Hand gripping the hilt of her sword, Thorne descended the stairs. She paused on each step, wary eyes watching for any sudden movement. When she reached the bottom, she nudged Bodhi with the toe of her boot.

Bodhi didn't bat a single eyelash. One eye looked like it had swollen shut, the area surrounding the socket shaded in hues of blacks, blues, and yellows. There was a cut on her cheek that was infected, red streaks radiating out from the wound. Her hair was matted down at the temples, beads of perspiration pooled on her upper lip, and the front of her tunic was drenched in sweat.

Thorne's hand shifted from her sword grip to her knife hilt. She took a knee beside Bodhi. She tentatively reached out, placing two fingers against Bodhi's throat as she checked for a pulse.

A low growl caught her attention and Thorne turned to look. A big, half-naked barbarian was coming toward her, his ankle shackles clinking with every step. He also wore wrist shackles and he was winding the length of chain over his knuckles as he approached.

Thorne tried to stand, fingers scrambling for the pommel of her sword. Her movement was hampered by the proximity of the wall. She looked up the staircase. The guardsman was standing on the platform, his fingers wrapped so tight about the grip of his sword that his knuckles were clenched white. His eyes were wide and unblinking and he looked as though he couldn't move a muscle.

"No," said a raspy voice.

The barbarian halted.

Thorne risked a glance down. Bodhi had one eyelid cracked open and a bloodshot eye rolled up and peered at Thorne. It looked like it took considerable effort, but Bodhi turned her head to the side and fixed her eye on the barbarian.

"It's fine." Bodhi rolled her head on her neck until she was looking back at Thorne as she said, "But don't go far."

The barbarian retreated a few paces. He took up a position in the shadows of the staircase. His beefy arms were folded over his massive chest, there was a scowl on his face, and his eyes were fixed on Thorne.

Thorne warily shifted her gaze from the barbarian watchdog to the warrior.

"You made friends? In here? With him?" Both Thorne's brow and voice rose in surprise.

"What can I say? I'm a charmer." An unexpected cough racked Bodhi's frame.

Thorne's eyes drifted down to Bodhi's forearm. The bite marks were coated in dried blood, dirt, and Spirits only knew what else. The puncture wounds had festered and were oozing pus. Thorne placed her palm to Bodhi's forehead. She was hot to the touch.

"The prison surgeon will have something to break the fever."

Thorne gripped Bodhi's jaw and forcefully turned her head for a better look. She sensed movement and cast a look over her shoulder. It wasn't until she released her grip on Bodhi's jaw and dropped her hand away that the barbarian melted back into the shadows.

"That cut needs stitching. He'll probably irrigate your arm, too."

"Ah." Bodhi's lips cracked as she smiled. "Wouldn't want to disappoint the crowds by my being too weak to stand at my own trial."

"Actually," Thorne had to admit to herself that it hurt to say it, "wouldn't want to disappoint a certain maid that came by my office."

"Gwen?"

Thorne saw something come alive inside the warrior. With a grunt of exertion, she worked her feverish, beaten body up into a sitting position. Wrist chains clinked as she tried to rise up enough so that she could see past Thorne and up the stairs.

"She didn't come."

Thorne placed two hands on Bodhi's shoulders, easily pushing her back down. She heard an audible sigh escape Bodhi's lips, almost as if she were relieved that Gwen wasn't there.

"Where is she?" Bodhi suddenly asked.

Thorne shrugged and looked toward the arrow-slit window.

"It's near dark. I'd imagine she's on shift at The Dirty Duck."

"You can't let her."

"If she wants to be a tavern wench, that's her choice. How she lives her life isn't your concern. Nor mine."

"Listen to me." Bodhi gripped the front of Thorne's tunic and pulled herself halfway up off the floor. There was a wild look in her feverish eye. "You don't like me. I get that. I think you fancy Gwen, though."

Thorne blanched. She didn't want to. *Someone like her, I can't.*

Bodhi must have read into Thorne's reticence.

She leaned forward, her clammy face so close to hers that Thorne could smell the stench of illness on her breath. "I don't know what you might think of her, but Gwen's not some tavern wench. She's a good girl." She leaned around Thorne, staring at the guard at the top of the steps. "First chance he's got, that bastard of a sergeant is planning on having a go at her like she's a common tavern whore, willingly or not."

Thorne slowly turned and looked at the guardsman standing inside the doorway. He was at attention, looking straight ahead. He blinked beneath her stare, though, and Thorne was convinced he knew what Bodhi had confided in hushed tones.

"Guardsman, where's Sarge?"

"Supper break, I think." He shrugged. "He and the corporal left together."

"Your Corporal Ernest has a sweetheart at The Dirty Duck." Bodhi began coughing again.

Thorne grabbed her wrists, forcing Bodhi to let loose the grip she had on her uniform. Thorne pushed her back against the wall.

Tears were streaming from Bodhi's good eye, her face turned crimson, and her entire body lurched with each cough.

"I'll send the surgeon." Thorne paused halfway up the stairs, turned and looked down on Bodhi. "Don't think I'm going to allow you to die a heartbeat before your execution."

Chapter Sixteen

Somewhere in the distance, a rooster crowed.

Gwen glanced out the window. It was well past dawn, the morning already gone. *Even their city chickens don't wake up properly. Back home, the roosters cock-a-doodle-doo at the crack of dawn. By that time, I was already up, dressed, and feeding slop to the pigs. I had to be; it was the only way to get all my chores done before nightfall.*

In Chatham, the day ended properly, too. Work till dark, have supper around the table, and wash up the dishes. Then, it was straight off to bed and peaceful, dreamless slumber that lasted until the next rooster crow heralded the start of a new day.

Not in Fairhaven. Not so far as Gwen had seen. Here, it seemed as if everyone started the day later. Folk stayed up later, too, crowding into public houses, away from their families, as though they preferred to eat supper with strangers. Then, it was drinking, gambling, and anything else they pleased deep into the night. When sleep did come, it was full of tossing, turning, and restless dreams that, by the light of day, left the sleeper exhausted.

Rachel, Fauna, and her guardsman, Ernest, were seated at a table near the hearth. Wisps of smoke curled above their mugs of steaming cider. There was a trencher filled with salted pork and gravy in front of Ernest and even though he was chewing, his eyes were closed, and he appeared to be nodding off.

"Morning, luv." Rachel used her foot to kick the fourth chair out from beneath the table.

"Is it? My body insists it must still be the middle of the night," Fauna said between sips of her cider.

"Much as I hate to admit it, you city girls have corrupted me. I don't think I've ever stayed in bed this late in my life." Gwen grimaced as she sat down and her back popped in response.

"In all honesty, luv, when I didn't see you here in the common room, I thought you'd already snuck out."

"Rachel. Gwen wouldn't leave without telling us farewell. Would you, Gwen?"

"Of course not, Fauna." *Days ago, I might have. In truth, I know I would have, without a second thought.*

Last evening, she'd gone to settle things with Roe. He'd surprised her by gifting her some fruit, nuts, and dried meat from the kitchen. He said he wouldn't see her off in the morning, but made her promise if she were ever back that way again, she'd stop by.

She'd gone to her room and packed her gear. Twice. Even slept in her traveling clothes so she'd get a quicker start.

Then promptly spent the night tossing and turning, undesired thoughts in her mind and unwelcome images in her dreams. Her sleep was filled with troubling flashes of Bodhi, Gerald, Thorne, and finally, of Karyn, all with their throats slit and pointing accusing fingers at her.

What Bodhi said about looking down my nose at them, judging them...she was right. It's like Rachel said, they all used to have plans, hopes, and dreams. Who did I think I was to judge Karyn or anyone given the things I've done?

"Still, with the curfew lifted and the lockdown ended, I thought you'd be on the first horse out of here."

"Rachel!"

Ernest started at Fauna's raised voice. She patted him on the sleeve and he settled back down in his chair. He put his spoon in his mouth and chewed as if he'd never missed a bite, even though Gwen was certain he'd been woken from a sound sleep.

"Gwen, you have to forgive Rachel." Fauna shot the other tavern maid an admonishing look. "She's hardly civilized before her third mug."

"It's fine. You forget, I've seen Rachel after that third mug and I'd hardly call her civilized even then."

"This from the wench raised on a pig farm." The lines at the corners of Rachel's eyes and mouth crinkled as she gave an uncharacteristic smile.

"In truth, I meant to be on my way by now," Gwen stifled a yawn, "but I couldn't get my lazy bones moving."

"I know why I'm exhausted, luv. I thought you turned in early, though. Unless, of course, you weren't alone…"

"Oh, I was alone and thankful for it. I owe Roe for stepping in and staring down a guardsman that way." Gwen suppressed a shiver. "I swear, if I ever see that sergeant again I just might go up to him, grab his chest in both my hands, and tweak his nipples. See how he likes it."

Gwen saw Rachel, Fauna, and Ernest all exchange looks.

"Um, luv, I don't think that's such a good idea."

"You're right. He'd probably enjoy it." Gwen noticed the same exchange of looks. "What? What have I missed?"

"Sarge didn't report back to post after our supper break last eve. We spent the night searching, but didn't find him until after dawn," said Ernest around a wide yawn.

"So, he found another willing, or not-so-willing, maiden. Can't say I'm surprised that he'd shirk his duty for a little poke and tickle. I hope Commander Thorne gave him what-for."

"Actually, Gwen. I don't think she had to." Fauna reached out, taking Gwen's hands in hers and clasping them the way someone might when they had sad news. She looked to Ernest and jerked her head at Gwen as if he should be the one to explain.

"Sarge's throat was slashed. He's dead."

Gwen felt her eyes widen and her mouth drop open. It was the last thing she expected.

"It was a street peddler that found him and summoned the guard." Rachel braced herself on the arm of her chair and leaned forward, eyes gleaming. "Rumor is that Sarge was murdered by the same beast that killed all those women."

"That's not official," Ernest was quick to point out. "No one said that."

"No, luv, you only said that he was killed the exact same way as all the rest."

Ernest looked both flummoxed and annoyed. Fauna placed a hand upon his, as if to calm and reassure him. At his perturbed expression, Rachel flashed him a smug look and turned to Gwen with more juicy gossip.

"Commander Thorne's been summoned to the magistrate's office. She may have to let your friend go."

Bodhi freed? Thank the Spirits.

To Ernest, Gwen said, "When she's released, will you tell her she can pick up her weapons from Roe?"

"That's not official, either," protested Ernest around a mouthful of salted pork. "No one's said that. Besides, if she wasn't already locked up in gaol, I would've thought Bodhi had killed Sarge."

"What for, luv, that beating? If she wasn't chained up in that gaol in the first place, he'd never had the chance."

"For her." Ernest pointed to Gwen.

He looked from Rachel to Gwen and back again. His expression gave away how pleased he was that for once during this conversation, he seemed to know something the tavern maid didn't.

"That's why Bodhi took that beating. Sarge told her he was going to…" Ernest looked at Gwen and he blushed all the way to the tips of his ears. "…make advances on Gwen. She nearly choked him to death."

"You hear that, Gwen? Your hero defended your virtue. Again." Rachel winked and nudged Gwen.

"Yes, I suppose she did." Gwen chewed her bottom lip.

"Pardon my saying so, Gwen, but you don't seem overjoyed by anything we've told you. Not that I would expect you to be pleased by the death of anyone, not even Sarge," said Fauna. "But, I would think you'd at least be glad about Bodhi."

"I am. I'm glad she might be freed. I wish her nothing but happiness." Gwen nodded.

She saw the furrowed brows and speculative looks around the table. She released a sigh and rolled her eyes at having to tell them.

"When I went to visit Bodhi, she told me how she feels." There was a hitch in Gwen's voice and she had to swallow before continuing, "She never wants to see me again."

The room was filled with awkward silence. Gwen looked from face to face, seeing varying degrees of discomfort and pity. Gwen wished she could be anywhere else but right here, right now.

There was the sound of a *crack* from beneath the table.

"Ye-ouch." Ernest bent over, grabbing his shin, and glaring at Fauna.

She glared right back at him. Once again, she signaled with her eyes and jerked her head in Gwen's direction.

He shot Fauna back a questioning look.

She jerked her head at Gwen again.

"Go on, tell her," Fauna mouthed.

"Tell me what?" asked Gwen, not entirely certain she truly wanted to know.

"That stuff that Bodhi told you in the cell..." Ernest's voice trailed off and his eyes left hers. He squirmed awkwardly in his chair before looking back at her. "...she only said that to protect you. She thought that if you came back again, Sarge would...you know...force you...and she wouldn't be able to stop him."

"Oh." Gwen blinked. She didn't know what to say. *Really, what is there to say?*

"Um, I've gotta go. With Sarge dead and Commander Thorne unavailable, I'm the senior officer in charge of the gaol. I've gotta go."

Ernest was already scooting his chair back, the wooden legs scraping on the floor. He stood up and adjusted his tunic, smoothing out his uniform and checking his sword in its sheath.

"I'll bring your supper by later." Fauna gave him a peck on the lips.

Ernest blushed scarlet and ducked his head, a goofy smile upon his lips. He gave an enthusiastic nod, turned around, and promptly fell over the chair he had pulled out. He leapt up and dusted himself off, his eyes never leaving Fauna's face the entire time he walked backward toward the door.

I want to go, too was what Gwen thought of saying, but didn't.

Gwen didn't know what she would do when she reached the gaol, what she would say to Bodhi when they were together in the cell. Despite Ernest's explanation, Bodhi's accusations rang in her ears, and she doubted if the warrior truly did want to see her.

Perhaps she should wait at the tavern until Bodhi was released. After all, she had to return for her weapons and traveling gear. That way, if Bodhi really didn't want to see her again, they would both be free to walk away.

Gwen waited so long in her indecision that Ernest was out the door, the little bell above the frame tinkling with his departure.

Gwen still didn't know what she should do. All she knew for certain was that she couldn't leave Fairhaven now.

†

"All of them?" questioned the ironsmith.

"You heard me. All of them."

With her hands clasped firmly behind her back, Commander Thorne walked up and down the line of prisoners. They were a ragtag group, in varying stages of dishevelment. Most of them half-starved and half out of their minds. Still, somehow, they'd been organized enough, if only for a little while, to attack the guards that had come with their midday rations.

They'd risen up, en masse, out of the pit, charging up the stairs, Bodhi and her barbarian leading them. The plan seemed simple enough—overpower the guards and make it out of the gaol, even if it meant taking the door off its hinges. Thorne looked at the door hanging askew and it appeared that they were very nearly successful.

"Chain them up. Fetter them to the walls." Her order had been the only logical course of action.

She knew there were, of course, already iron rings mounted in the walls throughout the cell. It was, after all, a very old gaol. All that was needed were shackles and chains to secure the prisoners in place.

The guardsmen held swords and spears at the ready, trained on the prisoners as the ironsmith fixed the shackles in place. Some of the prisoners were luckier than others, depending on whether he fixed the iron about their wrists or ankles. The ones with ankle restraints still had enough length in their chains that they could sit or lie down on the floor. The ones with wrist restraints were forced to stand in place. Some of the iron rings were fastened low enough that their arm was merely at their side. Others were positioned above their heads and their shoulders were popped out of joint to reach the rings.

Thorne watched as the poor bastard the smith was affixing to the wall now only had a short chain on his wrist shackles. The chain had been stretched through an iron ring located so far above his head that he had to stand on tiptoe, stretching first one side of his body and then the other to keep his arms from being yanked out of their sockets.

"I'll need more chains," said the ironsmith.

"Take two men with you to your shoppe. Bring back as many as you think necessary and then double that number," ordered Thorne.

The ironsmith nodded, half-bowed, and rushed for the stairs.

Thorne motioned for two guards to escort him.

Thorne paced to the end of the row and back, looking each prisoner up and down the way she might inspect troops. At the head of the line, she stopped and stared for long heartbeats, reveling in a feeling of deep satisfaction.

The two ringleaders, she'd had them put on display so that everyone else in the cell might see their punishment. She'd had them done first, knowing it would cow the others into submission. It worked. No one had made so much as a peep since Bodhi and her barbarian were made examples.

She'd had them fitted with collars about their necks and personally selected chains a length of no more than six inches apiece. They could hardly move, let alone sit, lie down, or sleep. They were, in short, chained like ill-kept dogs.

They'd been chained for about a candlemark now and as of yet, neither showed any sign of strain. Thorne knew it wouldn't last. First, the discomfort would set in, the shifting from leg to leg to relieve the pressure off aching knees. Second, fatigue would begin to creep in. Their eyes would close. They might even slip off to sleep until their chains jerked them up short and their choking brought them back to wakefulness. Then, the cycle would start all over again. Fatigued sleep, sudden alertness, and fatigued sleep again until they choked one too many times to come back from it.

The barbarian, Thorne didn't care about. He could choke on his own vomit and be done with it. Bodhi, on the other hand…

"Guardsman."

A guard rushed to Thorne's side, drew up short, and saluted.

"Fetch a bucket of water. She starts to fall asleep, you douse her with it." Thorne briskly slapped Bodhi's cheek with her fingers as if to rouse her.

"Yes, ma'am." The guard rushed to the trough to dip out a bucket of scummy water.

Thorne reached out, gripping Bodhi by the top of her hair and pulling her face up. One blue eye peered back at her. Her eye was clear and appeared focused; lacking the glazed look it had held when Bodhi had been at her most feverish. However, her skin was still clammy and Thorne had no doubt that infection still raged throughout her body.

"No one, no one escapes from my gaol," said Thorne.

"That's fine. I'll wait for the official letter of release." An indolent smirk formed on Bodhi's lips.

"Pardon?"

"That would be my guess. I suppose the magistrate's gonna want you to give that letter of commendation back, also." Bodhi's smirk had turned into a full-on grin.

Thorne frowned. No doubt, she'd overheard conversation between the guardsmen. It seemed the sergeant's death was all any of them could talk about. *As well it might be, considering that it was a fellow guardsman that was murdered.*

"I see that rumors run rampant even through the solid stone walls of a gaol. Rest assured, that's all it is—gossip."

"Then, you weren't summoned to the magistrate's office?"

Thorne's jaw clenched. Her eyes flashed. *When I find the guardsman feeding information to the prisoners...* "As a matter of fact, your little attempted rebellion has made me late for a meeting with the magistrate. Don't fear, I'll be certain to tell him you're the reason for my delay."

"I'm certain he'll be lenient, considering I'm about to be released, anyway."

Enough. Thorne leaned in closer, pressing her face so close to Bodhi's that their noses were nearly touching and she could smell her foul breath and the stink of her unwashed body. "Listen carefully." Thorne dropped her voice so that no one else, prisoner or guard, might overhear. "Those were nothing more than dirty little tavern whores that got their throats slashed. Sarge was a member of the guard. His death isn't related to theirs."

"He was—" Bodhi's voice was cut off.

Thorne twisted the length of her chain about her fingers, tightening it until Bodhi choked.

"Killed in the same manner," Bodhi still managed to rasp out.

"I'll convince the magistrate it was someone who copied the crimes, maybe one of your trollops in a futile effort to see you freed." She gave Bodhi a poke in the chest that elicited a satisfying grunt in response. "You'll be executed, I'll see to that, even if I have to have your tongue cut out to prevent you lying through your teeth at the trial."

That's when it fell into place for Thorne—Gwen. *She held nothing but contempt for Sarge. And, she pleaded numerous times for Bodhi's life.* "What power do you hold over her?"

Bodhi blinked back at her, as if she had no idea what Thorne was talking about.

Gwen wasn't the only one, either. She'd seen her with that last tavern whore that had been murdered. *Two more of them were fawning all over her, too.*

Fawning. Fauna. She'd seen the girl on the arm of her corporal, flirting with him. Fauna was a comely maid. She could have her pick, no doubt. While Ernest, well, to call him homely would be a kindness. There were only two things a wench like her could want from a lad like him—his coin or information. And, a corporal in the city guard didn't earn much.

Ernest is the leak. Poor, dumb bastard probably doesn't even realize it. Thorne glanced toward the arrow-slit window high on the wall. The candlemark was growing late, she had to meet with the magistrate, and Ernest hadn't yet arrived. *When next I see him, I'll set him straight.*

†

Gwen was livid. She'd finally made up her mind and gathered enough of her courage to come to the gaol to face Bodhi. The condition she'd found her and the other prisoners in—no matter that Bodhi did look like she was no longer at Death's door—was appalling. Chained, shackled to collars, unable to reach either food or water, or even afforded the simple act of being able to relieve themselves.

Gwen stopped her pacing back and forth. She scuffed the sole of her boot against the stone floor in an attempt at scraping off whatever that was she'd stepped in.

"This is unacceptable. No one should be forced to live like this."

"Doubt it'll be for much longer."

Gwen looked up, staring at Bodhi. Her eyes widened and her mouth dropped.

"No. No, she wouldn't?"

Bodhi nodded and the iron collar slid up and down her neck, rubbing her skin raw.

"I'll appeal. I'll go to the Office of the Magistrate."

"Won't do any good. Can't you see; he has to go along with it? Otherwise, he'll look like a fool for giving Thorne all those accolades. The citizens would call for his resignation, if not his head."

"I don't care. I'll make him listen. I'll go to his home tonight. I'll drag him from his supper table and force him to come down here if need be." Gwen was pacing in tight circles as she laid out her plans.

"That your virgin maiden?" The barbarian leaned as close to Bodhi as the length of his collar chain would permit.

Gwen stopped pacing and turned to look at the barbarian, wondering that he hadn't recognized her from the tavern brawl. *Guess if you've punched one maid...*

Bodhi nodded.

The barbarian frowned. "I thought maidens were supposed to be sweet, soft-spoken, virtuous, and pure of deed and heart."

"Gwen's not that sort of maiden."

"She's not even at all like any of the wenches we keep at home," said the barbarian.

Gwen glared at the broad grin on Bodhi's face. She was going to make a sharp retort, until Bodhi's smile unexpectedly fell, to be replaced by a grave expression.

"Gwen, listen to me." Bodhi's tone was serious—life-and-death serious. "They'll put on a sham of a trial. They'll have to have one to quash the rumors about Sarge's murder."

"There are enough of us that know the truth. We won't be silent."

"Listen. Please."

Gwen fell silent. For Bodhi to plead with her in that manner… *How much more dire could it be?*

"They'll behead me or hang me or whatever it is they do here and pat themselves on the back for executing a dangerous killer. I don't want you to see that. Before they…before they…I want you to get out of town. Take my horse. Or, purchase one. I'm sure the livery master will sell you one now."

"I won't leave you, Bodhi."

"Get out of Fairhaven, Gwen. Get out and don't come back."

"In Chatham, you didn't leave me. I won't abandon you now."

"As I recall, you tricked me into staying."

The nerve. "No one forced you to stay." She narrowed her eyes, glaring at Bodhi, daring her to contradict her.

"Being chained up in that temple put a stop to my leaving." Bodhi's dimples briefly showed through the dirt, blood, and grime, until she sobered again.

"Leave, Gwen. Go now." Bodhi performed as much of a head jerk toward the door as her restraints would allow.

"In a bit. I just want to stay a while longer."

To her surprise, Bodhi didn't put forth any further argument.

✝

"Gwen?" Bodhi's soft voice washed over her.

"Hm?"

"Wake up." Bodhi's voice was no longer so soft, nor soothing.

"'m awake."

Gwen's head bobbed. She was tired, so tired that she'd nearly fallen asleep on her feet, with her arms folded, and her chin resting on her chest. No matter how exhausted she was though, nothing…nothing could bring her to sit on the filthy floor or lean up against Spirits-knew-what that was coating the wall.

"Gwen." Bodhi's tone was insistent.

She cracked one eye open and looked at Bodhi.

"You must go. Now. Someone's coming."

Gwen turned to see Ernest entering through the awkwardly hanging gaol door. Rachel was behind him and they were both rushing down the stairs and into the lower level of the cell.

"The guardsman said you were here." Ernest's face was flushed and he sounded out of breath.

"I meant to stay only a while." Gwen stretched, her joints popping with the movement.

"Is Fauna with you?" Ernest grasped Gwen's upper arms in a tight grip.

"No." Gwen shook her head and looked past Ernest to Rachel.

The older woman was wringing her hands and had a decidedly frantic look about her.

"What's happened?" asked Bodhi.

"Fauna left the tavern candlemarks ago to bring plates for Ernest and Gwen for supper," said Rachel. For once, her characteristic *luv* was absent from her speech.

"I haven't seen her." Gwen shrugged and looked to Ernest.

"I haven't either," he said. "I thought she'd gotten busy or simply forgotten what she'd said about supper."

"She didn't forget you." Rachel reached out a hand and cupped the lad's cheek. "She hasn't returned to the tavern, though. Roe sent me to fetch her back."

Gwen felt a queasiness in her stomach.

"What time is it?" asked Bodhi.

Gwen looked at her and shook her head. It was already nearing dusk when she'd set out for the gaol and she'd been with Bodhi for several candlemarks.

"Oh, no," Rachel said.

"You shouldn't have let her come alone." Ernest was staring at Rachel and there was a hard edge to his voice that none of them had ever heard him use before.

"It's not her fault. The curfew was lifted—"

"We all knew it wasn't safe. We knew it wasn't the real killer locked up in here." There were tears glistening in Ernest's eyes as he gestured wildly at Bodhi.

"This isn't helping Fauna. Someone needs to be out there searching for her." Bodhi placed a hand to her collar, as if signaling that someone should free her.

"I can't do that. I don't have the keys. Even if I did, I can't just let prisoners out of gaol. And, I can't go myself. The commander hasn't returned from the magistrate's office, yet." Ernest looked and sounded tortured.

"Gwen, you have to do it."

Gwen turned and gave Bodhi an incredulous look.

"She's a hunter. She can track anything." Bodhi looked at the others.

"Bodhi, I can't."

"You can. You tracked that ogre, didn't you?"

"That wasn't difficult. Big, lumbering ogre trampling through the countryside and all."

"I couldn't have done it."

Everyone was looking at her. Rachel, Ernest, Bodhi, and the barbarian chained to the wall beside Bodhi.

Gwen released a heavy sigh.

"I can't track through the city, on cobblestone streets."

"Start back at the tavern, track her from there."

"It's not possible."

"Gwen. Gwen."

Damn Bodhi's soft voice calling my name, making me look at her. Rot her eyes for looking back at me with those baby blues.

"Gwen, you're that girl's only hope. I believe in you. You can do this."

"I can send some guardsmen to accompany you," offered Ernest.

"No," said Gwen. "In order to have any chance of tracking Fauna, I can't have anyone else trampling on the trail. If I go, I go alone."

Chapter Seventeen

Gwen followed her instincts, scarcely paying heed to where they were leading her. She was on the scent now, she was certain. When it came to tracking, it was about feeling and not thinking of which way the trail led.

She had stood outside The Dirty Duck Tavern, staring at the ground, turning about in circles, uncertain which way to go. She was convinced she'd never be able to pick out a single trail amongst the trampled footsteps. Then, she stopped—just stopped. She closed her eyes and waited and when she opened them again, she knew which way to go.

It was the way Fauna would have gone. She'd been carrying supper to gaol for me and Ernest. She'd take the shortest route.

Gwen hadn't been in Fairhaven long, but over the course of the past few days, she'd certainly learned the quickest way to the gaol. Out the door, to the left and down the first side street on the right was where Gwen started. The farther away she got from the crowded tavern front, the less foot traffic there was likely to be. True, the curfew had been lifted, but only just. There were still plenty of folk afraid to be on the street. That helped her track Fauna.

So did the accursed misting rain that seemed to forever linger in Fairhaven. The excess water drained off into runnels between the cobblestones. But, there was still enough moisture on the stones that the dirt and ash formed an oily surface on the streets and alleyways.

The grime from soles of shoes left enough of a trace that she was able to pick out and follow a trail. The tread appeared to be from a small foot and Gwen prayed that it was Fauna's tracks. *If they aren't I won't be able to backtrack and...* Gwen put that disconcerting thought out of her head. This was the right path. She would find Fauna. People were counting on her, people that she couldn't let down. Fauna, Rachel, Roe, and Ernest.

Bodhi believed in her.

That's what she had said. Bodhi couldn't do it, but she believed in her. That admission coming from the arrogant, cocky, and jaded warrior was what had spurred her to try.

Gwen knelt down, feeling the moisture seep into the knee of her britches. Eyes darted over the surface of the cobblestones. She saw Fauna's tread. She touched her fingertips to the outline of her shoe.

There was another shoeprint. This one was larger and it crossed over Fauna's path once and then came back again further up. Gwen could see where Fauna's footsteps were left first, then the larger ones followed after.

Gwen climbed to her feet. She clutched her bow firmly in her grasp. She drew an arrow from her quiver and nocked it on her bow. Steeling herself, taking a deep breath, she followed the trail.

She turned a blind corner and came up short. There was one brazier, burning low, barely casting enough illumination to see by. The light was certainly too dim to pierce the darkness more than a distance of three or four feet. Gwen looked skyward. Heavy clouds sporadically blew in front of the full moon, offering little help.

This is it.

She knew it was.

She could hear breathing, deep and guttural like an animal's. She heard a frightened whimper of response. Despite wanting to run the other way, Gwen took one hesitant step forward and then another.

Her eyes adjusted to the darkness and—*there.* She saw the shadows move.

Gwen couldn't believe her eyes. *It's just what they'd said it was, an animal. No, not an animal...a beast.* Hunched over, it appeared to be mauling at its prey on the ground.

It looked up, blood dripping from its open maw. There was the shine of a blade clutched in a curved claw. Nostrils flared as it sniffed at the air. Then, gleaming eyes looked directly at Gwen.

The beast rose from its crouched position and Gwen could see that it wore human clothes. Gwen gasped. More than that, it wore the distinctive crimson tunic of the city guard.

It drew closer, more lumbering than walking.

Gwen took a reflexive step back.

The moon came out from behind the clouds, its light reflecting off the wet cobblestone and illuminating the alley.

Its back was hunched. Its face was scrunched up into an ugly scowl. There was an untamed mass of hair, the strands sticking out at all different angles from its head. It was ebony black all over, except for a wild shock of solid white.

Gwen gasped aloud. "Thorne?"

The beast snarled and charged.

Gwen backed up, but then drew her line and stood her ground. She drew a deep, steadying breath. She found her anchor position, fixed her sights. The flax string bit into the flesh of her fingers. She released her aim.

It…Thorne…was running at her. She made a powerful leap, Gwen's arrow flying beneath her lengthening frame. Thorne…the beast…landed upon Gwen, knocking her backward. It tore the bow from Gwen's grasp and snapped it in half.

Gwen was on her backside, scooting backward, crablike, as she tried to regain her footing. The cobblestone was too oily, too slick, and she couldn't get any purchase.

Thorne pounced upon her. She landed hard, knocking the breath out of Gwen. She was leaning in close, her teeth bared and at Gwen's throat. There was a sniffing sound as Thorne inhaled deeply.

"I can smell it on you. You reek of it." The beast's voice was guttural, its words nearly indecipherable.

"I don't fear you."

"It's not your fear I smell. It's your guilt."

The knife was in Thorne's hand, the blade flashing as she slashed at Gwen's throat.

The blade sliced her. Gwen felt the warmth of her blood upon her flesh. She brought her arm up, her fingers gripping about Thorne's wrist as she tried to keep the bestial commander from cutting her again.

Her other arm was pinned at her side, Thorne's knee pressing into flesh and muscle. Gwen screamed and tugged her arm free. Her hand went to the quiver belted at her waist. Fingers fumbled, dropping one arrow before securing another.

She gripped the shaft, brought her arm up, and plunged the arrow deep into Thorne's side. The beast howled. Gwen twisted the shaft, burrowing the barbed head in deeper.

Thorne let loose her knife and clutched at her side. She snapped the shaft in half. Flinging it over Gwen's head, it landed against the far alley wall. Hand pressed against her wound, arrow sticking from between her fingers, her blood poured over her hand and tunic.

Green eyes flashed.

Thorne backhanded her across the face before bolting.

Gwen turned over, propping herself up on her elbow. She reached for the discarded knife, her hand closing about the grip. She crawled to the side of the alley, bracing her hand against the stone, using it to help her climb to her feet.

She was lightheaded. There was blood running from her cut throat, down her neck, and beneath her clothes. She clutched a hand to her wound. Leaning against the wall for support, she turned her head and looked down the alley at Fauna's still form.

✝

Gwen sat at a table, hunched over a mug of cider, her head cradled in her hands. Roe was moving about behind the counter, gathering supplies. Rachel and Fauna were at another table, speaking in lowered tones and placing items into a wicker basket.

Ah, youth. Or, perhaps it's only Fauna's nature. She'd been attacked, bitten by an inhuman beast. Gwen had seen the blood on her blouse and the mauled flesh of one breast. The wound had required stitches and would no doubt scar. Fauna had seemingly taken it all in stride, even jesting about how she could tell everyone she had an overly amorous lover. Today, she was up and about, a smile on her face, showing no signs of being the worse for wear.

Gwen, however, was aching all over. It had taken every bit of strength she'd had to drag herself and Fauna back to the tavern. A full night, the next day, and another night in bed, and she still felt as if every part of her body hurt. She experimentally swallowed, feeling the tender bite of pain in her throat.

She placed a hand to her throat, fingers patting at the bandage. Rachel had summoned the old crone from the herbal shoppe. She'd looked Gwen over, um-humming and ah-ha-ing as she'd gathered cobwebs from the corners and placed them on Gwen's throat. Then, she mixed crushed purple-belled foxglove and ground together all sorts of other foul-smelling ingredients until she'd formed a paste. Then, she slathered the concoction on Gwen's throat and wrapped a strip of cloth around it.

"Leave it be for three days," the crone had said.

Other than minimal discomfort and sounding like a strangled frog, Gwen couldn't fault the old woman her remedy. If it hadn't been for Rachel enlisting the crone's help, she could have very well bled to death.

Gwen's eyes darted to the door as she heard the creak of its hinges, the brass bell tinkling above the frame. As the door opened, a flash of late afternoon sunlight intruded into the dim lighting of the tavern, momentarily chasing away the gloom.

The sunshine filtered in, silhouetting an image in the doorway. Gwen blinked against the brightness. There was a halo of golden hair and broad shoulders. It was still a powerful build, even if somewhat more gaunt looking.

That's to be expected, though.

The door closed, revealing Ernest standing behind Bodhi.

"I think this belongs to you," he said, guiding the warrior into the common room.

It attested to the state of Bodhi's health that she allowed him to lead her to the table where Fauna and Rachel were working and pull out a chair for her. Bodhi collapsed into her seat.

Gwen saw Fauna and Rachel exchange looks, wrinkling their noses a bit. As if by some unspoken agreement, they both stood up and edged away from Bodhi. Bodhi was nearly slumped over the table and didn't seem to notice their aversion.

Gwen wouldn't say she was weak—she'd never say that about Bodhi. Bodhi was strong. Stronger than anyone she'd ever met and she doubted if she were a lesser woman that she would have survived her ordeal in gaol.

She sniffed, at last realizing what had driven Fauna and Rachel away. *Well, what should any of us expect; that a body would smell like a dozen roses after being locked up in that cesspool of a gaol?*

"Thanks for returning her," croaked Gwen.

"Yeah, well, don't forget our arrangement," said Ernest. "She's your responsibility now. See if you can manage to keep her out of trouble."

"I don't need a nursemaid," groused Bodhi.

"What about the other prisoners?" Gwen asked.

"Better. Not everything can be remedied overnight. But, the gaol door's been fixed. They've been unchained and I'm working on implementing better prison conditions," said Ernest.

"Look at you, in charge." Fauna wrapped her arms around Ernest's neck.

She placed a kiss on his cheek that had him blushing scarlet. Fauna took him by the hand and led him to sit in front of the hearth.

Bodhi peered into the wicker basket. She dipped her fingers inside, only to quickly pull them back as Gwen slapped her hand.

"Out of that. They're making a basket for Karyn's family."

"But, I'm hungry." Bodhi affected a childlike pout.

"There's always mutton stew, luv." Rachel edged close enough to pack another bundle into the basket.

"Ugh." Bodhi scrunched up her nose. "They serve the same thing in your gaol here."

"Sounds like torture," said Gwen.

"Hey, there's nothing wrong with my stew," Roe protested.

"Maybe the first day. But after the third?"

"You didn't seem to mind it when Karyn was spoon-feeding you," reminded Gwen.

"Only because she drugged me." Bodhi had the nerve to look indignant.

"So, now you believe me?"

Gwen watched as Bodhi eyed the basket. Her fingers crept along the tabletop and slipped into the edge of the basket. She idly moved objects about with her fingertips.

Gwen grabbed her by the wrist and removed her hand.

Bodhi glared at her.

"Come on, we'll feed you. I promise. After you've bathed and burned those clothes."

"But…"

"But nothing. You reek." Gwen playfully held her nose. After all the time Bodhi had spent in gaol, she wasn't exaggerating.

Gwen sauntered away from Bodhi and approached Roe. The tavern keeper gave her a nod and reached beneath the counter. He pulled out a wrapped bundle and laid it on top of the bar.

"Guess you'll be wanting these back now." He began unwrapping the bundle.

Bodhi looked at the package with interest. On obviously shaking legs, she made her way to the bar. She placed both hands on the counter, fingertips reverently tracing the hilts of her swords.

"You gave my swords away?" Bodhi turned to stare accusingly at Gwen.

"Well, what was I going to do with them? They're too big for me to wield." Gwen defensively placed her hands on her hips.

Bodhi looked Roe over from head to foot, as if she were sizing him up. "Well, I suppose he wasn't the worst choice you could've made." She cast a look at Ernest. "You could have given them to him."

"Hey, I was gonna sell them to the ironsmith." Roe shrugged.

"You gave my swords to someone that was going to have them melted down?" Bodhi's voice rose in pitch with each incredulous word.

"Can't speak now," Gwen said, patting the bandage wrapped around her neck. "Must rest my throat."

Bodhi looked at Gwen and curled her lip up into a snarl.

Chapter Eighteen

"I think I can understand it."

"Understand what, Bodhi?"

"Your Commander Thorne."

Gwen stiffened in the saddle and felt the horse beneath her react in kind. She reached out a hand, smoothing her palm over the mare's coat in an attempt to calm the both of them. It worked. Gwen felt her anxiety lessen.

"In the north, there are men that can turn into wolves."

"Wolves?"

"Wolves." As if to demonstrate, Bodhi bit at the air, her teeth making a gnashing sound as they closed on nothing. "Has something to do with the full moon triggering their transformation."

"There wasn't always a full moon on the nights of the killings. And, Thorne wasn't a wolf."

"Well, you yourself said she turned into…something."

"I said it was like she became someone else."

Bodhi gave a shrug, as if there were no difference.

And, Gwen supposed, *maybe there wasn't.* Commander Thorne had been intelligent, meticulously disciplined, and professional. That…thing…she'd tracked had been…a savage, mindless beast.

They rode in silence. Gwen was thinking about life-changing events—those that had occurred in the city and those that had set her on a path to Fairhaven in the first place. Bodhi was—Gwen cast a sidelong glance at the warrior—there was no telling what Bodhi was thinking. They'd been through two life-and-death situations together now and the warrior was still just as inscrutable to Gwen as the first time they'd met.

They came to a fork in the road. Gwen's horse veered to the right, traveling the path between two fields of wild wheat. She closed her eyes and tilted her head to the sky, bathing in the warmth of the sun's rays.

Fairhaven had been her first city and while she was sure her experience had been marred by the persistent rain and murders, there was also a perpetual gloom and fetidness that seemed to cling to the air there. Fairhaven had been dreary, cramped, crowded, and loud.

Here, on the road well away from the city, Gwen felt safe, secure, and warm. In the countryside, there was fresh air, freedom, and quiet. *Maybe too much quiet.* Gwen realized she only heard one set of hooves on the path. She slowed her horse and turned in the saddle, looking about. She spotted Bodhi riding on the other path.

"Bodhi, where are you going?"

Bodhi wordlessly pointed north.

"You're going the wrong way."

Bodhi reined in her horse. "How can I be going the wrong way when I have no particular destination in mind?"

"Because I'm going east," reasoned Gwen.

"And, I'm going north." Bodhi tapped her instep against her horse's side and started off again.

"Wait. You can't."

"I…can't…?" Bodhi tugged on the reins yet again, turning the horse in a tight circle, and meeting Gwen at the fork in the road.

Gwen felt her nerve slip beneath that icy gaze, but the words came tumbling forth from her mouth regardless. "I paid your bond. You were released into my custody."

"There shouldn't have been any bond to pay. I was innocent."

"Of murder, yes, but there was also the matter of drunk and disorderly conduct, tearing up the inn—"

"I paid Roe for the damage done to The Dirty Duck."

"That didn't cover the municipal fine." Gwen continued to tick off on her fingers, "Resisting arrest, assaulting more than one guard, inciting a gaol break…oh, you didn't think I'd heard about that one? Your freedom cost me nearly all my purse."

"Your purse that came from the ogre's lair."

"Same as yours," said Gwen. "So, if you'll please settle your debt, I'll willingly part company with you now."

"I shouldn't have to repay coin that wasn't yours to begin with." A low growl rumbled up from Bodhi's throat. She sat atop her horse and folded her arms over her chest. Gwen placed her hands on her hips. They stared at each other for long heartbeats, neither willing to be the first to blink.

Finally, there was extensive below the breath grumbling that ended with, "I don't have it."

"Oh, Bodhi. I knew the coin was flowing as freely as the ale in Fairhaven, but you spent it all already?"

Bodhi opened her mouth as if to say something, but then huffed loudly and clenched her jaw.

"Fine. Seeing as how you've spent mine as well, you're stuck with me until your debt is paid."

"Fine."

Gwen had fully expected to spend the night and half the next day arguing the point with Bodhi. Gwen hid her blossoming smile behind the palm of her hand so Bodhi's pride wouldn't be stung by how easily she had won their disagreement. She picked up her reins and nudged her horse down the trail to the east.

To her consternation, she turned in her saddle to find Bodhi on the wrong path. Again. With an exasperated sigh, she turned her mare, veering her off across the wheat field until she came to trot alongside Bodhi's horse.

Gwen forlornly looked to the east. There was flat land and wild wheat growing as far as the eye could see. To the north, she saw hillocks and in the far-off distance, white-capped mountain peaks.

"Bodhi, I want to head east."

"No one's stopping you."

"I thought you didn't have a particular destination in mind."

"I don't, as long as it's north."

Gwen blew out a huff of heated air. *So, this is how it's to be, is it? Bodhi's stuck with me until she repays her debt, but only so long as I go where she goes.*

There was no point in arguing about it. Bodhi wasn't the type to change her mind, nor her direction, once it had been set. So, the maid rode beside the warrior, silently fuming, trying to calculate how many seasons it would take for a sword-for-hire fighter to repay the amount of coin she owed.

The sheer number made Gwen's head spin. *I should cut my losses and head for the nearest tavern. I'd be rid of her then and I could make a decent wage as a serving maid...*

†

Gwen knelt on one knee, bracing herself on her fingertips, at the edge of the riverbank. She reached out, cupped her hand, and brought the cool liquid to her lips. Her eyes darted behind thick lashes, scanning the copse of greenery along the opposite side of the river.

Long before her first hunting lesson, before she'd picked up her first bow, her father had taken her out into the forest surrounding their land and taught her how to listen to the sounds of nature. *Everything belongs and everything has its own sound*, he had told her.

Gwen distinctly heard and identified the sound of the water lazily moving along its course, gurgling as it passed over stones along its bank and around a tree whose branches had grown so long they resembled gnarled hands, their curved fingertips dangling and dipping down into the water. There was the overhead rustling of leaves as a gentle wind stirred the air.

Somewhere behind her, she heard the whickering of their mounts, and the sounds of Bodhi unsaddling, feeding, and brushing down the horses. She had offered to help, but Bodhi had insisted on doing it herself.

Is she actually humming? As she'd set up the rest of the camp, unpacking their gear, and building a fire, Gwen had surreptitiously watched Bodhi. The swordswoman had been dutiful and efficient in her care of the horses, with the exception of their brushing. With that, she took her time, giving them long, languorous strokes of the brush. Gwen had watched as with each stroke, the furrow was no longer on Bodhi's brow, the tension left her shoulders, and her entire body seemed to relax.

Perhaps that's all she needs to relieve her burden. A bath, new clothes, food in her belly, and Bodhi seemed none the worse for wear.

Despite Bodhi calling an early stop to the day and Gwen's relief to be out of the saddle, despite the beauty of their surroundings, Gwen couldn't shake a feeling of restlessness. It was like she *needed* something to happen. It was as if, after all the troubles and hardship she'd endured in her travels since setting out from home, that there had to be something *more*. She found herself starting at every noise, looking about every curve in the road, expecting an ambush by bandits, bloodthirsty trolls, or any number of ugly beasties her imagination could conjure.

Across the river, leaves on bushes rustled. Gwen tensed, but remained still, except for her eyes that darted about the thick foliage on the opposite bank. She made a showing of cupping her hand and taking another drink from the river. Her hand slowly dropped to her thigh, then drifted to her side, until her fingertips brushed against the shaft of her new bow lying on the ground beside her. Her fingers inched along the wood until they curved comfortably about the familiar grip.

That was the one thing she'd decided she liked about Fairhaven. It had a marketplace. The biggest one Gwen had ever seen. She'd had her pick of an entire stall of new bows. She'd spent nearly a half candlemark sorting through them all until she decided on precisely the one she wanted.

There was more movement, then the subtlest shade of brown against green. There was a flickering of an ear and Gwen identified the black eyes, the white muzzle, and ruff of a deer. She looked beyond the bush and saw two smaller forms in the clearing behind their mother, eating foliage.

Gwen eased her hand off the bow. There was a time when she might have taken the shot. Hunting had always been a means for Gwen to relax, to work through whatever was bothering her. For her, nothing else compared to tracking through the forest. On the trail of wild game, she became lost in the hunt, following her prey for candlemarks on end.

Not today. Today, she was…tired. There was no other word for it. Even though there was tenseness about her and she felt as if in any heartbeat she might find herself under attack, she couldn't summon up the energy to kill. Anything.

We can eat dried meat. Gwen thought back to the rations Roe and the girls at The Dirty Duck had packed for them. It was more than enough food to see them comfortably to the next town.

She looked down, her gaze catching her reflection in the surface of the water. Brown eyes stared back at her. There were dark circles beneath her eyes and her mouth was set into a fine line. Chestnut hair framed her face, falling over both shoulders of her pale green tunic.

Gwen shifted on her haunches and flipped her hair back over one shoulder, revealing the bandage about her throat. Fingers reached up, touching the dingy piece of cloth. She pressed in, wincing as she felt a tiny stab of pain. She stared at her reflection, watching herself as she experimentally swallowed. There was still some slight discomfort, but it was bearable and, thankfully, her voice had returned to its natural cadence and she no longer sounded like a strangled frog.

Fingers picked at the edges of the bandage. Gwen stared unblinking at her reflection as she peeled back the cloth, exposing her throat. She dipped the cloth into the cool water, bringing it to her throat, timidly wiping away the remaining concoction the crone had slathered on her neck.

Gwen leaned in closer to the surface of the water, tilting her head to the side, craning her neck for a better look. The poultice had closed the wound, leaving behind a long, jagged line stretching from the base of her jaw diagonally down to her collarbone. It was pink in color and the skin around it was smooth and flat, lacking the puffiness and redness that would indicate infection.

She'd been lucky. The wound could very well have been fatal. If the crone hadn't been a skilled healer, it might have festered and cost Gwen her life. Her hand shook as she watched her reflection touch trembling fingers to her upper chest. The tip of her index finger curled about her collarbone, just shy of touching the dark pink line.

Unbidden, memories of the alley returned. Flat on her back, pinned to the ground, Thorne breathing in her face, her teeth bared as she bent her head to Gwen's throat. Thorne had been a savage beast, bent on ripping out her throat. As she relived the moment, Gwen felt her heartbeat increase and her breathing quicken.

She was a wild animal, but this time, I wasn't the hunter, I was the prey. Gwen wondered if her encounter with Thorne wasn't the true reason why she didn't raise her bow against the doe. *Will I ever again derive the same satisfaction I once did from hunting?*

"It'll fade."

Gwen turned, startled to find blue eyes, entirely too close, peering back at her. Gwen's heart skipped a beat. She'd been so absorbed in her thoughts that she hadn't heard Bodhi's approach. She was surprised to find Bodhi kneeling on the bank beside her.

"Pardon?"

"The crone did a fair job. I doubt if the scar will be very noticeable. In time, it'll fade." Bodhi's arm came up, her hand extended. Her fingertips lightly grazed Gwen's throat.

Gwen recoiled from Bodhi's touch.

Bodhi's hand dropped, but she didn't move away.

Gwen averted her gaze, finding it difficult to look directly at Bodhi. She studied their dual images in the water. She was dark; dark hair, dark eyes, dark expression to match her mood. Bodhi's reflection was light. Her golden blonde hair fell about her shoulders. Her features were breathtaking, from her sparkling eyes to those dimples to that devastating smile of hers.

We're exact opposites.

There was a time that Gwen had thought Bodhi, being a seasoned swordswoman, would be jaded, cynical, and world-weary. Just as the barbarian in the cell beside Bodhi had assumed Gwen, being a virgin sacrifice, should be sweet, innocent, and pure. Instead, Bodhi had turned out to be more of a free spirit and Gwen had developed a pessimistic side.

I suppose if nothing else on this journey, I've learned that appearances are not always what they seem.

She traced her fingertips over the jagged line marring her throat.

"Do you think they've found her?"

Bodhi's reflection shrugged.

"Ernest had squads searching all of Fairhaven. They'll run her to ground, if she doesn't have someone aiding her or managed to make it out of the city on her own."

Gwen had heard Ernest and the others back at The Dirty Duck, speculating on what had driven Thorne to kill. Rachel had suggested that too much discipline had made her snap. Ernest had speculated that the beating from the bandits and the blow she'd taken to the head had caused some sort of damage. Even Bodhi had thrown in her opinion, stating that she was so down on tavern whores because she was a prude and they were the easiest targets to take out her frustrations on.

Gwen frowned. Certainly, Bodhi was probably the closest in her theory to what had truly motivated Thorne. Most of her victims had been tavern maids. But, Gwen wasn't convinced it was because she was repressing her urges or she thought tavern whores were dirty or a blight on society or any of the other reasons she'd heard put forth.

Gwen figured she had a better idea than the rest, having heard Thorne's tale from her own lips, but she didn't reveal her theory to the others. She couldn't. It wasn't her story to tell. Besides, told from Thorne's perspective, it made the commander sound like a victim, as well. And, that was something Gwen couldn't reconcile with herself allowing Thorne to be.

Her words…the beast's words…from the alley haunted her.

"It's your guilt I smell."

Gwen knew that an animal could smell its prey's fear. She suspected that perhaps the scent of the tavern wenches' guilt had been what drove the beast to kill them. *Perhaps it's also what drew Thorne to me. Even when she wasn't the beast, she could smell it…and it attracted her to me…* Gwen shook her head, banishing the memories of Thorne in her room, her lips at her neck and then of the beast in the alley, pinning her down, her teeth bared in a mirrored position at her exposed throat. Her hand reflexively closed about her throat and she swallowed convulsively.

She saw Bodhi's reflection watching her, a concerned expression on her face, but she couldn't speak her fears aloud, not even to Bodhi. *What if there are others, like Thorne, out there?*

"I'm sorry. I know you haven't had the best of luck. Despite what you told me, a maiden's first time should be special."

"If I don't die, that'll be special enough." Gwen recalled precisely the words she had used. *But, what's that got to do with...*

"Bodhi—"

"No, it's true. You didn't have a proper bedding by me." Bodhi cast a look at Gwen and then quickly looked away, downing her head. Her fingers plucked at blades of grass growing along the riverbank. "Then, your next lover turns out to be a monster. For what it's worth, I'm sorry about that."

Gwen heard the underlying note of sincerity in Bodhi's tone and when she looked up, Gwen saw it reflected in her image in the water. It was clear in her eyes—*pity.*

Gwen hated it when Bodhi had assumed she was working as a tavern wench in Fairhaven. She loathed it now that Bodhi apparently thought she was so hapless when it came to matters of love.

Her anger flamed. Nostrils flared. Blood boiled. Fists clenched and unclenched. Jaw tightened. She spun around, her movement so quick that she bumped against an unsuspecting Bodhi.

Bodhi got up, dusted off her black pants and tunic, and extended a hand to Gwen as if to assist her to her feet.

For Gwen, it was the final straw. All those times she was made to feel inadequate, guilty, and defenseless; all that tension that had been kept carefully bottled up, under pressure, building and building...finally exploded.

"Do you think I'm so helpless?" Gwen slapped Bodhi's hand away. "Hapless? Hopeless? Such an undesirable damsel-in-distress?" With each question, Gwen used both arms to give Bodhi a double-handed thrust against her chest and upper arms. "Do you think I need, or desire, your pity?"

To her consternation, Bodhi didn't raise a hand in protest, or to defend herself. She allowed Gwen to continue to push her, her boots sliding backward on the slick grass beneath her feet, causing her to lose ground to Gwen. Bodhi's apparent attempts at gallantry only infuriated Gwen all the more. "Do you think I'm so pathetic that I can't, or won't, take what I want?"

"Gwen—"

Gwen lunged forward, her fingers gripping Bodhi by the back of the neck as she roughly tugged her face down to meet hers. Her tongue plunged into Bodhi's mouth. It wasn't the gentle, sipping kisses that poets wrote of and minstrels sang about. It wasn't anywhere near what Gwen envisioned as being romantic. What it turned out to be was deep and bruising, passionate, full of want and need, and hotter than anything she could have ever imagined. By the time Gwen ended the kiss, they were both short of breath.

Bodhi's hair was mussed. Blue eyes had gone dark with desire. Bodhi raised a hand, her fingers wiping at her lips, her lips that looked kiss-swollen. Her breasts rose and fell with each breath. The leather cording at the eyelets of Bodhi's tunic were loose, revealing the delectable curve of a breast.

Gwen surged forward again. She pushed, backing Bodhi up against a tree. Her mouth locked onto Bodhi's. Bodhi's lips opened beneath hers and Gwen's tongue delved deep. This time when she withdrew, she dragged her teeth across Bodhi's bottom lip and sucked it into her mouth, nipping at the swelling flesh.

She felt Bodhi's arms come up, around her waist, her hands gripping her by the shoulders. Then, Bodhi was kissing her. It was Bodhi's tongue in her mouth, Bodhi's hand at the back of her head, Bodhi's fingers fumbling at the belt about her waist.

With a sharp gasp, Gwen broke off the kiss. Bodhi was attempting to take over. Bodhi was trying to wrest control away from her.

"No more." Even to Gwen's ears, her voice sounded much huskier than she'd ever heard it before. She liked the sound of it; it made her feel as if her tone brooked no argument.

Her aggressive manner, her authoritative tone, both must have taken Bodhi by surprise. How else to explain that a novice maid like Gwen had a seasoned rogue like Bodhi backed against a tree? How else to explain that Bodhi didn't raise a finger to prevent her from divesting the swordswoman of her dual harnesses and braided leather belt in record time?

Gwen's hands were beneath Bodhi's tunic, traveling over an expanse of flat stomach and ribs until she was cupping firm breasts. She gripped the pliant flesh, squeezing, thumbs working over hardened nipples. She pinched and tugged.

Bodhi moaned.

Gwen glanced at Bodhi's face. Her eyes were closed. White teeth were biting her bottom lip, leaving distinct impressions in full, pink lips. The color of them reminded Gwen of Bodhi's nipples, the way they had looked by morning's pale light.

Bodhi had been in bed with Fauna and Rachel, then. The thought of it annoyed Gwen. Impulse overtook her and she gave Bodhi's nipples a sharp tweak.

Bodhi hissed between gritted teeth. Her hands were down by her sides, her palms against the tree, thick fingers clenching and unclenching, short nails biting into bark. She brought one arm up, her hand gripping the hem of Gwen's tunic, fingers twisting the fabric.

Gwen used her boot to kick Bodhi's feet apart. She thrust her thigh between Bodhi's open legs. Her hand smoothed over the front of Bodhi's leather britches, cupping her fully. She pressed in and up, rotating the heel of her palm against Bodhi's heated flesh.

Bodhi's entire body jerked. Blue eyes flew open, piercing Gwen with a look.

Gwen pressed in harder, faster, and received a sharp gasp for her efforts. This time, Gwen wasn't certain if the sound had been wrenched from Bodhi or herself.

Touching Bodhi like this, taking her like this, seeing and feeling the effect she was having on the swordswoman's body…hearing the shallow, ragged breathing…smelling the arousal thick in the air…Gwen had never felt so stimulated in all her life.

She pressed her body fully into Bodhi's, putting all her weight behind her hand. Her mouth was at Bodhi's ear and she knew Bodhi could clearly hear every ragged, moist breath she exhaled. She could feel Bodhi straining, her hips attempting to rock against Gwen's thighs, unabashedly thrusting herself on Gwen's open palm, despite Gwen's full weight pressing into her.

Gwen felt it, knew it was coming. She could feel Bodhi tensing beneath her. She stilled her movements, pressed in harder, feeling Bodhi throbbing beneath her palm. Head thrown back, mouth open, corded muscles in her neck straining, a long, low groan rumbled up from Bodhi's throat.

Putting her weight behind it, Gwen pressed herself in firmly, frantically rubbing herself against the back of her hand that was still cupping Bodhi. A few quick thrusts was all it took. Gwen screamed out her release.

✝

Gwen felt calloused fingers upon her face, touching the smoothness of her cheek, tracing down the line of her jaw. The pad of a thumb passed over her bottom lip. Then, she felt fingertips on her throat and her eyes flew open.

She was on her back, on the ground, and she was ready to fight or flee until she realized the eyes looking down at her, intently studying her features, were blue and not green. Bodhi stilled her by lowering her mouth upon hers.

The kiss was soft and gentle, beginning with just a tentative flickering of Bodhi's tongue along her lips, coaxing Gwen to allow her in.

Gwen moaned as Bodhi's mouth moved away. Bodhi leaned in, pressing her forehead against Gwen's. Bodhi's breathing was ragged and to Gwen's surprise, she realized hers was no less labored.

Bodhi was just as gentle in the rest of her seduction. Smooth caresses and deft fingers soon had Gwen divested of her clothing. The rays of the midday sun warmed her flesh; the touch of Bodhi's lips and tongue overheated her senses. Bodhi's mouth closed upon Gwen's breast. She licked and kissed and sucked and made Gwen's hands uncontrollably reach up until her fingers were entwining themselves in blonde locks and she was incoherently mumbling Bodhi's name.

She felt Bodhi's hands upon her hips, her palms traveling over the length of her thighs. Then, she was touching the inside of Gwen's thighs and Gwen was opening her legs, inviting Bodhi's touch higher.

She opened her eyes, seeing Bodhi looking down upon her, all of her. Blue eyes moved higher, meeting Gwen's, holding her gaze. Fingertips grazed Gwen's sex, touching her, opening her. A finger slipped inside her.

Oh, blessed Spirits.

Gwen felt the added pleasure of a second finger.

Her gasp was silenced by Bodhi's mouth covering hers.

†

"Well, I suppose that answers the question you posed about being woman enough to take what you want."

Gwen turned her head so she could look up at Bodhi. The swordswoman was definitely smirking, a self-satisfied look upon her face. They were stretched out upon the grass, Gwen's head tucked in the crook of Bodhi's arm.

Gwen pulled the blanket Bodhi had fetched up to her chest. The sun had started its descent and the air was growing chill. She glanced toward the ring of rocks in the center of their camp, thinking one of them would soon need to tend to the fire.

That brought to mind the heat that had occurred between them. Now that the moment was past, Gwen felt herself blushing to the tips of her ears. Spirits, the way she'd behaved...

"What happened earlier, Bodhi, that was only a way of relieving tension, frustration. I needed release. It was only a physical coupling, nothing more. It changes nothing between us."

"Of course." Bodhi was much too agreeable in her answer.

"I mean it, Bodhi. It won't happen again."

"So you say." Bodhi rolled them over, pinning Gwen to the ground beneath her. "Yet, here you are, still in my arms."

Bodhi's eyes were heavy-lidded. Her fingers were inching the blanket lower, exposing Gwen's breasts. She pressed her lips to Gwen's sleepy nipples, coaxing them back to wakefulness. Her fingers wandered down Gwen's body. "Open for me."

Arms around Bodhi's neck, fingers laced into her hair, Gwen responded, feeling Bodhi nestle her body between her spread legs.

"And, don't think for a heartbeat this changes our arrangement in the slightest."

"Don't fret, sweet Gwendolyn." Bodhi's body began to move against Gwen's. "I always repay my debts."

✝

The sound of children's giggles, accompanied by women's voices, was what drew the matron's attention. Gnarled fingers stopped stirring the pot of water flavored with a single carrot and two leeks. She placed the wooden spoon on the stone hearth and picked up the stick she used as a walking cane.

Her frame was bent with age. Her clothes were nearly as thin as her frame. She used one hand to hold her threadbare cloak close around her chest. With aching joints that equally protested the chill in the air and every step she took, she made her way into the front room of the tiny house.

She was just in time to see the front door being closed. She went to the window, drew back the covering, and peered out. Two women were walking away, their shoulders hunched and their heads ducked against the drizzling rain. There was no one else to be seen on the street.

"Who was that? What did they want?" The matron turned and asked the children.

She stared at the boy and girl. Even at three- and five-summers-old, they clearly took after their parents. They had their father's blonde hair and Karyn's brown eyes and her nose, too. She saw the excitement in their eyes as they gathered around the table.

"Rachel and Fauna. They said they know Momma," answered the boy.

"Brought dat." The girl, the younger of the two, stopped sucking her thumb and pointed at a handbasket perched on the tabletop.

The old woman drew back the covering on the basket. Inside were fresh vegetables and enough packets of dried meat to see them through the coming winter. There was also a wedge of cheese and two loaves of bread. *Oh!* She hadn't been able to bake her own bread in ages.

"Mitt, go fetch the knife from the kitchen."

She reached into the basket and picked up a loaf, intending to cut off a hunk for each of them.

As she did, she heard a jingle, then another. She moved aside the other loaf of bread and peered inside the basket. There was a burlap bag, tied closed with twine. Aged fingers were unable to work loose the knot. Mitt ran in with the knife and she used the blade to cut through the cord.

The matron's eyes went wide as the contents spilled out onto the table. Trembling, gnarled fingers sifted through the coins, eyes widening as she counted more gold coins than she could ever spend in the next twenty winters.

✝

"Stop staring."

"Huh?"

Gwen was walking beside her horse, her backside, thighs, and calves vehemently objecting to sitting in the saddle a heartbeat longer than necessary. At first, even the

231

simple task of walking had seemed arduous. With each new step she took, she felt cramped muscles ease up a little bit more.

Something else she felt—Bodhi's eyes upon her.

Bodhi had dismounted almost as soon as Gwen had. Instead of walking beside her, though, the warrior's stride had been slower, and she'd fallen several paces behind. Gwen hadn't thought much of it at first. But, now…

She stopped, turned, and looked at Bodhi.

"Stop it," she said.

Bodhi shrugged, her expression a mixture of innocence and bewilderment.

"You're staring. Again. You've been looking at me, watching, staring…ever since…we…" Gwen's voice trailed off as she gestured between the two of them.

"Well, after what happened," Bodhi stepped closer to Gwen and waggled her eyebrows suggestively, "mayhaps I'm seeing the fair maiden in a new light."

"Because I wasn't quite the shy, demure virgin you were expecting, hmm?"

"From the first day I met you, fair Gwen, I knew there was nothing shy or demure about you." Bodhi gave a hearty laugh. "You do have considerably more…talent…than I expected, given your experience. I suppose your commander wasn't quite the prude I figured her to be."

Gwen's brow furrowed. Then, she remembered the night she'd made certain Bodhi saw her taking Thorne to her room.

"Bodhi, there's something you should know." Part of her had never intended to tell. But, after what had happened and how she'd behaved, she felt she owed Bodhi at least that much honesty. She reached out and touched Bodhi's forearm and waited for blue eyes to look down at her before she admitted, "Thorne never…I didn't…we didn't…"

"No?" Bodhi frowned.

"There was an attraction there and I had every intention…" Gwen could feel the heated blush rising to her cheeks. "I must have sensed there was something wrong with her…with the situation."

"I see." Bodhi smiled, her dimples showing.

"Yes, well, there you have it."

"Uh-huh."

"Truly, Bodhi," she said. "That's all there is to it. It just…didn't feel right. I couldn't go through with it."

"Of course."

Gwen rolled her eyes. Bodhi was practically strutting about the henhouse like a proud rooster.

Oh! The arrogance. I can't believe I…she…we… Gwen gave a groan of exasperation. In a huff, she gripped her horse's reins tightly, turned and stormed off. She was several paces down the road when she heard Bodhi behind her, her words calling after her.

"It's okay to admit the truth, Gwen. It's because she wasn't me."

"Believe me, Bodhi, that's what I found most attractive about her…"

THE END

About the Author

Del Robertson

To those who know her best, Del is an unapologetic jokester. Her wicked sense of humor can be found throughout her numerous award-winning stories on the net. As a military brat, Del has lived all over the world and has been exposed to many different people and cultures. It is from these past travels that she draws the characters that populate her stories. Del currently resides in Texas.

Other Books from Affinity eBook Press

Desert Blooms—Dannie Marsden

Luce's story continues in DESERT BLOOMS…

When we last met Luce Velazquez in Desert Heat, she went through hell and back to salvage her soul and reputation. Hoping to get her life back on track with lover Beth Ryan, a woman who understands her pain and can relate on every level. Instead, Luce is in the hospital, and Beth in protective custody.

Jessica Sullivan, Luce's friend and ex, has big doubts about the sincerity of Beth's love, and is in no hurry to release her from custody.

Can Luce's new found happiness last, or is Jessica correct in her doubts?

A heart stopping romance that will fill you with the wonder of friendship, anger of betrayal, and the everlasting vision of love.

Bayou Justice—Ali Spooner

Hell hath no fury like a woman scorned. When Kara, Sasha's, new lover is taken hostage as a diversionary tactic to allow the drug dealing Bellfontaine brothers to escape justice, Sasha springs into action.

Kara is released physically unharmed, however, her emotions, and budding career in the District Attorney's office are left in shambles when she is held blame for their release,

Appalled, by the failure of the criminal justice system, Sasha exacts her own brand of justice for the acts committed against her lover. From the Bayou's of Louisiana to the jungles of South America,

Sasha plots her revenge.

HER—Lisa Ron

Fox has been looking for that one person who will make her feel complete-her perfect match.

Together with her friends, Megan and Tree, Fox continues her quest while dodging exes and clingers, laughing a lot along the way.

When she meets Madeline, she instantly knows that she finds HER.

Madeline has her own problems-notably a domineering husband.

Can Fox win her heart? Can they make a life together?

This story will make you laugh, cry, and hold your breath as the story unfolds.

With the right person love can conquer all.

Through the Darkness—Erin O'Reilly

Becca Cameron is a loner—by choice. She lives in a hundred year old farmhouse built by her great grandfather. A tragic accident in her home a year earlier drove away her lover, and Becca tries to accept what she cannot change and hang on to the belief that love can conquer all.

Chase Hunter, had a meteoric rise in the Eastman Corporation and was, at thirty-four, the youngest vice-president. To Chase, her work was all consuming leaving little time for friends or lovers. There was simply no place in her life for anything but her job.

When Becca and Chase meet at their work place, the attraction is spontaneous. Life begins to look brighter for both women as work takes a second seat to romance.

Unknown to either woman, someone is watching their every move…

Will passion outweigh doubt? Can love conqueror fear?

Letting Go—JM Dragon

A failed relationship puts Stella Hawke's life on the brink of chaos.

When her grandmother falls gravely ill in Ashville, Stella ends her army career to take care of the woman during her last weeks. Little does she know that an old army comrade, socialite Reggie Stockton, whose family owns the local newspaper, also lives in Ashville.

Will she allow herself to accept Reggie's help to turn her life around and let go of the past?

This is a journey where both women re-evaluate what they want out of life.

Will that path lead to happiness or to a parting of the ways?

Requiem—JM Dragon & Erin O'Reilly

In the final book of the When Hell Meets Heaven Series, Olivia and Amelia reluctantly join forces with Parker and Remington to save their lives and those of the ones they love. The only problem—will three alpha females and an ex-nun be able to work toward a common goal and not kill each other before they complete their mission.

The four women are up against the formidable strength of DOCO along with a corrupt politician, bent on mass destruction. Can they complete their mission knowing that a requiem will be the harbinger of their end should they fail.

McKee—A.C. Henley

Private Investigator Quinlan McKee has returned to Los Angeles after a three-year absence, only to find herself embroiled in a world of child slavery and police corruption.

Finding Her Way—Riley Jefferson

Is it love or just great sex?

After ending an abusive marriage, Jerrica Kerrison is finally alive and she's apologizing for nothing! She has a job with a financial firm in Boston, a townhouse in Newburyport, and a sports car she drives way too fast. Jerrica has everything except that indefinable emotion called love.

Madison Jeffrey is a lost soul. A PR job in the south has always protected Madison from the pressures of her family. But one day, fate brings her back to New England, forcing Madison to face her long buried demons, and a sister who despises her.

When a chance meeting brings Jerrica and Madison's separate worlds crashing together, the attraction is instantaneous. After one passionate night together, Jerrica retreats into the safety of her world, leaving Madison to figure out what happened.

Will Jerrica open up her heart to the idea of love? Can Madison finally believe that she is worthy of unconditional love? Or will a devil hiding in the shadows tear them apart?

Denial—Jackie Kennedy

Time spent in Somalia has Doctor Celeste Cameron accustomed to living and working in a war zone. Coming back home to America, Celeste is glad to see the end of the peril she has been in—or so she thinks. Danger seems to follow Celeste and she finds it in the shape of Amy. What Celeste feels for Amy scares her more than anything she has faced in war zones. Amy has the same feelings, but is in denial and vows to marry Josh, Celeste's twin brother, no matter what. When fate brings them together again, will they give in to their mutual attraction or will they once again deny what they feel.

Out of Retirement—Erica Lawson

Melanie Stokes was a doctor—a very good one, or so she hoped. She was calm and cool under pressure, and very little fazed her. Until…

Caitlin Joseph ran a small retirement home for older women in need. The fact that everyone in the house was gay was a coincidence, although it did cut down the number of women agreeing to live there.

Mel took up an offer to do some relief work for a local community center when their regular doctor was away on holidays. As soon as she arrived at the home she knew something was different about the place. Was it the little old lady chasing the paper boy down the street or the sign saying "Dykes Retirement Home"?

But there was something about the place that also appealed to her. Sure, Caitlin was cute as a button, but it was more the fact that she took very good care of her charges, despite their rather bizarre behavior.

The older women seized the opportunity to introduce a woman into Caitlin's lonely life, using any means possible to keep Mel coming back. Their plans were boosted by the introduction of another woman into the house, who set hearts a fluttering and blood pressure rising. Now if she was a lesbian it would have been perfect…

Galveston 1900: Swept Away—Linda Crist

On September 7-8, 1900, the island of Galveston, Texas, was destroyed by a hurricane, or 'tropical cyclone', as it was called in those days. This story is a fictional account of Mattie and Rachel, two women who lived there, and their lives during the time of the 'great storm'. Forced to flee from her family at a young age, Rachel Travis finds a home and livelihood on the island of Galveston. Independent, friendly, and yet often lonely, only one other person knows the dark secret that haunts her. Madeline "Mattie" Crockett is trapped in a loveless marriage, convinced that her fate is sealed. She never dares to dream of true happiness, until Rachel Travis comes walking into her life.   As emotions come to light, the storm of Mattie's marriage converges with the very real hurricane. Can they survive, and build the life they both dream of?

This second edition of one of Linda Crist's best-loved novels maintains the original story, while incorporating some reader-pleasing passages that were cut from the first edition. As an added bonus, the short story "Something to Celebrate" is included at the end of the novel, detailing further adventures of Rachel and Mattie.

Rapture: Sins of the Sinners—A. C. Henley & Fran Heckrotte

A serial killer is targeting young lesbians throughout the state of Texas.Texas Ranger Cochetta Lovejoy is assigned to the case. Convinced she knows who is committing the murders, Ranger Lovejoy is willing to do whatever it takes to put the perpetrator behind bars--even if it means stretching the limits of the law by manipulating the judicial system. Detective Agnes Kelly-Elliott is one of Ft. Worth Police Department's finest investigators.   When Ranger Lovejoy appears on the crime scene of a recent murder, Agnes fears a dark secret that, if revealed, could destroy her family ties, and end her career. This is a dark, gritty, graphic tale of desire gone awry, and flawed characters looking for redemption in all the wrong places.

Taming the Wolff—Del Robertson
ONLY ONE WOMAN...
As devastatingly beautiful as she is headstrong, noble-born Alexis DeVale abruptly finds her preordained life in upheaval. Abducted at sword-point, held for ransom, thrust into a maelstrom of lawlessness and piracy...
HAS THE POWER...
The strength of her passion, the depth of her love...
TO TAME THE WOLFF...
Mayhem. Brutality. Murder. These are the tools of the trade - and Kris Wolff is the master of her profession. Captain of the high seas, a roguish pirate, her heart hardened by life, her passion tightly controlled by the secret she's forced to keep. Faced with a new danger, The Wolff finds herself unable to guard her heart from the tumultuous desires that Alexis DeVale has awakened.

A Window in Time—JM Dragon
When Julia Stokes undertakes a dare organized by her friends days before she leaves for University, little does she know that the peculiar events that night would have a profound effect on her life.

The mystery women she met that night named Evelyn , reappears, or so Julia thinks, in her life several years later. Then a mystery begins to unravel before her eyes creating even more questions that she has no answers to.

A Window in Time is a light romance with a strange twist.

Fire and Ice—Gaelle Cathy

After a vicious encounter in New York City, the Beckett family, including twenty-year-old college student Emma, retreats to New Hampshire. They are seeking a place to heal and for more peaceful surroundings.

Turns out, the move creates more upheaval when Emma meets glass artist Charlie Campbell. The spark is immediate but Charlie's reluctance and Emma's personal history make for a bumpy start to their romance.

Just as their love blooms, a dark family secret is exposed that threatens to destroy not only Emma and Charlie's relationship, but Emma's relationship with her family.

Will Emma and Charlie's love survive the secret's exposure?

Does love really conquer all?

Private Dancer—TJ Vertigo

Reece Corbett grew up on the mean streets on New York City, abused, used and in trouble with the law. Faith Ashford grew up wealthy, with all the creature comforts that money provides. When they meet fireworks begin.

Miss Match—Erica Lawson

Clancy Fitzgerald is twenty-nine, single, and a virgin. According to her aunt, she is as good as dead.

Minerva Goldberg has used all her matchmaking wiles to make a conventional match for Clancy. Now it is time to use an unconventional one.

Fashion editor, Carmen Pratka does Minerva a favor by going on a blind date with Clancy. Clancy refuses to acknowledge what the rest of the world knows. Carmen makes it her personal mission to not only convince Clancy that she is a lesbian and she, is the right woman for her.

E-Books, Print, Free e-books

Visit our website for more publications available online.

www.affinityebooks.com

Published by Affinity E-Book Press NZ LTD
Canterbury, New Zealand

Registered Company 2517228